The Royal Throne

LEAGUE OF RULERS, BOOK THREE

JENNIFER ANNE DAVIS

REIGN PUBLISHING

Published by Reign Publishing

Cover Design by Phoenix Design Covers
Proofreading by Allyssa Painter and Leah Alvord
Map by Annika Jost

ISBN (paperback): 979-8-9864009-7-6
ISBN (ebook): 979-8-9864009-6-9

Library of Congress Control Number: 1-15026813951

CASTLE
CUSP
PALACE
LYNK
AVONI
PORT RITE
GATE
GATE
LEAGUE HOUSE
PALACE
CARLON
SKYFALL RIVER
NISK
LARK
LY FOREST
N
W
E
S
BAKLEY
CASTLE

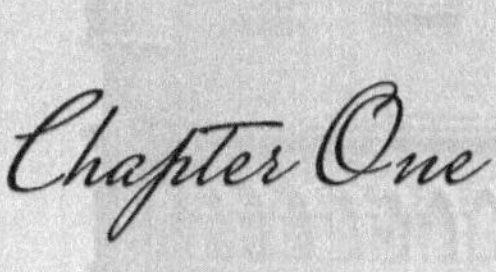

Chapter One

At the bow of the ship, Sabine gazed toward the coastline where rows of Lynk soldiers held their formation with rigid precision. Just ahead of them, Rainer stood clad in leather armor, a sword strapped to his waist. He looked every bit the formidable and unyielding king he was known to be.

"I didn't expect to receive this sort of reception," Otto mumbled as he leaned against the railing next to Sabine.

"King Rainer wants to remind us of his military might," Markis quipped.

"As long as he isn't here to arrest me, I can handle him," Sabine said. For days, she'd been crafting different plans to keep Rainer from waging war. But seeing her husband in full military attire sent a chill of foreboding through her—and at the same time, it strengthened her resolve. Now, she knew exactly which path to take.

"He doesn't have anything to arrest you for," Otto insisted. "Regardless, that's why I'm here. As a League representative and a fellow ruler, I can help you." He squeezed her shoulder in reassurance.

While her brother might think he had sway with Rainer, Sabine knew better. Rainer did what he wanted. In order to stop him, she'd have to beat him using his own tactics. The only reason she'd allowed Otto to accompany her was so that he could escort the stolen Bakley children home.

The ship pulled up next to the dock, and the anchor was dropped. Bakley soldiers finished bringing in the sails before extending the gangplank. Sabine approached it, her hair tossing in the wind.

"I'll go first," Markis said, easily making his way across the narrow strip of wood.

Sabine followed her guard, her legs wobbly. Once on the dock, a wave of nausea hit her. It seemed like everything around her was moving up and down. The last time she felt this way, Evander had given her some sort of root to chew which instantly calmed her stomach. She wished she had it now. Shoving all thoughts of Evander aside, she focused solely on her husband as she walked along the dock. She would not—*could not*—think about Evander and how much she missed him. Such dangerous thoughts would only get her killed.

As she made her way to shore, Rainer kept his eyes trained on her. She had no idea what he was thinking or what he planned to do once they reunited. She needed to stick to the story Anton had told him—that she'd left to see her brother. Under no circumstances could she reveal that Evander had kidnapped her.

Markis stepped off the dock, then turned and held out his hand for her. She took it, allowing him to help her onto the sandy beach. Keeping her focus on the king, she assumed her brother followed her as she headed straight for Rainer. His dark hair, chocolate eyes, and the strong cut of his jawline made him devastatingly handsome. But looks could be deceiving.

When she was about three feet away from him, she stopped and curtseyed, taking note that neither Anton nor Axel were in attendance. She straightened and looked Rainer in the eyes. "It is good to be home," she said by way of greeting, choosing her words carefully while trying to keep her voice strong, as if nothing were wrong. Right now, she needed to appear young, innocent, and naive. It was one of the reasons she chose to wear the dress she did. It was from Bakley, so by Lynk's standards, totally inappropriate since it covered her from neck to ankles.

Rainer's eyes remained locked with hers for an uncomfortable minute before he glanced over her shoulder.

She stepped aside and gestured to her brother. "May I present Prince Otto Ludwig of Bakley."

Otto bowed his head in a polite gesture. "King Rainer Manfred, it is a pleasure to finally meet you."

Captain Higman stepped around them. "Your Majesty."

"Report," Rainer ordered.

"We spotted the Bakley ship sailing north in the river. I boarded, found our queen, and remained to ensure her safety."

"Besides these two, are any other royals on board?" Rainer demanded, his right hand clutching the hilt of his sword as if ready to pull it out and decapitate someone.

Cold terror slid down Sabine's spine as she realized he was referring to Evander. If her husband believed the Avoni prince was aboard that ship, it explained the unusually large number of soldiers assembled. For now, she'd feign ignorance and hope he had no proof she'd traveled alone with Evander. She'd been meticulous about erasing every trace of their time together.

Higman shook his head. "No, Your Majesty."

The king turned in Otto's direction as if just seeing him for the first time.

"This is quite the greeting you have for us," Sabine said, wanting to recapture his attention. Now it was time for her to make her move. "I'm glad you're taking my safety seriously after what your sister did."

"My sister?" He tilted his head to the side, his brows pulling together.

"Yes. I still can't believe Princess Lottie hired an assassin to kill Princess Alina and myself." She kept her voice loud and articulate so the nearby soldiers would hear.

Rainer's eyes narrowed. "The assassination is still being investigated," he said, a tightness to his words indicating he was irritated.

"I don't understand." She glanced at those around her. "Your sister—"

Rainer took an abrupt step forward, pinching her elbow and cutting her off. "We'll discuss this matter in private."

They stood there staring at one another.

She'd pushed him far enough for now. "Very well. I am eager to know what you've done to ensure my safety." She lifted her chin in the air, glad his soldiers had overheard that his sister was guilty of treason. The first seed had been planted.

"Your orders, Your Majesty?" the soldier to the right asked.

Rainer looked at Sabine, his eyes searching hers for something. She forced herself not to flinch or cower.

"Ensure our queen makes it safely to the palace," Rainer said, releasing her.

"Aren't you accompanying me?" she asked her husband.

He shook his head. "I'm not done here." He raised his right arm, and a unit of twenty soldiers moved to surround her.

Glancing at the Bakley ship, she noticed two Lynk vessels had blocked it in. "Brother, do you need to get any of your things?" She feared for the lives of the men on board. If Rainer decided to kill them, as he had the Avoni delegation, she'd feel personally responsible.

"Prince Otto," Rainer said, "please remain here with me." Then to Sabine, "I will have his things delivered to the palace. When you arrive, tell Claire to prepare a room for him." He turned his back to her.

She began walking, knowing Markis would remain with Otto. For now, she was on her own. Or, as on her own as she could be with a unit of soldiers accompanying her. After being aboard the ship for so long, it felt good to walk and stretch her legs, though she could do without the ridiculous humidity. It was worse than she remembered.

By the time they reached the top of the mountain where the palace was located, Sabine was drenched with sweat. It was the perfect excuse to find a seamstress in town.

As they walked through the center of the business district, she spotted a shop with brightly colored fabrics and she headed for its entrance.

"Your Majesty," the soldier closest to her said, "we have orders to escort you to the palace."

"And you will," she replied. "However, I'm hot and wish to put something lighter on."

The soldier opened his mouth to respond.

Sabine held up her hand. "You are permitted to check the store before we enter and you may remain with me. The rest will stay outside."

He nodded before barking out orders for the soldiers to spread out. Once he was satisfied the shop was safe, he escorted her inside.

The storekeeper curtseyed. "Your Majesty." She was a pretty woman in her early thirties with dark skin, black hair, light brown eyes.

"I am in dire need of something to wear," Sabine said,

perusing the fabrics. "I'd also like to commission you to make some new outfits for me."

"It would be my honor."

"Do you have anything readily available for me for today?"

"I have nothing suitable for a queen. However, I am more than capable of making you whatever you desire."

"Can you come to the palace tomorrow so we can discuss my wardrobe?" Her new and improved wardrobe.

"It would be my honor, Your Majesty."

Sabine turned and exited the shop, pleased another part of her plan was already underway.

Without acknowledging the soldiers, she headed toward the palace. When they reached the cliff at the end of the town, the wood planks lowered to form a bridge. No matter how many times she'd witnessed this, she still found the entire construction fascinating.

The sun remained high overhead, no clouds in sight. Thankfully, only a slight wind blew. Sabine started across the bridge as a group of palace guards headed straight for her. They each wore the traditional black tunic, pants, and mask.

At the half-way point, the soldiers accompanying her stopped. Sabine left their protection, stepping closer to the palace guards. When she was five feet from them, she paused and spoke loud enough to address both groups of men. "Who is responsible for making arrests?" she asked. "Does that jurisdiction fall to Lynk's soldiers or to the palace guards?"

One of the soldiers spoke. "It depends on the situation. Normally, the soldiers handle such matters. However, if the incident takes place inside the palace walls, the palace guards handle it."

She tried to hide her smile, knowing she was about to infuriate Rainer. Facing the palace guards, she spoke loud enough for the soldiers behind her to hear as well. "Princess Lottie hired an assassin to kill Princess Alina and myself. Since she committed treason, I want her arrested."

"The princess is currently in the palace, so we will handle the matter," one of the palace guards said.

Turning to face the soldiers, she said, "Thank you for escorting me." She needed these people on her side, so she smiled kindly at them. Then she joined the palace guards.

At the end of the bridge, she stepped inside the palace and was immediately greeted by a man she recognized and despised.

"Your Majesty," Captain Lithane said. "These men will escort you to your room."

One of the guards briefly spoke to Lithane about Princess Lottie.

He looked at Sabine. "This is the first I'm hearing about it."

"Really?" she replied. "I'm surprised my husband would keep that information from you." She met his gaze deliberately. It was easy since Lithane didn't wear a mask like the others. "Will you do me the honor of personally handling the matter? I trust my safety to no one else."

There was a moment of silence before he replied, "Yes, Your Majesty. I will see to it."

"Thank you. I'll feel better knowing she is locked up, unable to hurt me."

He bowed to Sabine—a first for him.

As she glided down the hallway, she said loudly, "Captain Lithane does an exceptional job. I hope he gets promoted soon." She knew he held the highest position in this palace, but she needed him to soften to her. Earning the loyalty of all these men was paramount.

On her way to the royal wing, she traversed through the

pristine white hallways of the palace and across the lush courtyards. When she reached her door, she threw it open hoping to find—and there she was. Curled up on her bed was Harta. The dog's head flew up. As soon as she spotted Sabine, her tail wagged and she jumped off the bed, running to her. Sabine dropped to her knees and let the dog lick her face. She couldn't help but laugh. Her dog always made her feel better.

"Queen Sabine," Claire said with a smile as she came out of the bathing room. "It is good to see you. I have your bath ready."

After instructing Claire to have a room prepared for Otto, Sabine placed a kiss on Harta's nose. "It's good to see you."

Standing in front of the mirror, Sabine evaluated her outfit. The mistake she'd made when she'd first arrived here all those weeks ago was not fully understanding what the people expected of their queen. The vast differences between Bakley and Lynk had been so overwhelming that she hadn't fully embraced the culture here. And she'd been brokenhearted over her sister. Now, things were different. She knew what she was dealing with, had a better grasp on the rules, and she understood the customs.

While it would be difficult playing the part and behaving the way she needed to, she knew she could pull it off. Growing up, she'd always been one to bend the rules. Push them even. This was no different.

Turning slowly, she took in her appearance, barely recognizing herself. Until the seamstress from town visited and designed clothes to Sabine's specifications, this would do. And this was a good segue to what she had planned. Fabric went from her waist up and over her breasts and shoulders, cascading down her back, leaving the entire area between her breasts down to her naval exposed. At her waist, the fabric hung in four sections: one in the front, the back, and on each side. When she walked, her legs showed.

If she twisted too quickly, she feared she'd expose something she shouldn't. She'd need to move carefully and keep her shoulders up and back. When Otto saw her, he would be furious. That was the only part of her plan she hadn't accounted for.

Sabine pulled her long brown hair into a knot at the base of her head, exposing her neck. Her makeup accentuated her gray eyes nicely. She decided against jewelry since she didn't want it to detract from her skin. Satisfied, she went over to her door and stepped out into the hallway. Since her guards all wore masks, she couldn't see their reactions to her appearance. However, they were used to women dressing this way and no one probably thought anything about it. While she had worn the outfits in her closet, she'd always chosen ones that covered as much as possible. The one she had on now, she never would have considered before.

But that was then.

Now she was at war—and this was her armor.

"Your Majesty," one of the guards said, stepping forward. "Where can we escort you to?"

While she needed to speak with Rainer to get a better sense of what he was thinking and planned to do, she decided against facing him right now. "I wish to go for a walk." She headed down the hallway, not deigning any more of a response.

At the main courtyard, she stopped in the center near the water fountain, tilting her head back and reveling in the warmth of the sun on her skin.

"Your Majesty," Claire said, coming up to her. "Your brother is in a guest room. He wishes to see you."

After traveling on the ship, Sabine didn't want to be holed up in a room. "Bring him here."

Claire curtseyed and hurried away. Sabine turned to her guards. "Has Princess Lottie been arrested?"

"We haven't received word," one of the men answered.

"If one of you can please see that it's being handled, I'd appreciate it."

"Consider it done."

As Sabine strolled through the courtyard, she paused at different rose and flower bushes, pretending to smell or admire them. Her goal was to get as many people to see her as possible. In her peripheral vision, she spotted others moving through the courtyard. She heard the sound of doors closing and spotted people walking on the second floor balcony above. The palace seemed abuzz with activity. It wouldn't take long for word to spread that she was home.

She didn't know how many people were still in residence. With war brewing, the palace was probably the safest place for most nobles and high ranking officials. Plus, Rainer would want his commander, generals, and captains close for planning purposes. Of course, the planning was probably done. They were in the execution phase now.

"Well, well, well," a deep voice drawled from above.

Sabine glanced up and found Axel leaning on the railing of the second level, watching her.

"I was wondering what the servants were scurrying around for." He smirked.

Taking a deep breath, Sabine smiled seductively as she lifted her gaze to Axel's, making sure one of her legs was slightly forward, exposing as much skin as possible.

"Welcome...home?" he said, making it sound like a question. Testing her.

She lifted a single eyebrow. "It's good to be home. I

brought my brother with me." She kept her voice strong and level, trying to reveal the truth in what she said.

His brows drew together. He opened his mouth to speak, but his head snapped to the side.

Sabine followed his line of sight to see Rainer storm out of the far archway, headed straight for her.

Chapter Two

Even furious, Rainer was attractive. The leather armor showcased his toned arms. His tousled, wind-blown hair only added to his appeal. Sabine had always found him handsome. Too bad when he opened his mouth, he ruined it.

He stopped a few feet from her, his chest rising and falling as he curled his hands into fists, attempting to rein in his temper. His eyes closed for a few seconds, and when they opened, his anger was gone. A slow smile slid across his face, and his eyes darkened as they took her in.

Now she understood that he used his allure as a weapon. At least two could play that game. "It's good to see you, husband." She lowered her chin, batting her eyelashes as she smiled coyly at him.

Besides Axel, a handful of people stood on the second level overlooking the courtyard, along with several couples passing through. This was one of the many reasons she'd chosen this area—she wanted witnesses.

Rainer took a step closer, his hand sliding to her waist. He leaned in toward her, whispering, "You are not to give my soldiers or my palace guards orders." His warm breath brushed her ear. He leaned back, not expecting her to respond.

Making no attempt to lower her voice, she replied, "Are you saying I'm a queen in name only?" She tilted her head, pulling her brows together in an attempt to look confused.

He pinched her side. "This is Lynk, not Bakley. This is *my* kingdom. I will protect it."

Her eyes narrowed as she took a step back, pulling away from his grip, her hand going to her chest in shock. "I took an oath to protect Lynk," she said loudly enough for those nearby to hear. "Lynk is now my kingdom. These are my people, too."

Rainer's eyes narrowed. "Lottie is my *sister*." His voice remained low, like water running over pebbles.

"That makes her betrayal even greater," Sabine replied, her voice loud and articulate, carrying through the courtyard. Everyone in the palace needed to know Lottie was responsible for Alina's death and that she'd hired an assassin to kill Sabine. Lottie was trying to take Rainer's throne. It surprised her that he would continue to defend his sister given what she'd done.

He glanced around, as if taking note of those witnessing this spectacle. "I don't know what game you're playing at," he said, his voice a harsh whisper. "But let me make one thing abundantly clear. You have no say in what happens with my family."

Tears filled her eyes. "I thought I was your family. That *we* are a family." Her loud voice echoed through the courtyard, shaking as if on the verge of tears. Turning away from him, she kept her head held high, blinking back tears. "I believe that as the rulers of this great kingdom, we have a responsibility to enforce its laws. I don't think we can let someone break the law just because you know them or they're special to you."

Then she turned back to face him, pointing at his chest. "If you won't enforce the laws, if you won't put Lottie in the dungeon and see justice served, then you're not the king I thought you were. You're not the king Lynk deserves. I no longer feel safe here and must leave." She raised her eyebrows in challenge, hoping she'd hit the right nerve with him.

"Leave?" His voice dropped to a low, almost menacing tone as he stepped closer, his hand reaching for her arm.

Sabine knew he couldn't afford for her to leave again. They didn't have long to procreate and produce an heir. Otherwise, he'd forfeit the throne and Lottie would claim it.

She was about to respond when Commander Felix entered the courtyard, heading straight for them.

He bowed. "King Rainer, I need a moment of your time."

Rainer kept his focus on Sabine, his voice soft so it wouldn't carry as he said, "We'll finish this discussion tonight. Until then, go to your room. You will not give any orders until after I've outlined your duties." With that, he turned and walked away with Felix.

Her temper flared, making her want to yell after him. However, she schooled her features, making sure to keep her anger and resentment locked beneath the surface. Too many people were watching. Instead, she let hurt and sorrow consume her—which wasn't hard. All she had to do was think about Alina's death to feel hurt, and about leaving Evander to feel sorrow. Tears fill her eyes.

Her dear, sweet sister was buried beneath the ground in Bakley. Sabine had sworn to seek vengeance for the murder, and she wouldn't rest until Lottie paid for her crime. The time Sabine had spent with Evander helped mend her heart, but they could never be. She was married, and he was the Avoni prince and leader of a ruthless assassin guild.

To move forward with her life, Sabine needed to focus on

Rainer, even if she couldn't love him. Not when he treated her like this. Like a child. He would never see her as an equal, let alone treat her as one. Their age difference was too great. Lifting her hand, she wiped the tears before they could fall. While she wanted to garner sympathy from those nearby, she didn't want to appear too weak.

"Your Majesty," one of her guards said, "shall we escort you back to your room?"

It would be so much easier to gauge his reaction if she could see his face. She hated that the palace guards all wore black masks, hiding their emotions.

"I just need a moment," she mumbled, closing her eyes and taking in a deep breath, letting it out slowly.

"Sister," Otto said as he neared. "What's the matter?" He stepped around her guards and stood in front of Sabine, his eyes looking her over and widening ever so slightly at the sight of her clothing.

In Bakley, women wore dresses that covered everything except for their hands and head. It was taboo to show any other skin. However, here in Lynk, the weather being hot and muggy, the clothing was at a minimum to make life comfortable. She knew the outfit she wore was hard for her brother to see her in. Thankfully, he was seasoned enough in court politics to keep his features schooled.

"Sabine," Otto whispered. "What's the matter? You never cry or show your emotions like this."

"I'm playing my part," she whispered back. "Ready for our performance?"

He nodded. "So long as you are truly okay, I'm ready."

Late last night, they'd discussed various scenarios such as this one, so at least Otto had some inkling what she intended to do and what she needed from him in return.

Looping her arm with his, she led him along the pathway

in the courtyard. Loudly, she said, "I'm so glad you're here in Lynk with me, brother."

"Ever since I heard of the assassination attempts against you, I've been eager to help you in any way I can. Losing one sister is hard enough; I don't intend to lose another." He squeezed her arm in encouragement.

As children, they'd played games such as this in an attempt to manipulate their parents into getting what they wanted. Most of the time, their parents saw right through it. Sabine hoped they were more successful now, especially since they were older, more experienced, and the stakes were infinitely higher.

She sighed dramatically. "King Rainer doesn't want to arrest Princess Lottie, even though she is responsible for having Princess Alina killed and hiring the assassin who tried to kill me."

"Why won't he arrest her? Didn't she commit a crime?"

"She did. Princess Lottie is guilty of treason and should be in the dungeon, awaiting punishment for her crimes." She steered them toward a more crowded section of the courtyard, wanting as many people as possible to overhear this conversation—or rather, performance.

"Do you think it's because she's his sister that he doesn't want to uphold the law?"

Sabine shrugged. "I don't know. He just scolded me for questioning him and told me to go to my room. He said I am not allowed to make any decisions with regards to this kingdom."

"But you're its queen."

"Apparently, in name only." Glancing furtively at those they passed, she saw looks of shock and outrage on many faces. She had to withhold her smile.

"That's against the law as well." Otto stopped walking

and faced his sister. "King Rainer crowned you the queen of Lynk. You took an oath."

"I know," Sabine replied. "I have to do what's best for the people of this kingdom."

"Not only do you have a legal duty, but you have a moral obligation as well. If King Rainer won't protect his citizens, then you must."

She nodded. "I am the queen of Lynk and will behave as such. Even if my husband doesn't agree."

One of her guards approached. "Your Majesty," he said, bowing. "I hope it isn't too bold of me, but if your life is still in danger, if there is a credible threat, I think you should meet with your personal guards. We can discuss the best way to keep you safe, given what we're dealing with."

Otto squeezed her arm. "I think that is a wise idea. I'm appointing Lieutenant Markis to your protection as well. I will meet with Prince Anton and Prince Axel to discuss the matter further. I'll help you get to the bottom of this." He hurried away.

She was about to insist that her brother have guards assigned for his own protection when four men bearing Bakley's colors hurried after him. It was wise of him to bring men he trusted into this palace of lies and deceit.

Sabine stood in the library by the window, her guards spread out before her. "Who's in charge here?" she asked.

One of the men pulled his mask off. "I am, Your Majesty. My name is Drew." He had dark brown hair shorn close to his head. His light brown eyes matched his skin. Sabine guessed his age to be around twenty-eight or so.

"It's nice to meet you, Drew. Since I know Lieutenant Markis, I am making him the head of my guard while he's here in Lynk. You will be his second in command. Once he returns to Bakley, you will resume your position."

"Of course, Your Majesty," Drew responded, about to replace his mask when Markis reached out to stop him.

"I'd like to make a change," Markis said. "Everyone, remove your masks. I need to see your faces." The men did as he said. "Good. Queen Sabine, please take a look at these men. These are the only men who I entrust your safety to. No one else."

She looked each one in the eyes, trying to memorize their faces.

"When you are on duty, you will no longer wear a mask," Markis instructed. "Queen Sabine, please address any concerns you have regarding your safety."

She took a deep breath, then began. She told her guards everything, starting with her perspective of the assassination attempt in the seamstress's room, then how she married Rainer at the castle to gain protection, followed by what she overheard between Lottie and the assassin during the masquerade. She explained that she'd left the palace that night out of fear—fear that Rainer knew the truth and hadn't confronted Lottie. When she was away, an assassin had hunted her, but he was dead now. Once Sabine had received word that the missing children from Bakley had been found and were in Lynk, she returned with her brother to ensure the children made it home safely.

"So while we don't know if there are any active assassination threats against the queen," Markis said, folding his arms and pacing near the table, "Lottie is an issue. She wants the throne and isn't afraid to hurt the queen to get it."

"We didn't know Princess Lottie was involved before," one of the guards said. "Now that we do, we can be better prepared."

"And no one who isn't vetted will be allowed near you, Your Majesty," another said.

She nodded, still standing near the window. "I suppose that's all we can do for now."

"Maybe the king wishes to perform an investigation first," someone suggested. "Just to make sure it's his sister who's behind this before he arrests her."

"Regardless," Markis said, "laws are laws. The princess can't be given endless chances to kill our queen. She's already struck once with Princess Alina. We can't allow her to succeed a second time."

Sabine shivered despite it being warm.

"Tell me, Drew," she said, "does the queen of Lynk traditionally have no say here in this kingdom?"

He shifted his weight as if uncomfortable. "We haven't had a queen in over fifteen years," he said. "But traditionally, our queens are more often considered an art piece, looked at rather than heard," he replied. "I'm sorry."

"I asked for the truth." She took a seat at the table, drumming her fingers on it.

"However," Drew continued, "we have laws. Laws that must be obeyed by everyone—royals included."

And that was what Sabine had been counting on.

"We'll do whatever we can to keep you safe," Drew added. "But if I'm being honest, I'd like to do a little reconnaissance. I want to ask around and see what I can discover about the situation."

"I think that's wise," she answered. "Then it won't just be my word you have to go by."

She glanced at Markis who nodded his approval. Everything seemed to be going according to plan. That should have been her first clue that things were about to get messy.

Rainer burst into Sabine's bedchamber without knocking or being announced. "We need to get a few things straight," he said, not bothering with pleasantries.

Sabine remained sitting on her bed, petting Harta, waiting for Rainer to get to the point of this conversation. Or rather *visit* since she doubted there would be much conversing going on.

"I want to make one thing perfectly clear. You do not have any authority whatsoever over my family."

Her eyes narrowed. "You're saying that in Lynk, the princes and the princess have power over their queen?" That was ludicrous.

"No, that's not what I'm saying." He folded his hands behind his back. "You are the queen, but Anton, Axel, and Lottie are my siblings. I will take care of them—not you."

She continued to stroke Harta's head. "And what about once we have a child? Will I have no say in how that child is disciplined?"

He mumbled something under his breath as he came farther into the room, heading to one of the archways leading to the balcony, his back to her. He stood there, unmoving. "Speaking of my heir," he said, his words clipped. "We will not be sharing a bed until I am certain you are not pregnant."

"In case you forgot, we haven't consummated our marriage." There was no way she could be carrying a child.

He peered over his shoulder at her. "Exactly."

Shock rolled through her at his implication. "I didn't know it was possible for a virgin to suddenly become pregnant. How does that happen?"

Rainer turned to face her. "I have it on good authority that you've spent time with another man."

Her heart beat rapidly. There was no way he could know

that she'd traveled alone with Evander. "I've been with my brother," she said slowly. "Surely you're not implying anything untoward?"

"No, not Prince Otto. Someone else."

"Why don't you tell me who you think I've been with?" Even though she had traveled alone with Evander, she'd remained true to Rainer—regardless of how difficult that had been or how much she wanted to be with Evander.

"Let me ask you this. Who did you leave with the night of the masquerade?" His eyes remained watching her every move.

While petting the dog, she thought back to what Anton had told her he'd said to Rainer. "No one. I left by myself."

"How did you get out of the palace unseen?" He raised his eyebrows.

"That was weeks ago," she mumbled, still stroking Harta's head. "I was frantic that night. Terrified. I don't remember all the details."

"Which way?" he asked again, clearly annunciating each word.

The best answer would be a combination of truths infused with lies in order to protect Evander and Avoni. "That was the night I learned of Lottie's treachery," she said. "I was so scared."

Rainer rubbed his face and sighed. "Let's try another question. How did you discover this supposed treachery?"

She leaned back against the headboard, Harta moving her head to rest on Sabine's legs. "The night of the masquerade, I snuck into the servants' passageways. I went to the Avoni delegation's suite. There, I overheard Lottie with a man whom I assume is an assassin based upon what he said. I rushed to find you, but you were gone. No one knew where you were." It was the night Rainer had been on a mission of his own.

"Then what did you do?"

"I ran into Anton," she said. "He mentioned something about a League meeting, and I knew my brother would be there." Her family had sent her letters, but she hadn't received any of them. She suspected Rainer was responsible for destroying them. "Since I hadn't heard from my family in weeks, I thought something must be wrong." His shoulders stiffened ever so slightly. If she hadn't been looking for it, she might have missed it. "So, between me being terrified for my life and worried about my family, I was frantic and not thinking clearly. I assume I went out the way you showed me, but I'm not sure if it was the same way or not. Like I said, it was late, dark, and I was frightened—especially when no one knew where you were. I needed you, and you weren't there."

"And you did this alone? With no one helping or guiding you?"

"Looking back, I wish I'd taken Lieutenant Markis with me. But like I said, I was afraid and not thinking clearly." The more she spoke, the easier the lies came.

"And once you exited the palace? Then what did you do?"

That was a very good question, and here was where things would get tricky. "I headed to the water where I found a boat. It was small. I have no idea who it belonged to. I'm so sorry if I stole someone's boat—I wasn't thinking. I used it to travel along the coastline. When day came, I found a dock. After tying the boat up, I traveled south on a road to the League's house in Nisk." In truth, she never would have been able to make it on her own back then. Now, she probably could thanks to everything Evander had taught her.

"And you did all of this alone?" He sounded skeptical.

"Yes, alone. Without the aid of another person." She folded her arms, annoyance setting in.

"Why not travel with Anton?"

"The thought never crossed my mind."

"Even though he's the one who told you about the League meeting?"

She shrugged. "All I could think about was getting away from your sister and the assassin. I needed protection, and I went to the League and my brother for that."

"You are the queen of Lynk, and I will protect you." His words sounded cold and lifeless.

"Then Lottie is in the dungeon where she can't hurt me?"

"I ordered for her to be locked in her room, and two men are guarding her. She won't hurt you."

Sabine pursed her lips, unconvinced that locking Lottie in her room would prevent her from scheming to seize the crown.

"Speaking of which," Rainer continued, "I'd like for you to remain in here as much as possible."

"Why?"

"It's the safest place for you."

She didn't respond because she had no intention of hiding in her room all day. Instead, she said, "Now that I've answered your questions, I'd like you to answer mine. Where were you the night of the masquerade? Why couldn't I find you in the palace?" As soon as she asked the question, she realized her mistake. If she'd escaped from the palace on her own and found the boat as she claimed, she would have run into Rainer and his men. Evander had a decently sized ship, so he hadn't traveled along the coastline. That was how he made it undetected.

Regardless, Rainer wouldn't admit what he had done that night. He would never reveal that he assassinated the Avoni delegation.

"Do you know Prince Evander?" He moved to the foot of the bed.

"Yes. I met him at the League's house." She needed to

tread carefully. "I also met the League members from Carlon and Nisk."

He tapped the footboard. "Until you've had a bleeding and I can be certain you're without a child, we will not be together as husband and wife."

A strange sense of relief filled her. "And once I have my cycle?"

"Then you will do what needs to be done to ensure I have a proper heir."

"Then you better make sure neither Lottie nor an assassin harm me. Otherwise, you'll be without an heir, and Lottie will take your throne."

He stilled. "You honestly think my sister is trying to overthrow me?"

"I don't think—I know."

A smile slid across his face. "How little you think of me to believe my own baby sister could outsmart me. I pray you don't make the same mistake." He sauntered to the door and paused. "I'm leaving first thing tomorrow morning. I won't be back for a few days." Without waiting for her to respond, he left, closing the door behind him.

Chapter Three

Between the stifling humidity and Sabine's restless thoughts trying to decipher what Rainer knew about her time with Evander, sleep eluded her. After tossing and turning for hours, she finally gave up and got out of bed before the sun had even risen. Since the king had left the palace, she needed to be as productive as possible and not squander this opportunity. She sent word to her brother and Markis to meet her at the front of the palace in thirty minutes. Then she searched through her closet until she located the bag she'd given to Markis to hide there. She opened it, pulling out her crown. Since the late queen's personal journal was still tucked inside, Sabine shoved the bag back behind her clothes, out of sight.

She quickly dressed and placed the crown atop her head. Satisfied with her appearance, she exited her room and headed to the front of the palace, her guards trailing her. It felt strange to walk the halls so early in the morning. While there weren't any nobles about, there were plenty of servants cleaning, carts of food being brought in, and the smell of baking bread wafted through the corridors.

Otto and Markis were already there waiting for her. They all quickly made their way across the bridge to the dirt road opposite it.

"Rainer didn't say where he was going or how long he'd be gone for?" Otto asked.

"No, he did not." Sabine couldn't imagine her father treating her mother that way.

"Since Rainer isn't here, there's no need for me to stay," Otto said. "Once we're done with this, let's make arrangements for me to return to Bakley with the missing children."

Sabine froze. "You don't think he's marching south right now to wage war, do you?" Her stomach rolled with nausea at the mere thought.

"We'll find out soon enough."

They reached the last building, the one right next to the edge of the cliff. Markis knocked on the door and an elderly woman opened it, granting them entrance. The room was lit by a single torch. The old woman knelt and opened a door built into the floor, revealing a steep staircase. Two of the guards began the descent.

"Are we going down there?" Otto asked, pointing at the opening.

"We are." Sabine remembered the first time she came here and how afraid she'd been to go into the ground like that.

Markis went next, waving for Otto to follow him.

"Thank you," Sabine said to the elderly woman, smiling at her.

The woman grunted.

Sabine went next, the remainder of her guards after her. Cold air wrapped around her as she descended the staircase. She'd only been down here once before, and she didn't remember it being this cold.

When Markis reached the door at the bottom, he knocked three times, then kicked it once. The door swung open, revealing an enormous cavern. Sabine prayed soldiers were there training and not marching south with Rainer.

"This is unbelievable," Otto mumbled as he stepped inside. He hadn't traveled through the lava tunnels like Sabine did, so there were a lot of things he didn't know about Lynk. "Is this *under* the town itself?"

"It is."

"If Bakley had something like this," Otto said, "we'd have a large army too." He went to the railing that overlooked the floor of the cavern twenty feet below where hundreds of people were running drills and training.

Relief filled Sabine—the soldiers were here. "If Bakley had this, then we'd have no flat land. I'd take hundreds of farms over this any day." She hated the heat and humidity and missed her horse, her barn, and even the flower fields.

"Now that we're here," Markis said, "how would you like to proceed?"

Focusing on the task at hand, she gripped the railing, trying to decide if she should just announce herself or give some sort of speech first.

"Your Majesty," a deep voice said, gaining her attention.

Sabine turned and spotted Felix approaching. "Commander, it's good to see you again."

He bowed. "What can I do for you this morning?"

"King Rainer thought it would be a good idea for the soldiers to swear fealty to me as soon as possible," Sabine said, the lie sliding right from her mouth.

He gave a curt nod. "Yes, excellent idea to do it at this hour. Almost everyone in the area is here."

"Are there many out of the area?" she asked, hoping Rainer hadn't taken a group of men to invade another kingdom or carry out some nefarious task.

Felix folded his arms. "At any given time, I'd say about half our forces are out on patrol or stationed throughout the kingdom. The rest remain here to be used at the king's discretion."

Relief filled her. It sounded like everything was proceeding as usual today. "I trust you can help me with this?"

"Of course, Your Majesty. Follow me." He led the way down to the bottom of the cavern.

The smell of sweat mixed with something else Sabine couldn't pinpoint hung heavy in the thick, stale air. She stood at one end of the cavern, her guards fanning out behind her. Commander Felix put two fingers to his mouth and whistled, garnering everyone's attention. He was about to say something when Sabine stepped forward, placing her hand on his arm.

When those present saw her, they dropped to one knee and bowed their heads.

"Please rise," Sabine said. "I would like a moment of your time."

Everyone stood, facing her.

Clearing her throat, she spoke loudly so everyone could hear. "I came here today because it is important to me to know those in my army. I want to make sure our kingdom remains strong, and you are all taken care of accordingly." She scanned the crowd, holding each gaze for a heartbeat, wanting to gain their trust.

"Since King Rainer and I married at the castle instead of here in the palace, you have not had a chance to swear fealty to me." In Bakley, only those holding a rank or high position in the army swore fealty. She wasn't sure how it was handled here in Lynk. Regardless, she wanted everyone to feel important, valued, and connected to her.

"If I may?" Felix asked her, his voice low.

She nodded, giving him the floor.

"I am honored to be able to swear my loyalty to my new queen." He knelt on one knee, swearing his allegiance to her. Then he stood and arranged everyone into two lines. Someone brought a chair for Sabine to sit on.

One by one, each soldier, dressed in casual training gear, came forward, saying the same words Felix had. It felt as if hours passed, her hand became sweaty from so many people touching it. However, she sat there, a smile on her face, the queen's crown atop her head. Otto, Markis, and Felix remained near her, overseeing it all, her guards checking each person before he or she stepped forward to make the declaration.

This was Rainer's army. He'd trained with them for years. Sabine was an outsider, a newcomer, and she needed to do everything in her power to show them that she could be the queen they needed her to be.

She sat there until every single person in the cavern swore fealty to her.

When they finally headed back to the palace, the sun was already high in the sky indicating half the day had passed. Her stomach growled with hunger, and her muscles ached from sitting for so long. If only she could ride a horse or run through a field. However, Lynk had neither of those things. Her mind, like it usually did, thought about Evander. If he were here, he'd probably stroll right up to her with that cocky grin of his. He'd say something to make her laugh—he always seemed to be doing that. Since she'd left him, had she laughed once? A genuine laugh? She missed him terribly.

"Is everything all right?" Otto asked as they crossed the bridge, returning to the palace.

"Yes," she replied. "I'm just tired after this morning."

He rubbed her back. "You did well today."

They were just about to step off the bridge when Captain

Lithane appeared in front of them. "Where have you been?" he demanded.

Sabine blinked, shocked by his blatant disrespect for her. Something would have to be done about this.

Otto took a step forward, into Lithane's personal space. "If we were in Bakley, I'd have you arrested."

Lithane's head jerked back.

"I am a prince," Otto scolded him. "And this is your queen. I can't imagine King Rainer putting up with this sort of behavior."

Lithane rolled his shoulders, as if irritated. "Forgive me, Your Highness."

Otto stepped back, rejoining Sabine.

"Queen Sabine," Lithane said. "Someone is here to see you. She is a local seamstress from town. Normally, I wouldn't have admitted her, but she said she had an appointment with you."

"Yes, I do."

"She's in the receiving room," Lithane said.

"Thank you." Eager to meet with the woman, Sabine hurried along. She spent the next several hours going over clothing designs and looking at fabric samples until she was certain she'd ordered everything she'd need.

Sabine headed to the library where she'd asked Axel and Anton to meet her. Both were already there sitting at one of the tables, waiting for her.

"It's not often I'm summoned to the library early in the evening," Axel said by way of greeting.

"Is that normally how you address your queen?" Sabine said, half-teasing as she slid onto the chair across from him.

Axel chuckled. "No, but that is how I address my sister-in-law." He winked.

"Anton, it's good to see you." *Alive.* "How was your journey back to Lynk?" A simple enough question that he could answer as he saw fit with Axel present.

"Eventful," Anton replied, scratching behind his ear. "It was good you traveled home by ship instead of accompanying me."

Sadness gripped her. The decoy must have been killed.

Anton patted her arm. "I'm glad you trusted your instincts," he whispered.

She hadn't even considered using a decoy until Evander had shown up with one at the house. It wasn't her instincts —it was Evander's.

"So, *sister*," Axel said, "why are we here?"

"I have a few questions," she started. "Do you know if Lottie is allowed to leave her bedchamber?" Rainer had said he'd put her there and had guards posted. "Or if she's allowed to receive visitors?"

"All I know is that Rainer refuses to have her arrested. He's sequestered her to her bedchamber. Beyond that, I have no idea," Anton said.

"Have either of you tried to see her?" she asked.

"Nope. It's only been a couple of days," Axel shrugged. "Maybe I'll feel the need to visit her in a month or two."

Sabine shook her head, wondering if he ever took anything seriously. "Do you know why Rainer won't have her officially arrested and charged with treason?" Was it simply because Lottie was his sister? Or was there more to it than that?

Anton shrugged. "One never knows with Rainer."

She nodded, as if she understood. "Tell me, what happens here in Lynk when a king, the person who is supposed to enforce laws, refuses to?" Could Rainer be arrested for failing to do his duties or did it not matter?

"That's a muddled notion," Anton said. "Technically, with Lottie, the only one accusing her of anything is you." When Sabine went to argue with him, he held up his hand. "If Lottie did something and everyone saw, it would force Rainer's hand. But this is more of a personal, family matter."

Sabine simmered with anger. None of this was fair.

Axel slouched in his chair, his head resting against the back of it as he stared up at the ceiling. "I've learned firsthand that a king can be above the law." His voice was quiet but sharp.

She recalled reading the journal from the late queen— Anton and Axel's mother. The journal had revealed that the late king was not Anton and Axel's father. When the king found out, he had his own wife killed for what she'd done. If that was within his rights, Sabine didn't know. "How are your laws made?"

Anton looked at her. "Are you serious?"

She didn't understand why her question would warrant that reaction from him.

"Do you honestly not know?" Anton asked, leaning forward on the table.

"I have not studied Lynk," she admitted, hating that she'd neglected her studies growing up. In her defense, she'd never thought she'd leave Bakley, let alone become a queen of another kingdom.

Anton tilted his head to the side. "Didn't you study how Bakley's laws are made?"

She pursed her lips. "No." She hated to admit it, but it was the truth. There had been no need for her to learn such things. Especially not when she had a horse to ride, a new dance to learn, or a possible suitor to charm.

Axel chuckled but didn't respond.

Anton rubbed his face. "The general gist of it is that the League created certain laws that all kingdoms must follow. The point is to prevent a war amongst ourselves. We must remain friendly and united should trouble arise from another continent. As such, certain laws are indisputable."

"I had no idea."

"Lynk can have additional laws made by the king and queen, but they can't negate or contradict rules the League sets forth."

Sabine sat there staring at Anton. She'd had no idea the amount of power he'd held by being a League member. "Thank you for explaining it to me," she said, her voice soft. This was another area she would have to read up on so she understood which laws were made by the League versus which ones were unique to Lynk.

"I must go." Anton stood. "I have a meeting to attend." At the exit to the library, Anton paused and looked pointedly at her. "While Rainer is away on his trip, use your time wisely." And with that, he left.

Axel chuckled, tilting his head to look at Sabine. "I have a feeling things are going to get interesting around here." He stood.

"Where are you off to?"

He shrugged, sliding his hands into his pockets. "Here... there. But I agree with Anton about time and using it wisely and all that." Whistling, he strolled out of the library.

Since Sabine didn't know when Rainer would return, time was of the essence. She dispatched a letter to Duchess Cassandra requesting her immediate assistance. The duchess arrived at the royal sitting room only minutes after receiving the letter.

"Your Majesty," Cassandra said with a curtsey.

"It is good to see you. Come, sit." Sabine motioned to the sofas. "Please help yourself." Plates with fruit and bread had been placed on the low table between them.

Cassandra took a small plate, adding a few grapes and a piece of rosemary bread. "Thank you for inviting me to the royal sitting room." Her lips pulled into a smile. "I'm glad you're back." She took a bite of her bread. "And you're the queen of Lynk."

"It is good to be back. I had a much needed visit with my brother," Sabine responded. "He returned to Lynk with me. I hope you'll get a chance to meet him before he leaves."

"May I speak freely, Your Majesty?"

"Please do." She folded her hands together.

"There's been a lot of speculation about what happened and why you left." She set her plate down. "Some say you were kidnapped, others say you ran away to be with your lover from Bakley, and there are even some who claim the king was forcing you to marry him against your will. Many are wondering why the two of you had a private ceremony. Everyone thought there would've been a big celebration. So when you disappeared, there were rumors galore."

A laugh escaped Sabine though she'd been trying to hold it in. "Those are all fanciful rumors, and none of them are true."

"Can I ask what really happened?"

"I went and visited my brother. That is all."

Cassandra peered over her shoulder, then lowered her voice. "After the masquerade, it was a bit of a spectacle around here. At first, the king acted as if you'd been kidnapped. He sent half the army out looking for you. Then, a few days later, he formally announced that the two of you had married and you'd been crowned queen. A few days after that, he announced that you were homesick and had gone to see your brother."

"That's the general gist of it," Sabine said, not wanting to give any more details on the matter. The less people who knew, the better. "Which is why I've asked you to meet me today. In Bakley, when one is crowned, people line up to swear fealty. Is that something done in Lynk?" She knew it was common practice across all kingdoms. She might not know how laws were made, but she knew how queens were.

Cassandra chuckled. "Yes, it is something we do. We've all been eagerly waiting for word of when it'll happen. It's one of the reasons so many of us are still here in the palace and haven't returned to our homes."

This was working out better than she'd hoped. "Perfect. Will you help me organize it? Let's hold it in two days in the throne room. Will that be enough time to inform everyone?"

"I would be honored. You write a decree, and I'll make sure that it's circulated properly."

Sabine stood and went over to the desk off to the side. She pulled out a piece of paper and a quill and began writing the decree, hoping she worded it correctly. Being from Bakley aided her in situations like this—if she made a mistake, she claimed it was how things were done in her kingdom. When she finished, she handed it to Cassandra.

"It is my pleasure to take care of this for you, Queen Sabine." She curtseyed.

Chapter Four

The following day, Sabine met privately with each of the dukes who were staying in the palace. She sat and listened to what each had to say, asking questions about their land, family, and if there were any issues she needed to be aware of. Most spoke carefully, supporting Rainer while expressing concern over going to war and not receiving the food shipments they were promised. Some even mentioned the high taxes they were forced to pay the crown—all for a good cause, of course. Regardless, Sabine had been able to read between the lines.

Exhausted, she put her nightdress on and curled up in her bed. Harta jumped up, snuggling near Sabine's feet. Since it was still early, she'd decided to read through the late queen's journal to see if there was any useful information in there. Right when she opened the cover, a knock resounded on her door.

"Your Majesty," Markis called out.

"Enter," she responded with a sigh.

He poked his head in. "Prince Axel is here to see you."

She'd had a long day and didn't want to deal with anyone. However, since Axel was her brother-in-law, she waved him in.

Axel sauntered inside, his hands in his pockets, his gaze roaming about the room.

Markis entered behind him, closing the door.

Axel peered over his shoulder. "You don't need to be here," he said to Markis. "The *queen* doesn't need a babysitter." He smirked.

"She doesn't, but you do," Markis said, not missing a beat. He stood next to the door, making it clear he'd remain there throughout this conversation.

"Suit yourself." Axel went out onto the balcony, his back to Sabine.

She rolled her eyes at how annoying Axel could be. After sliding off the bed, she carefully placed the journal under her mattress before straightening and pulling on her robe, tying it around her waist.

She went over to the archway, leaning against it as she watched Axel. "Why are you here?"

He shrugged. "No one has seen you all day. I just wanted to make sure you're still alive." He turned to face her. The sun had only just set, the sky casting an eerie glow across the balcony.

Sabine glanced back and spotted Markis diligently standing at his post, Harta now sitting beside him, both of them watching Axel. She tried to hide her smile.

"I'm alive. No one managed to kill me today." She folded her arms, waiting for him to get to the point of his visit.

He took a few steps closer to her. "Where were you today?" he asked, his voice low, barely above a whisper.

"I was utilizing my time wisely." He didn't need to know anything beyond that.

Axel chuckled. "Good. I'm glad." He didn't say anything else, as if waiting for her to elaborate.

"Is that all?" she asked.

"Yes, I just wanted to make sure you were alive." He winked, then strode past her.

Markis opened the door, letting Axel out.

"That was—" Markis didn't get to finish because Claire rushed into the room carrying a tray laden with food.

"Your Majesty," Claire said, setting the tray on the small table. "One of your guards said you hadn't eaten supper."

There'd been no time since she had back-to-back meetings all day. Her heart swelled from this kindness. "Thank you."

"Also, several packages were delivered for you today. After the guards went through them, they were brought to your room. The delivery boy said he was from a local seamstress's shop and that you'd ordered them?"

"I did."

"I put the new items in your closet for you."

"Thank you," Sabine said.

Claire curtseyed, then left the room.

"I'll leave you to yourself," Markis said. "You have a big day ahead of you tomorrow."

"Wait," Sabine said. "Have you heard anything about where Rainer went?"

"I haven't."

"Keep asking around. I'm more concerned with when he'll return than where he is."

"I'll see what I can find out."

As long as she made it through tomorrow before Rainer returned, she didn't care when he came back. The longer he stayed away, the better for her. "And if you can, train with the soldiers. I'd like to know what they think about their new queen and the state of the kingdom. I assume they'll speak more freely during a training session than if asked directly."

"Consider it done." He reached for the door handle.

"There's one more thing."

He paused.

"When Otto returns to Bakley, you're going with him." Even though she trusted Markis implicitly and wanted him at her side, he needed to go home to his family. He'd already been gone too long.

"Are you certain?"

"I think it's for the best." The people here would accept her more if there weren't any reminders of where she came from.

"I'll make sure your personal guards are up to par before I leave."

"Thank you."

He nodded and left the room.

Sabine and Harta stood there, staring at the door. "I think it's for the best." Reaching down, she pet her dog's head, trying to convince herself that she didn't need anyone from home to be there with her. Her wants didn't matter—all that did was keeping Markis safe.

The next morning, Sabine stood on her balcony, a light rain falling. Since it so rarely rained in Lynk, she came out here to revel in it, and it reminded her of Avoni. Tipping her head back, she could almost imagine she was on the canal with Evander.

Tears welled in her eyes, but she refused to let them fall. She had no idea if she'd ever see Evander again. Thinking about him would do her no good. Her focus had to be on

Lynk and stopping Rainer from going to war. The king claimed he'd rescued the Bakley children from ships manned by Avoni people. The children were supposed to be here in Lynk. It was time for her to find out where they were and prepare them for their journey home to Bakley.

But just for a moment, here in the silence, in the rain, she would allow herself to think about Evander. Her assassin-pirate-prince. His smile, piercing green eyes, and dark red hair. His laugh, him nudging her, the feel of his hand in hers. The way he made her feel, his friendship, their banter.

Forcing herself to take a deep breath, she shoved all memories of him away. There was a lot she had to do today, and she needed to focus on that. She just wished the fog wasn't so heavy and the rain so misty. It reminded her too much of where she wanted to be. Of where she'd left her heart.

She went back inside—it was time to get ready for the day.

After having a small breakfast, she dressed, saving her new outfits for when Rainer returned. Satisfied with her appearance, she placed the crown atop her head and exited her room.

As she headed to the throne room, her guards trailing her, Markis came to her side.

"I have some of the information you requested," he said, his voice soft so it wouldn't carry.

"And?" she asked.

"The soldiers I spoke to don't seem to have a strong opinion one way or the other about you." At each intersection, he scanned the hallways before allowing her to cross.

"Anything else?"

"The king left with a dozen soldiers. Word is he will be back in a week."

"But no location or destination?"

"No."

When they reached the throne room, Sabine paused and faced Markis. "And what is my brother up to?" She hadn't seen him at all yesterday.

"He and I are going to do a little reconnaissance while everyone is distracted," he whispered. "The rest of your guards will escort you inside and remain with you. Prince Otto and I will see you after."

"Very well." She turned and strode into the throne room, wishing she was going on a mission with Markis and Otto rather than attending this formal event. However, this was important, so she would force a smile on her lips and get through it.

Much to her delight, the throne room was already filled with people. She glided along the aisle. When she reached the dais, she gracefully went up the steps and stood before the royal throne, facing those gathered.

Anton separated from the crowd and joined her on the dais. "If I may?" he asked her, his voice a whisper.

She gave a curt nod.

"Thank you all for gathering today to celebrate our newly crowned queen," Anton bellowed so everyone in the room could hear.

Sabine didn't think she'd ever heard him make a speech in public before.

"At Queen Sabine's coronation, I pledged my fealty to her. Today, I will stand as witness as you all pledge your loyalty to her as well. We'll begin with the dukes and duchesses."

Sabine sat as people began lining up.

Anton took out paper and a quill. "I'll record everyone who attends today," he murmured close to her ear.

"Thank you." Markis had already informed her that one of her guards was compiling a list of everyone presently in the palace. Anyone who didn't show today would be watched.

Anton gestured for the first couple to approach.

Duchess Cassandra and her husband came forward and pledged their fealty, followed by the remaining dukes and duchesses. After they were done, anyone with a title came forward in no particular order. There were far more people in attendance than Sabine had realized. Once the nobility finished, the rest of the people in the palace began swearing their fealty to her. Even some of the servants came forward to take her hand and kiss her ring. After several hours, the room finally emptied out.

"I'll make a copy of this and get it to you," Anton said. "I'm sure Lieutenant Markis will want to see it."

"Thank you for coming today and for your help."

"Of course. This should have been done a long time ago. I'm glad it's finally taken care of. As Lynk's League member, I am responsible for making sure these things are handled properly." He bowed, then left.

Sabine returned to her room and found she'd already received a handful of invitations. Anyone of importance either invited her to supper or was throwing a small party in her honor to celebrate her coronation. Sabine immediately responded and accepted each invitation.

When Otto and Markis joined her that evening, they told her they'd discovered the location of the Bakley children in the palace. The two of them had spent the day talking with them, trying to find out the truth of who'd taken them and what really happened. Otto said he was fairly certain he knew the culprit but wanted to refrain from saying who until he had solid proof. He asked Sabine how well she knew the commander and if he would be willing to speak to her on the matter. She wasn't sure, so she sent a letter to Felix, summoning him to a meeting.

The following days were filled with Sabine attending gathering after gathering. She always made sure to dress in appropriate Lynk attire, she wore her crown, and she tried to get to know each of her subjects on a personal level. Her goal was simple: to win each and every one of them over. While she knew it couldn't be accomplished with a single event, it was at least a start.

Sabine and Otto were seated in the royal family's dining room enjoying breakfast, Axel and Anton nowhere in sight, when Markis announced Commander Felix's arrival.

"Come in and join us," Sabine said, motioning for him to take a seat at the table.

He did so while Markis remained next to the doorway.

"What can I do for you, Your Majesty?" Felix asked.

Sabine set her fork down and observed the older man. He'd probably been a soldier in the king's army for at least three decades. As the commander of the army, he should be aware of the king's plans.

"Now that I'm the queen of Lynk," she began, "I am trying to get up to speed on the state of affairs. I'd like a detailed report of all orders the king has given to the military over the past year."

He nodded. "I can put that together for you. However, it'll take me some time to gather everything."

"The sooner the better," she replied.

"Is there anything specific you're looking for?"

"Like I mentioned, I want to be brought up to speed on the kingdom's affairs." She took a sip of tea. When she set the cup down, she said, "I am curious if there's anything in there with regards to Bakley. Specifically, the children that were taken, then subsequently found."

"I spoke with some of the children," Otto said. "They claim they were used to make arrow tips."

Felix didn't respond.

"Commander," Sabine said, "is that true?"

"Yes." One word. Nothing more. He kept his focus on her, as if waiting for a follow-up question.

"Did Lynk steal the children from Bakley?" Sabine held her breath, afraid of the answer.

"Yes."

Otto cursed, shoving his chair back from the table. Sabine reached over, placing her hand on his arm, letting him know he needed to be quiet so she could get more information from Felix.

"Why did Rainer tell me he found them on a boat?" Sabine had lost her appetite, so she shoved her plate away.

"After the children were used to make the necessary weapons, they were put on a boat and brought here to the palace."

"When I spoke to them," Otto said, "they seemed confused as to who had taken them."

Sabine knew Felix wouldn't answer unless she forced him to with a direct order. "What were the children told about those who had taken them?"

The corners of Felix's mouth turned up, and Sabine knew she'd asked the right question.

"They were told the men who stole them from their homes were from Avoni. They were told they needed to make weapons because Avoni had none. Then, when the job was done, Lynk soldiers miraculously found them, put them on a boat, and brought them here."

Rainer had lied. He'd sent word to her father that he'd found the children on ships manned by Avoni soldiers. But Avoni had nothing to do with this. Relief filled her—Evander hadn't been a part of it at all. Back when she'd first heard about Avoni's possible involvement, Evander had been furious that she'd even questioned him.

Regardless of what had happened, at least the children had been found and were safe. Her priority was getting those children home to their families before anything else happened to them. "Prince Otto will be escorting the children home," she said.

"I'll make sure Prince Otto has everything necessary for the journey."

Sabine took another sip of her tea.

"Is there anything else I can do for you this morning?" Felix asked.

"What does Rainer plan to do with the army? Does he plan to invade Carlon and Nisk? Is he going to declare war?"

Felix took a deep breath, letting it out slowly as he sat back in his chair, watching her. After a moment, he rubbed his eyes. "Yes," he replied.

Although Sabine had guessed this was what Rainer intended to do, hearing it confirmed by the commander of the army turned Sabine's blood cold.

"Do you know why the king wishes to invade the kingdoms to the south of us?"

"We're told we need food," he answered. "But I've heard the king mention wanting to get rid of the League. Beyond that, your guess is as good as mine."

"Can I ask you a personal question?" Sabine inquired.

"Yes, Your Majesty."

She rubbed her temple. "Do you agree with what King Rainer plans to do?"

He sat there staring at her for a long minute before answering. "My wife likes you. She believes you're what this kingdom needs. I'm a commander, my son a captain. Neither of us wants to see a war. We'd both be at the front lines. And, well, there are other, more personal reasons. I've been around for a long time. I'm in my fifties. I'd like to live the rest of my days on my land. I'd like my family—my *entire* family—to be with me. I believe the League was put in place for a reason and wish our king would follow and respect the rules set forth by the League."

Unease filled Sabine. While she'd known Rainer was breaking the League's rules, she hadn't fully realized he'd wanted to dismantle the League entirely. The other kingdoms would ban together against Lynk. But Lynk had the strongest army of all. "I'm told we have ships off the coast of Carlon and tent cities with men ready to storm into Carlon and Nisk?"

"We do."

Sabine gripped her hands together. "Do I have the authority to give you orders?"

He smiled. "You are my queen."

Hope filled her. "I want the ships called back to Lynk, I want the tent cities torn down, and I want the soldiers to go back to wherever it is they're normally stationed."

Felix leaned forward, his forearms on the table. "You must understand what you're doing. If the other kingdoms decide to come against us, we'll be defenseless."

"But I don't want to go to war."

"Understandable. What about defending ourselves?"

She hadn't considered that.

"And what of the king?" Felix asked. "When he finds out what you've done, he'll not only be furious, but he'll undo your orders."

In other words, she needed to give different instructions. "What do you suggest?"

"No one has ever asked me that before."

"Are you not the commander? Wouldn't your advice be the most valuable of all?"

He leaned back, considering her. "Personally, I'd move the

ships north so they're still in play but off Lynk's shoreline, close to the border. I'd leave the tent cities right where they are—but I'd give them different orders. Perhaps focus on training, running drills, protecting our border—not preparing to attack. Then, hopefully, no one will discover their orders have changed. Does that make sense?"

She nodded. "That is a good idea." She chewed on her bottom lip, thinking it through.

"Prince Otto, if I may be so bold to offer a recommendation," Felix mumbled. "If I were you, I'd leave as soon as possible. When King Rainer returns, Queen Sabine is going to have a fight on her hands. You don't want to be used as leverage against the queen. The less people here who love or care about her, the better."

"How can you serve a king you think so little of?" she asked.

"You forget he is a new king. A young king. I served under another man for many years. A good man. When the old king died, the commander retired. King Rainer appointed me as the new commander. I thought it was a great opportunity. Now that I know the king better, now that I know his plans and what he's capable of." He shrugged. "However, I swore allegiance to him and the throne."

"Luckily for you, I am now on the throne and can help you."

He nodded. "More importantly, you can help all of Lynk."

Just then, a messenger ran into the room. "Your Majesty," a young man said as he bowed. "A letter from the king of Bakley."

Sabine took the letter, examining the seal. It was, indeed, from her father.

"I'll take my leave," Felix said as he stood. "I'll get that full report to you as soon as possible." He left the room.

Sabine tore the letter open and read it.

"What does it say?" Otto asked, leaning over her shoulder.

She read the words but they didn't register. "I don't understand."

"Our brother, Viktor, is getting married?" Otto said.

Sabine couldn't imagine her brother married. At least not Viktor. He wasn't even next in line to marry—Otto was.

"He is to marry Princess Carin, Evander's sister," Otto said. "She's the youngest of the three Avoni princesses, correct?"

"Yes," Sabine answered. During her stay in Avoni, she'd only spoken with Carin a couple of times. Sabine had been closer to Gemma since Gemma showed up to help when Evander had been injured.

"What do you know about her?" Otto asked.

"Carin is beautiful, but I don't know if her personality will match Viktor's since I don't know her that well." She couldn't imagine Viktor married to an assassin. "This is..." Surprising. Shocking. Unexpected.

"Viktor is probably upset I wasn't home to enter into negotiations instead of him." He chuckled. "Pity."

"Why the necessary union between Bakley and Avoni?" she mused.

"Read the letter again. Father has a coded message in there." Otto stood and began pacing the room. "It's genius really. Avoni and Bakley are aligned, just like Lynk and Bakley. Lynk can't make a move against Avoni now. The marriage ensures Avoni is safe from an attack."

"I thought that was the purpose of Prince Evander marrying Princess Lottie?"

Otto chuckled. "She can't marry him if she's in the dungeon or dead."

After she'd met and talked with King Kai from Avoni, she couldn't imagine him aligning his kingdom with Bakley's.

And, to be honest, a small part of her felt as if a knife had pierced her heart. If she'd been home, maybe she could have married Evander. Cursing her fate, she shoved back from the table and stood, needing to do something.

"Where are you going?" Otto asked.

She peered over at him. "Up for a little mischief?"

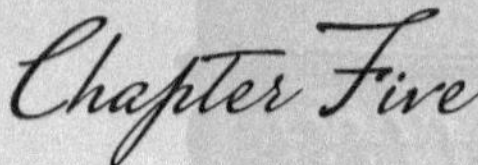

Chapter Five

Sabine and Otto crossed the bridge, her guards following close behind.

"I'm glad we're out of the palace," Otto said. "I've been wanting to talk to you."

She peered at him sidelong. "About what?"

He whispered, "You need to be careful with Rainer."

A dark laugh escaped her lips. "Trust me, I know—I'm married to him." While she didn't know him well, the fact that he'd had the entire Avoni delegation killed, kidnapped the Bakley children, and planned to wage war was more than enough for her not to like the guy.

"The longer I'm here," Otto said, "the more I hear about him that is disturbing."

"Like what?" She couldn't imagine what else there could possibly be.

"His temper is brought up repeatedly."

"By whom?" She wondered who he'd been talking to and where his information came from.

"Guards, soldiers, some of the nobles in the palace. Just be careful."

Sliding her arm around his, she pulled him closer. "Thank you for caring. But you don't need to worry about me. I've got this." He likely wouldn't believe her false bravado. However, she needed to assure him so he'd leave. The longer he stayed, the more she feared for his life.

He patted her hand. "I really hope so."

They stepped off the bridge and headed along the main road, into town.

"What, exactly, is your plan for today?" Otto asked, nodding at the first set of buildings they were about to pass.

She dropped her brother's arm and opened her arms out wide. "This is my kingdom; these are my people. I want to get to know them." She reached up, making sure her crown was in place.

"And why is this considered mischief?" he asked.

"Rainer asked me to stay in my room for my own safety. When he finds out I've been wandering the palace, he'll be upset. When he finds out I've been in the town, he'll be livid." A smile slid across her face.

"And your goal is to upset the man?" he asked incredulously.

"No, that's just a perk."

The streets were crowded and many began to notice her. The people moved to the sides of the street, bowing, allowing her and her brother to pass through the center untouched.

"All right," Otto mumbled, "you've got their attention. Now what?"

"We shop."

The two of them entered the blacksmith store on the right. Sabine introduced herself to the owner and asked about the swords and weapons he forged. A small dagger with a handle made for a woman caught her eye, so she bought it. The next store she went to sold jewelry. She perused through the necklaces and bracelets before buying a couple of items. Next, she went to a leather store where she bought a belt for Otto.

The two of them continued shopping, buying something from each store they entered. By the time they reached the end of the main street, her guards had their arms full with food, wine, clothes, bags, and other various items.

Word spread quickly that the queen was out buying goods. Many came to catch a glimpse of her while children began bringing her bundles of stonecrop. The beautiful pink flower was one of her favorite colors.

Seeing the citizens of the kingdom she ruled over made her realize she needed to make a point of shopping here at least once a week and employing some of these people in the palace. Since this town was so close to the crown, she wondered if all towns were as well off as this one, or if this was the exception. Once she figured out how to stop the upcoming war, she'd find a way to visit the other towns in Lynk. It was time she got to know all her people.

Back in her room, which was now filled with flowers thanks to the children from the town, Sabine plopped onto her bed, exhausted. Harta jumped up and lay beside her, licking her face. Sabine laughed.

Someone knocked on her door. She groaned, too tired to get up to answer it. "Who's there?" she called out.

Markis stepped inside. "Your Majesty, Prince Anton is here to see you."

She waved him closer. "Do you know what it's about?" she whispered.

"No. But everyone in the palace is talking about what you and Prince Otto did today. My guess is it has something to do with that."

If that was the case, then she could speak with Anton. "While we were out, were you able to do what I asked?"

"I'll discuss that with you later."

"Okay, let Anton in." She sat up but remained on her bed. It was probably better to use the royal rooms for receiving guests, but this was just Anton and those rooms felt like Rainer's, not hers.

Markis opened the door, admitting Anton.

"Queen Sabine, may I have a word in private?" Anton asked, eyeing Markis.

She nodded and Markis left the room, closing the door behind him. It surprised her that her guard would leave her alone with Anton but not Axel.

"Is everything okay?" she asked, petting Harta.

"There's not much that goes on in this kingdom that I'm not aware of," he said, coming farther into the room, his posture relaxed.

As the king's spymaster, Sabine assumed Anton knew a great deal about the goings on in the kingdom.

"Commander Felix dispatched two highly confidential letters today," he said.

Her hand froze on Harta. She blinked several times, not sure how to handle this situation. Not once had she considered Anton learning about her conversation with Felix.

"Obviously, I had my spies read the letters."

Closing her eyes, she wished she could go back in time and insist Felix send a single messenger to deliver her instructions verbally. Only, that would have meant even more people being aware of the changes she'd issued. The less who knew, the better.

"Rainer is going to kill you when he finds out what you did," he said, his voice low.

"If," she murmured, "if Rainer finds out." She kept her

focus on Harta, refusing to look at Anton and read the judgement that was sure to be on his face.

"How are you going to keep this from him?"

"No one knows."

"My spy who intercepted the letter knows. I know. The captains in charge of the army camps and on the boats know. That's at least six people."

And Otto knew but she kept that to herself. "There's no reason for any of those six people to willingly tell Rainer anything." If Anton decided to keep his mouth shut, she would get away with it. It all depended on the prince.

He perched on the side of her bed, near her feet. "What's your goal?"

"Peace." At that, she finally looked him in the eyes so he'd know she was serious.

His eyes remained on hers as if searching for something. "Even if you manage to pull this off—and that's a very big if —you may save the other kingdoms but destroy this one in the process."

"I don't think Lynk is so fragile that it can be ruined by peace." To stop this war, she needed Anton on her side and willing to help her. "And what about the League?"

"What about it?"

"Are you aware that Rainer intends to destroy it?"

His eyes narrowed. "What do you mean *destroy* it?

"He doesn't want it to exist any more. He wants to make his own laws instead of being under the League's rule." Harta jumped up and trotted out onto the balcony. Sabine pulled her feet under her, fidgeting with a string on her bed.

"Are you certain?" Anton asked.

"I am." When he didn't respond, she decided to push him. "Where do your loyalties lie?" She'd asked him this very thing back in Nisk when he'd questioned her about her own loyalty. Would Anton uphold the League's rules and stand with the League? Or would he side with and follow Rainer? At some point, he would have to choose because he couldn't be loyal to both.

He ran a hand through his hair, the only sign of his agitation.

"Why did you come here? To warn me? Arrest me?"

"Technically, no laws have been broken." He sighed. "I came to hear your side. That is all. I should go." He stood and started to head to the door.

"Wait." Sabine hadn't considered doing this until this very moment. "I have something for you." Reaching under her mattress, she pulled out the late queen's journal. She came and stood before Anton. "I found this at the castle when I married Rainer. This belongs to you. You and Axel." She handed it to him.

His hands shook as he reached for the journal. "Is this my mother's?"

"Yes. It was in the room I stayed in."

He took it, his eyes filling with tears as he carefully opened the cover and read over the first page. "Why are you giving this to me now?" He closed the journal.

"I don't know Rainer well like you do," she said. "At first, I didn't think he was like his father, but the more I learn, the more I wonder about that. And it scares me."

"My step-father was a monster."

"And Rainer?" she asked, her voice barely audible, afraid of the answer.

"He is the same."

A monster disguised as a handsome king made him all the more dangerous. "You should know that my plan is to stop the monster by any and all means," she whispered. "Even if that means sacrificing myself."

"You'd do that for Lynk?"

"For Lynk, Bakley, all the other kingdoms. I don't want a

needless war where fathers, husbands, brothers, and lovers die. The League has kept us at peace and it needs to remain in place."

"Can I keep this?" he asked, placing his palm on the cover.

"It belongs to you." While she'd wanted to read through it to discover more about the past, hoping it would give her insight into Rainer, this belonged to Anton since it was his mother's, and she had no right to keep it to herself.

"Rainer doesn't deserve you." He made no move to go. "Be careful. I'll do what I can on my end."

Hope bloomed in her chest since this meant they were allies on some level. He'd already proven he could keep a secret and was beginning to earn her trust. "Can I ask you something?"

He lifted the journal. "After giving me this, you can ask me anything."

"Did Rainer give the order to kill the entire Avoni delegation?" For some reason, she'd feel better knowing it came from one of the captains instead.

His face darkened. "Yes. I didn't know about it until after I returned from meeting with you in Nisk. It was a top secret mission that Rainer planned and executed with a handful of men. Not even the commander knew ahead of time."

Back in Avoni, Queen Serilda mentioned to Sabine that Rainer might have assumed Sabine was on that ship as well. It had been bothering her ever since. "Did Rainer think I was on it? Did he try to kill me?" At first, she'd assumed he wouldn't dare do something so bold. After all, he needed her alive in order to have an heir in time to keep his throne. But lately, she'd been reconsidering.

"Honestly, I don't know."

"How do we enforce the rules?" she asked, wondering if she had the authority to arrest Rainer. And if she did, would she be able to maintain control over Lynk and the military? "I want to stop him before he hurts more people."

Anton sighed. "It won't be easy to stop him, but it's possible. Messy, but possible."

That was what she'd assumed. In order to stop Rainer, she'd have to destroy him. The problem was if she took him down, she'd take down Axel, Anton, and Lottie with him. She might very well be willing to sacrifice herself for others, but she didn't know if Anton was, and she didn't think she had the right to ask that of him.

Sabine stood on her balcony overlooking the lush valley below. It had been an hour since Markis was supposed to be there to meet with her to go over what he'd learned from his investigation. It had been an hour of worrying and wondering where he was. Hopefully, he hadn't gotten himself into trouble. Unable to wait any longer, Sabine pushed off the railing and exited her room, heading to Duchess Marin's suite. The duchess was hosting a small gathering for only a few noble women to congratulate Sabine on her marriage and coronation.

As she made her way through the palace, she noticed only four of her regular six guards trailing her. She wanted to ask where the other two and Markis were. However, she didn't want to draw attention to the fact that she had fewer guards, and there must be some problem they were dealing with.

The duchess had a designated wing in the palace with several rooms, all westerly facing. The large sitting room opened to an expansive balcony. Tall vases filled with flowers of all kinds were spread throughout the room. Several tables with platters of food had been set up for today. Servants walked around handing out drinks.

A single sentry stood guard at the door. When he announced the queen, the approximately fifty people present bowed and curtseyed. Sabine greeted everyone and thanked them for coming to the gathering. Duchess Marin came forward, giving a heartfelt toast, and conversations resumed.

"Has there been any word on where our king is?" the duchess asked as she looped her arm through Sabine's, leading her out onto the balcony where there were less people.

"No," Sabine said. "It's rather sad that he just left without informing me or anyone else what he was doing." Sabine took a goblet from a servant and pretended to drink.

Lady Karmen came over, joining them. "Still no word on the king?"

Sabine shook her head. "I'm worried about my life and safety here in the palace." She leaned forward, taking these women into her confidence. "Princess Lottie hired the assassin who killed Princess Alina. I overheard her ordering the assassin to kill me. The king knows yet he's only sequestered his sister to her rooms. I don't know if he plans to do anything else."

Both women shook their heads.

"You'd think he'd want to seek justice for his new bride," Marin said.

"Maybe that's what he's off doing," Karmen suggested. "He could be hunting down the assassin to make sure our queen is safe."

That couldn't be the case since Evander had already taken care of the assassin. However, she guessed Lottie could have hired another one. Although, if anything happened to Sabine, everyone would know Lottie was behind it. The princess couldn't afford for something like that to happen right now.

Commotion came from the sitting room, and Markis

emerged onto the balcony a moment later. "Forgive me, Your Majesty," he said. "I need a moment of your time."

"Of course." She led him over to the side of the balcony where no one would overhear their conversation. "What's going on?"

"King Rainer is returning tonight."

She'd thought she'd have more time.

"Prince Otto is loading as many of the youngest Bakley children as he can fit onto his ship as we speak. The rest will travel with me by foot. We are going to leave as soon as possible."

"Will you be able to leave in time?" She feared for what would happen if Rainer returned and caught them.

"Yes, thanks to Commander Felix. He made sure all the necessary supplies were boarded earlier today."

"Excellent." Though she wasn't ready to part from Otto and Markis. It would mean that she was truly alone. The thought of not having Markis at her side unsettled her. However, he would be safer in Bakley, and she was certain his family missed him. His place was there, not here.

"I've spoken with your guards and told them I'm leaving. Captain Drew will be taking over for me. I've already gone over as much as I can with him, and I believe he wants to keep you safe and will do what's in your best interest."

"Thank you for everything." The words didn't seem adequate, since he had been with her from the start and had done so much to help her. She wanted to tell him not to go, that she trusted no one else but him. But she couldn't. He needed to go home.

"It has been an honor serving you." He bowed then left.

Sabine stood there, watching his retreating back until he disappeared from view. It felt as if she'd just fallen into a lake and didn't know which way was up.

"Is everything all right, Your Majesty?" Lady Regina said as she came to stand beside her.

"Yes." She forced a smile on her face, trying to keep her breathing slow and steady. "How's your husband, Commander Felix, doing?"

"He's doing well but wishes to retire," she said sardonically. "He wants to spend his days at home, playing with his grandchildren."

Sabine nodded as if she understood. There would never be a day where she could retire. But if she was able to, she imagined living someplace like where she'd grown up, surrounded by a loving family like hers. Evander's image came to mind.

"I don't want to monopolize your time," Regina said, "and it looks like there are others who wish to talk with you."

Sabine spoke to a few other people before excusing herself from the party. Out in the hallway, her guards stood waiting for her. Before Rainer returned that evening, she wanted to speak with someone. Squaring her shoulders, she said, "Take me to Princess Lottie's room."

Chapter Six

Sabine stared at Lottie's door, willing herself to find the courage to confront the woman responsible for Alina's death. The injustice of it burned—Lottie resting comfortably in her opulent bedchamber watched by only two sentries.

"Shall I knock for you, Queen Sabine?" Drew asked.

She shook her head, shifting her weight from foot to foot, trying to get her thoughts in order. Trying to keep her temper under control. The second she passed the threshold, her defenses had to be up. The purpose of her visit was twofold —get the princess to confess so Sabine's guards could overhear and try to understand why Lottie had Alina killed.

With Rainer's imminent return at any moment, Sabine couldn't wait any longer. Lifting her arm, she knocked.

The door flew open. "Oh," Lottie said, jerking back, away from Sabine. "I thought you were a servant delivering my food." Lottie wore a simple green dress, setting off her dark hair which hung in waves down her back. "What do *you* want?" The door remained only partially open, blocking Sabine's view into the room.

"Is that any way to greet your queen?" Sabine asked.

"What do you want, *Your Majesty*?" Lottie's voice dripped with sarcasm.

"We are now sisters," Sabine said. "Funny how that works. I had a sister, one I loved very much, and you had her killed. I was sister-less. Then I married your brother, and now you and I are sisters-in-law." Sabine stared into Lottie's cold, emotionless eyes. She clutched her hands together, afraid she'd reach forward and strangle the woman.

"Are you here to gloat?" Lottie asked, one hand on her hip, making no move to invite Sabine inside.

"Gloat? That I'm alive and the assassin you hired didn't kill me?" This woman was delusional if that was what she thought.

Lottie shrugged. "I suppose it doesn't matter now." She peered at the guards standing a respectable distance away. A slow smile spread across her face as she leaned forward and whispered, "I'm going to marry an assassin. Maybe I'll have him teach me the art of killing so I can finish the job myself." She straightened and folded her arms across her chest.

Red flashed across Sabine's vision—not for the threat to her life, but for the reminder that Lottie was going to marry Evander. She suddenly found it hard to breathe.

Lottie chuckled. "I heard stories from my contacts." She leaned against the doorframe. "I can see they must be true based upon your reaction. Interesting. I'm glad I said something to Rainer. He has a right to know you've been unfaithful."

Cold dread filled Sabine. "You're the one who told Rainer about..." She didn't finish that sentence since her guards could hear every word spoken. "I have not been unfaithful to my husband."

"You keep telling yourself that." Lottie suddenly straightened. "I'd ask you to come in, but I neither like you nor want to be in your company any longer than necessary." She started to close the door.

"Wait," Sabine practically shouted. "I just want to know why."

Lottie stopped, the door half concealing her body now. "Why what?"

"Why did you have Alina killed? Why send an assassin after me?" Not that having a reason would justify or make it better, but Sabine needed some sort of closure and for it to make sense. Some explanation other than power.

When Lottie didn't respond, Sabine took a step closer and said, "Are you jealous that your brother rules over Lynk instead of you?"

Lowering her voice, Lottie said, "You don't deserve to wear Lynk's crown. You're not even from here."

"I can understand that sentiment. But why de-throne your own brother?"

Lottie smiled, as if Sabine had told her a juicy tidbit of gossip. "That's for me to know and you to find out. Good luck."

The door slammed shut in Sabine's face, causing her to jump back in shock. The guards all looked to one another, not sure how to respond to the blatant form of disrespect.

Sabine addressed the sentries posted at Lottie's door. "Is the princess allowed to have visitors?"

"No, Your Majesty," the one on the right answered.

"Has anyone attempted to see her?"

"The princes have both visited her, Your Majesty."

"Does someone bring her food?" she asked.

"Yes, Your Majesty."

"Who inspects it?"

"Sorry?"

"Once the food arrives, do you or whomever is on guard check the tray for weapons, letters, or poison?"

He blinked, as if the thought had never occurred to him.

"The princess is in there because she killed Princess Alina and sent an assassin after me. Someone needs to be checking anything going into or coming out of that room in case she's trying to contact another assassin." Fury filled her because no one seemed to be taking this threat seriously.

"I'm sorry, Your Majesty. I will see that things are inspected from here on out."

"Thank you." She turned and strode away, irate for a host of reasons. The most illogical one was Lottie's betrothal to Evander. Deep down, Sabine knew that Rainer agreed to the union to get rid of Lottie so he wouldn't have to put her on trial for treason. It wasn't fair. And, perhaps, a deeper part of her heart was torn because she had grown rather fond of Evander. While she knew she was married to Rainer and nothing could ever happen between her and the prince from Avoni, she cared for him, loved him even. And Lottie—the woman who'd had Alina killed—was going to get to marry him. The unfairness of it gutted Sabine, making her want to scream.

When she reached the corridor leading to the royal wing, a handful of guards ran by. Drew stepped forward, next to her, his hand on the hilt of his sword.

"What's wrong?" she whispered, afraid to move or raise her voice.

Drew dropped his hand. "Those were King Rainer's men. My guess is he's either been spotted in town or he just arrived at the palace. His men are going to greet him."

With an irritable and heavy heart, Sabine couldn't face Rainer tonight. If she returned to her room, he would easily be able to find her. If he found her, he'd want to talk to her. She didn't have the energy for that right now.

Instead of turning toward the royal rooms, she headed the opposite direction to one of the smaller courtyards. Only, when she arrived, several couples were sitting in alcoves or on benches, not affording her the peace she craved.

As she turned to leave, she spotted Axel with his arm draped over the shoulder of a young woman. They were heading across the courtyard to one of the arches leading to the royal wing. Sighing, Sabine exited through a different archway, not wanting to run into Axel and his dalliance.

Back home in Bakley, one of her favorite things to do was ride her horse late at night through the fields when thousands upon thousands of stars dotted the sky. It had always soothed her soul and made her feel content. Lynk had no fields and only a few horses used mostly by the military—but it did have stars.

"I wish to go to the turret with the rooftop," Sabine said to Drew. "Can you take me there, please?"

"Of course, Your Majesty." He led the way along several corridors, bypassing the royal wing, until they came to a steep staircase. "Please wait here." He ran up the stairs, returning a moment later. "It's all clear." He stepped aside and gestured for her to proceed. "We'll wait here."

It surprised her that he was giving her a reprieve from her guards. Instead of questioning it, she ran up the stairs to the top of the turret. The stars shone brightly in the sky. A light wind made a few strands of her hair dance across her face. Tipping her head back, she smiled. It was so beautiful and peaceful up here that she could almost imagine she was at home in Bakley.

Gazing at the stars, she wondered what Evander was doing right now. Maybe he was even looking up at the stars like she was. Then she chuckled, remembering that Avoni had a constant cover of clouds. Most likely, Evander was off on some mission or maybe even at a tavern meeting with members of his assassin guild. She'd mistakenly hoped being here in Lynk with Rainer would have made it easier to forget about the Avoni prince. However, with each day, she felt his absence more acutely.

Going over to the railing, she leaned her arms on it, staring out toward the ocean in the distance.

"I thought I'd find you up here," Axel said from behind her.

She didn't bother looking over her shoulder at him. "What do you want?"

He came and leaned on the railing next to her. "I had nothing to do, so I came to check on you."

At that, she looked at him sidelong. "I thought you'd be busy with that beautiful woman I saw you with."

His lips curled into a smile and he shrugged, not bothering to give her an answer.

"Why are you really here?" He wouldn't have sought her out without a good reason.

"Rainer is back."

She nodded. "I know."

"Are you up here avoiding him?"

She chuckled because she was, but she wasn't about to tell him that. "Have you spoken with him?"

"No." He turned, his back leaning against the railing as he folded his arms across his chest. "Can I ask you something?"

"You can ask." She didn't know if she'd answer.

"What are you planning?"

"What do you mean?" She needed to tread carefully.

"Did your brother and Markis both leave?" He tilted his head, looking at her for confirmation.

"They did."

He nodded slowly. "Behind Rainer's back?"

Technically, yes. "I can't help it if he's not here when decisions need to be made."

He chuckled, looking up at the stars, as if they held the answer.

"So what are you planning to do?"

"Who says I'm planning anything?" He'd done nothing to earn her trust or confidence.

"Can I offer you some advice?" he said.

"You can offer."

"Be careful."

His words mirrored her brother's. "I always am." If Axel had a specific concern, then he needed to tell her instead of being vague.

"Rainer likes to carry grudges. He trusts no one, confides in no one, and *always* gets his way."

She nodded, filing that information away to dissect later.

"I spoke to Lottie," he said. "She admitted to hiring the assassin." His right hand rubbed the side of his face. "Honestly, I'm surprised she went to such lengths. Your sister…" His words hung in the air between them.

Her heart tightened. Her sister was dead because of Lottie.

"I get why she did it," he continued.

Sabine straightened and turned to face Axel. "You *get* why she did it?" she said, practically spitting out the words. There was no justification for killing her sister. "Lottie is nothing but a selfish, spoiled princess who wants to be the queen of Lynk. She intends to take the throne from her brother. My sister got in the way."

"True. But she also did it for Lynk."

Sabine started to protest.

Axel put his hand up, stopping her. "Hear me out."

She started tapping her foot, waiting for his excuse.

"Lottie told me she found out Rainer is going to wage war on the other kingdoms. She believes if she's queen, she can maintain peace and follow the League of Rulers like we're supposed to."

As to why Axel felt the need to tell Sabine any of this, she didn't know. No matter the reason, she'd never forgive Lottie. "You're trying to tell me that by breaking Lynk's laws and having my sister killed, trying to de-throne her own brother, your sister is really the hero in this situation? I don't think so." She faced away from Axel, not wanting to look at him. Nothing could justify what Lottie did. "You don't know what it's like to lose a sibling. You don't know what it's like to be hunted like an animal. You don't know what it's like to be sold like a piece of property to another person for an alliance to save your kingdom." With those words hanging in the air between them, she pushed off the railing and headed toward the stairwell. Her stomach twisted with nausea, and her arms shook with anger.

"No, I don't, Sabine," he called after her. "But I do know what it's like to lose my mother. I do know what it's like to have a man raise me, pretending to be my father, but abusing me any chance he got—physically and emotionally. And I do know what it's like to only have worth in the fact that I'm Rainer's half-brother. I can never inherit the throne. I have no position of authority here. I'm looked down upon because my father was a mere guard—a guard who Rainer's father slaughtered like an animal. I didn't have the kind, loving childhood you did. Maybe that's the reason I don't have high expectations of others since I'm constantly being let down. All I want is to survive, to protect my brother, and to try to find a little peace and happiness when possible. So no, I don't know what it's like to have gone through what you have, but don't you dare think that I don't know pain and suffering. It's insulting." Axel stepped around her and disappeared down the stairwell without looking back.

Sabine stood there, dumbfounded. This wasn't the first time she'd been put in her place by Axel. His carefree attitude and the way he carried himself masked the pain he held inside. Shaking her head, she went down the steps, not wanting to understand or sympathize with the prince. In order to bring Lottie to justice and stop the war, she couldn't be swayed by her emotions—emotions that could be manipulated and used against her.

She headed to her room, replaying her conversation with Axel over and over. Rounding the corner to the hallway before her room, she stumbled to a halt. Directly in front of her, Rainer stood with Heather at his side. A slow smile spread over Heather's face as she placed her right hand on her stomach—a stomach that clearly showed she was pregnant with the king's child.

Sabine forced herself to look Rainer in the eyes. He was staring right at her, as if daring her to challenge him. His arm slid around Heather, tucking her into his side.

Sabine's temper was about to snap, and she had to rein in her emotions, forcing her face to remain blank. Under no circumstances did she want Rainer to know how this affected her.

After rolling her shoulders back and lifting her chin in the air, she strode forward. "Welcome home, *husband.*" Her voice came out sounding sweet, but it was far from sincere. Without waiting for him to respond, she continued forward, expecting Heather to get out of the way and curtsey. When the woman didn't move, Sabine stopped two feet in front of her, her brows raised.

Drew stepped to the side. "Her Majesty, Queen Sabine Manfred of Lynk," he announced, pretending as if Heather didn't know who she was.

Heather glanced at Rainer whose focus remained on Sabine.

An uncomfortable minute passed. Drew placed his hand on the hilt of his sword and took a step closer to Heather. Finally, the woman stepped to the side and curtseyed, though not as low as she should have.

Sabine glided forward. As she passed Heather, she reached out and patted the woman's head as if she were a dog. "Good girl." She smirked.

She didn't stop until she reached her room where she began pacing, trying to tether this new information into something manageable. Rainer had returned with Heather—his pregnant mistress. He had to have done it to hurt Sabine. She blinked the tears away, refusing to cry over this situation. However, it hurt more than it should because of Evander. A man she'd fallen in love with, yet had refused to be with out of respect for Rainer. If only her own husband would show her the same courtesy.

With her hands on her hips, she continued pacing, trying to think this through. She couldn't live in this palace and share a man with another woman. It was insulting and degrading. Sabine was the queen, not Heather. With that title came respect. The problem was that Rainer only needed Sabine to have a child of noble standing. Once Sabine had Rainer's child, he would have no use for her. He could kill her just like his father had killed the previous queen.

But she was getting ahead of herself and needed to put things into perspective. None of this mattered if Rainer went to war. Her focus and concentration had to be on stopping the war. Once that was done, then she'd worry about everything else.

Her original plan had been to blend who she was with who she needed to be. It was why she had the town seamstress make those new clothes for her. They were in the Lynk style but covered more of her body so the Bakley part of her felt comfortable wearing the outfits. Now she understood how futile that was. To survive, to win, she needed as many people as possible on her side. In order to do that, she needed to embrace all things Lynk so everyone would think she was one of them.

Going over to her desk, she pulled out a piece of paper and a quill, quickly writing a letter stating what she wanted, hoping the seamstress would understand. She folded it, sealed it shut, and gave it to Drew, instructing that it be delivered tonight. Time was of the utmost importance.

Once that was done, she gazed at Harta who slept peacefully on the bed. It was time Sabine started thinking more along the lines of Evander. While she'd had Commander Felix change the course of the ships and alter the tent cities' purpose, there was more she could do. If she went before the nobles in the palace and formally accused Lottie of treason, Rainer would have to put Lottie on trial. The reason she'd been holding off on that was because it meant Lottie's bloodline would be punished as well. This meant that once Lottie was found guilty, Rainer, Axel, and Anton would be killed right along with her. It was a steep price to pay. While Sabine had no qualms with Lottie's death, she would feel immensely guilty for the princes' deaths.

If Sabine went through with this, if she had the entire royal family killed, it meant she would be the sole ruler of the kingdom. That was something she definitely didn't want. However, it might be the only way to prevent a war. Which meant that by going after Lottie and seeking justice for Alina, Sabine could save the entire realm as well.

She closed her eyes. If Lynk went to war, there would be countless deaths. Killing a few would prevent the deaths of many. While it sounded justified, she didn't know if it was morally right. She didn't know if she could go through with this. But right now, she didn't see any other way.

She wished she could discuss this with Evander. However, this was something she'd have to do on her own.

Chapter Seven

The following morning, Sabine awoke and found several crates had been placed in her room next to her closet. She climbed out of bed and went over, peering inside them. Each one was filled to the brim with clothing. The seamstress in town must have worked all night to create these outfits for her. She'd have to make sure the woman was heavily compensated.

After bathing, Sabine put on one of the outfits made from pale yellow silk. The top portion covered each breast and the bottom covered the front and back of her buttocks. Then a sheer material hung from tiny straps on her shoulders. A jeweled belt latched around her waist, holding the delicate fabric to her body. While it made her uncomfortable showing so much skin, this was exactly what she'd hoped for—it was Lynk through and through. The outfit would garner her the attention she desired.

When she exited her suite, she took in her guards' expressions. No one blushed and no one's eyes widened in shock which meant she wasn't dressed too provocatively. However, if her mother saw her like this, she'd receive a stern scolding. If her brothers saw her, they would take off their tunics to cover her. It was best Otto had left.

"Queen Sabine," Drew said with a kind smile. "You look exceptionally lovely today. I see you found your special deliveries."

"Yes, thank you for taking care of that."

Her guards led her to the royal dining room. When she entered, she found Anton and Axel both already eating breakfast.

Anton went still, his eyes bulging in shock.

A smile slid across Axel's face and he set his spoon down, admiring her. "I see you came to play."

Anton glanced at him, his brows pulling together in question.

"Our dear, sweet queen must know that our beloved brother returned with his mistress," Axel said as he leaned back in his chair, folding his arms.

With a sigh, Anton resumed eating, focusing on his plate as he spoke. "He's a fool. You'd think he'd be more worried about the state of the kingdom than who's in his bed."

It was embarrassing how everyone knew Rainer was sleeping with another woman. She took a seat at the head of the table, thinking about her own parents. Her father would never have treated her mother this way. Even her two brothers who were married loved their wives and wouldn't consider taking a mistress.

A servant entered, setting a plate before her.

"Perhaps the state of the kingdom wouldn't be so dire if the king weren't so eager to go to war and destroy the League." She plopped a blueberry in her mouth, her irritation growing. "Perhaps his own brothers could offer him counsel and encourage him to do the right thing."

"Maybe," Anton said. "If Rainer would listen to us, we

could do that. But Rainer does what he wants with no regard to our feelings. We're only half-brothers after all."

"He put you in charge of the League and his spies," she replied. "That has to mean he trusts you."

Anton rubbed his face. "The League position goes to a prince of the kingdom, so he didn't have many options. And as for the spies…" He chuckled.

Sabine so rarely saw Anton laugh that the sight made her pause. "Are you all right?"

Axel picked up his fork and resumed eating. "The late king caught Anton spying," he explained. "That's why he put him in charge of all that. Rainer has just kept the status quo since being crowned."

She took a sip of her tea. "How old were you when that happened?"

Anton shrugged but didn't answer as he took a bite of his toast.

"My dear Sabine," Axel said, his words taking on a sing-song quality "I'm glad you're here. You definitely keep things interesting." He took a bite of his eggs, winking at her.

She plucked a blueberry from her plate and chucked it at him, hitting him in the head.

Startled, his eyes widened. "See, I didn't expect you to do that." He picked up the blueberry, tossing it in his mouth.

Shaking her head, Sabine took another sip of her tea. She heard movement at the entrance to the room and suspected Rainer had finally arrived. He'd always gotten upset with her for dressing too demurely. Hopefully this outfit would please him and show him how hard she was trying to be the queen he wanted and needed. Although, that wasn't the real reason she'd chosen this dress. The real reason was needing the people here in the palace to see and believe she was one of them. In order to stop the war, she needed them on her side.

Nonchalantly, she peeked at Rainer to see his reaction and

almost dropped her fork when she spotted Heather walking in behind him. He sat in the chair opposite Sabine, not even bothering to look her way.

Swallowing her fury, Sabine set her cup on the saucer and decided to play dumb. "I need some fresh hot water for my tea," she said to Heather.

Heather sat in the chair to Rainer's left, not realizing Sabine had even been addressing her.

Axel chuckled, shaking his head, enjoying this far more than he should.

"The hot water isn't going to magically appear on the table, Heather," she said, using the woman's name to make it clear she was speaking to her.

"Excuse me?" Heather said, confusion showing on her face.

Sabine snapped her fingers and pointed at her tea cup. "I need hot water. And pregnant or not, sitting at the royal family's table is inappropriate. Servants have their own quarters. If you need to work less, take that up with your husband. Don't embarrass yourself in front of your king and queen by sitting down on the job."

Rainer's cheeks reddened. "Heather is not a servant," he said, his voice low, finally looking at Sabine. When he saw her outfit, he blinked several times, then looked away.

"Isn't Heather's sister, Claire, my lady's maid?"

"Yes, she is," Rainer ground out, the words sounding forced and strained.

"Claire told me her parents and sisters work in the palace. Is Claire mistaken?" She dared Rainer to say Heather was his lover. It was one thing for him to take Heather to his bed discretely, it was another matter entirely to parade her in front of the family and the court. She refused to be embarrassed like that.

"Heather is here as my guest," he replied, his knuckles turning white as he clutched his fork in his hand.

"Oh, I didn't realize we had guests. Please forgive me." Sabine turned her attention to Heather. "I assume your husband is here as well?" She smiled at the woman, wanting to put her on the spot and either embarrass her or make her leave. It was petty, but she didn't care. Her pride had been injured, and she wanted to make Heather hurt the way she hurt.

"He is, but he's working," Heather said, an eyebrow raised as she glared at Sabine.

"He's working," Sabine said, "but you're not?" She placed a single finger on her lips as if contemplating this.

Heather rolled her eyes. "Yes," she said, a bit too forcefully.

Sabine had to bite back her smile. She was finally getting under Heather's skin. "Is your husband working here in the palace?"

Heather set her fork down and turned to face Sabine. "He's at the military compound," she said, the words edged with anger. "Do you have any other questions? Or can I finally eat my breakfast in peace?"

Sabine opened her mouth to respond when Rainer said, "Enough with the questions."

Shock rolled through her that Rainer was defending Heather so openly. It made her want to chuck a blueberry at him, but she refrained from doing so. Now that she knew where Cutler was, she had more pressing matters to attend to. "If you'll excuse me," she said, standing slowly.

Rainer's eyes scanned her body, taking in every inch of her.

Sabine walked over to him and leaned down, placing a kiss on his cheek as her fingers trailed along the back of his neck. "Welcome home," she purred in his ear. As she stood, her breast brushed his arm. He stiffened. She smiled and strutted from the room knowing every single set of eyes watched her retreating form.

"She's quite stunning, isn't she brother?" Axel said. "Every man at court is jealous of you, including me. Anyone would be lucky to have someone so beautiful. You truly are a lucky king."

Sabine had moved too far down the hallway to hear Rainer's response—if he even had one.

Her hands shook, so she curled her fingers into two fists, refusing to let anyone see how much this incident had upset her.

"Where to, Your Majesty?" Drew asked, coming to her side as they headed along the corridor.

Unable to look at him for fear she'd see pity in his eyes, she simply replied, "The military training center." She headed toward the palace's main entrance.

"There's another, much easier way," Drew said. "It's the path the royal family uses."

She recalled hearing there was another way. "By all means." She gestured for him to show her.

He led her back the way they'd come from and to a corridor she'd never ventured in before. At a nondescript door, Drew unlocked it, pulling it open for her.

Sabine stepped onto a platform about ten feet by ten feet. To the right, a wooden staircase spiraled downward so far she couldn't see where it ended. Clutching the railing, she descended until she reached the bottom, where a long, tube-shaped tunnel stretched straight ahead, lit by torches. The air had turned cold. This underground tunnel must lead to the cavern used by the army for training.

Drew joined her, leading the way, until they reached a locked door. He pulled out a key.

"Why don't I have a key?" she asked. If this way was used by the royal family, she should have access to it.

He pursed his lips. "I don't know. You'll have to speak to the king regarding that matter."

"Do all the guards have one?"

"No," Drew replied. "Only those of us with clearance. Since I've been appointed as the head of your personal guard, I was given a key." He pushed the door open.

Sabine stepped inside the military cavern where dozens and dozens of soldiers were training. As people noticed her, they began to bow. "Please carry on," she said, not wanting to interrupt them.

Drew stepped to her side. "Are you wanting to train? Observe?"

She looked at him sidelong. "I wish to have a word with Captain Cutler." She feared she would see judgment on his face. However, he simply nodded. "This way." He led her along the side of the cavern, skirting around those training.

They passed a tunnel on the right where she heard dogs barking. She recalled Lottie saying they trained dogs here and that was where Harta had come from. Sabine would have to visit the kennels later.

"There he is," Drew said, pointing to the far end of the room.

Sabine spotted Cutler fighting with another man of similar height and weight, his movements jerky. If she had to guess, she'd say he appeared angry.

"We'll wait here to afford you some privacy," Drew said.

"Thank you." Sabine went over to the mat Cutler was fighting on, standing off to the side, waiting for him to finish.

The second Cutler twisted and caught sight of her, he ended his fight. His opponent patted him on the back before moving to the adjacent mat.

Cutler picked up a towel from the floor, wiping off his

sweaty face and chest. "Your Majesty," he said, slightly out of breath, his shoulders rising and falling.

"Captain," she replied.

He reached down and grabbed his shirt off the mat, putting it on. "Did you need something?" His hands went to his hips, his focus above her head.

No one was close enough to overhear their conversation. "I think you know why I'm here."

His focus finally settled on her face, his eyes searching hers. "Yeah, I suppose I do," he said in a low voice. "He promised me he'd leave us alone. That Heather could have her child in peace."

She'd been told the same thing. "Do you know why he changed his mind?" Perhaps it was the upcoming war. Maybe Rainer wanted Heather here in the palace where it would be safer. The fact that he felt the need to personally escort her meant he still loved her dearly. Sabine just wished it wasn't being thrown in her face.

"I do not. On the journey here, I was ordered to ride ahead of the party as a scout." His voice dripped with a bitterness Sabine understood.

"So you didn't have the opportunity to overhear any conversations that may be pertinent?" she asked.

He shook his head. "Is there anything else you need?" His attention shifted to her guards not far away.

"Why did you come here? Why not stay at the manor?" she asked, wondering why Cutler remained married and loyal to a woman who was in love with another man. Maybe it would help her to have clarity over her own similar situation.

"I'd rather be here training and working with my fellow soldiers than alone, holed up in my home, with nothing to do." Cutler looked Sabine over. "Forgive me for asking, but the king, is he not pleased with you?"

Her face went red with the implication that the king was

unhappy with her performance in bed, but then a laugh escaped her lips at the absurdity of it since she and Rainer hadn't consummated their marriage.

"Forgive me for even asking," Cutler said. "It's just that you're young and beautiful. I thought that once Heather was away from the king, you'd distract him enough for him to forget about her."

She appreciated the compliment. "Heather is beautiful as well." The woman was one of the most gorgeous people Sabine had ever seen. "And she is carrying Rainer's child. They have a history together. I barely know the king."

He sighed. "I guess I'd been hoping it was just a physical attraction between them and that once they were separated, it would end," he admitted.

"You mean instead of them actually being in love?"

He nodded.

It was time to get to the crux of why she was there. "Did you know the king's sister, Princess Lottie, hired the assassin to kill my sister, Princess Alina? She also hired an assassin who came after me."

His eyes widened. "Is that why she's sequestered to her rooms?"

"It is."

He turned and grabbed the towel again, rubbing it over his face as he took a step closer to her. "That's technically treason," he mumbled, his voice low.

"It is."

"What has the king done?"

"Besides sequestering her to her room? Nothing."

His eyes searched hers. "What proof do you have?"

"I overheard her speaking to the assassin."

He tossed the towel back to the floor. "Then it's your word against the king's."

"Unfortunately. I'd mistakenly assumed my word would

be good enough and he'd support me, his wife. However, I can see now that I was gravely mistaken. I am on my own. I fear another assassin will come after me."

"I need time to think over this," he said, glancing around the room. "My parents are having a small gathering this evening to welcome Heather and me back to court. Will you attend? We'll be able to speak freely."

"I'll be there."

She returned to her guards. "Drew, I'd like to go into town."

"Of course, Your Majesty." He led her to the second level where they took the stairs up, exiting through the building at the edge of town. They headed to the main road.

As soon as the townspeople spotted her, they approached, wishing her well, giving her flowers, asking if she wanted to come and shop in their stores. Sabine spoke to as many of them as she could as she made her way to the seamstress's shop.

When she entered the store, she found the woman asleep in a chair while a young girl who looked about twelve sat at the counter.

"Is that your mother?" Sabine asked the girl.

The girl nodded.

"Do you work here?" she asked, wondering if it was common for children this young to work.

"I only work here when my mom needs the help," she whispered. "My mom and aunts were up all night sewing your clothes."

"So you know who I am?" Sabine asked her.

She nodded. "Everyone knows who you are, Your Highness, I mean Your Majesty. Should I wake my mom? Do you need to order more clothes?"

"Don't wake her. I'm here because I need some help."

The girl sat taller. "I can help you."

"Excellent. I need a new lady's maid." She planned to let Claire go as soon as she returned to the palace. There was no way Heather's sister would serve as her attendant any longer. "I'm hoping you know someone who is trustworthy who can handle the job."

"If I were older, I'd do it," the girl said with a smile.

"I'm sure you'll make a lovely lady's maid one day. But you're right, I do need someone a bit older to assist me. She needs to be able to help me dress, do my hair, and handle social issues that may come up at court. Do you know of anyone who might be able to do that?"

"My one aunt might be able to. She's twenty-five and doesn't like working here cause she's not very good at sewing."

Sabine chuckled. "Is she around? I'd like to meet her."

The girl nodded and slid off her stool, running past the curtain that led to the back of the store.

Sabine waited a few minutes until the girl returned with a young woman who had tanned skin and long, dark hair. The woman was tall and rather striking.

"Your Majesty," the woman said. "My niece said you wanted to meet me?"

"Yes. What's your name?"

"Harper." She curtseyed.

"What do you know about royal protocol?"

"Um, absolutely nothing." Her lips pulled into a smile.

"Are you a quick learner?"

"I think I am, but my sister might not agree with me."

"I am in desperate need of a lady's maid," Sabine said matter of factly. "Would you like the job?"

Harper's eyes widened. "You want to hire me?" she asked, her voice louder than necessary in the small store, her excitement showing through.

"I do. I need someone I can trust."

"I'd love to work in the palace." Her smile got even bigger.

Sabine turned to face Drew. "Can you handle this matter for me?"

"Yes, Your Majesty. I'll speak with her family and make the necessary arrangements."

"Thank you." She faced Harper again. "I'd like you to meet Captain Drew. He is in charge of my personal guard and will be going over everything with you. I hope to see you later this evening."

"Thank you, Your Majesty. You won't be disappointed."

Sabine exited the store with the rest of her guards following close behind. A small crowd had gathered outside. While she didn't think she had room for any more flowers in her bedchamber, she took all the bouquets that were given to her, thanking every single person who'd taken the time to do something so kind for her.

Then she perused through the town, buying some bread, honey, and even a few pieces of jewelry. These people needed to know she was one of them. If that meant purchasing items frequently, she would do so. A lot of them were reserves in the army. Since she wanted to take control of that army, she needed them on her side.

A servant opened the door, granting Sabine entrance into a quaint sitting room. Even though the sun had set, the windows and doors remained open, allowing the warm air to pass through. Dozens of candles had been lit, brightening the space. A handful of people were present, all the men dressed in uniform which meant they were in the army. When she entered, her guards remained out in the hallway, probably because this was the commander's private rooms and she would be safe in his presence.

Lady Regina immediately rushed over, going into a low curtsey. Commander Felix joined her a moment later, bowing.

"Thank you for coming, Your Majesty," Regina said as she stood.

Cutler came over. "Queen Sabine." He bowed.

"Thank you for inviting me." A servant handed Sabine a glass of wine. She took it and went farther into the room.

Felix introduced her to everyone—they were all high ranking officers and their wives.

"We weren't sure if the king would be joining you this evening," Lady Regina said, glancing at Cutler.

Sabine smiled. *Let the games begin.* "Though the king returned last night, I have seen little of him. He seems to be preoccupied with personal matters that don't include me."

"That's a shame," Felix said. "He is lucky to have you by his side. I must admit, I haven't seen him since he returned. He hasn't been to the training center. Had my own son not told me, I wouldn't even know the king was here."

Cutler stood off to the side, leaning against the wall, a drink in hand.

Sabine rarely pitied anyone. However, her heart ached for Cutler. It was obvious Rainer and Heather had spent the day together. It was also clear that Cutler loved Heather. For Heather to throw that in Cutler's face, Sabine found it hard to stomach.

An uncomfortable minute stretched between those present. One of the wives said, "Your Majesty, I'm so glad you've returned to the palace yourself. We heard you'd been gone as well." It sounded more like a question.

Sabine understood the statement for what it was. These people wanted to know where she'd been.

"I'm thankful to be home after the horrible ordeal of facing an assassin." She took a seat on the nearby sofa, taking a sip of her drink.

"An assassin?" The woman said. "Was it the same one who…"

Not missing a beat, Sabine nodded. "It was. I just don't understand why King Rainer didn't arrest his sister once he found out she was the one who'd hired the assassin. Not to do anything, to let her send the assassin after me, I can't tell you what terror that caused."

"Princess Lottie?" another woman said.

"She wants the crown and is trying to overthrow her brother." Sabine looked around the room, taking in everyone's response to her words. A few looked skeptical, so she forged on. "King Rainer discovered his sister was behind Princess Alina's death. Since he's a new king, he thought it would look bad to have his own sister trying to usurp him, so he married me hoping that it would afford me the protection I needed. However, I then heard Lottie with the assassin telling him to end me so her brother would lose the throne. Fearing for my life, I fled the palace and went to see my brother. Once the assassin was dealt with, I returned. I only hope Lottie doesn't hire another one. I've tried talking to Rainer, but he barely speaks to me." She let her eyes fill with tears.

"That is horrible," Regina said, her hand going to her chest in shock. "Though, I'm not surprised. Our king seems to be preoccupied with his concubine instead of protecting what matters most."

Sabine nodded. "Sometimes I feel so alone here. However, since being crowned, I feel I have a purpose. I'm trying to learn as much as I can about Lynk and our army. I want to help lead this kingdom in any way I can. I want to help my subjects." She did her best to meet as many eyes as possible.

"I am your humble servant," she said. "If there's anything I can do to help, please let me know." She bowed her head.

Regina came and sat next to her on the sofa. "We're so glad to hear that," she said, rubbing Sabine's back. "You're young and shouldering a lot of burden."

She nodded. "Thank you for inviting me tonight. I miss being around my family and feeling loved and supported." While she hoped to garner sympathy, she didn't want anyone to think she was weak. These were the highest ranking members in the army. She needed them on her side. "You have to understand," she continued, "I grew up in a large family. It's hard not to have that any more." She reached out, taking Regina's hand and clutching it. "I'm sure you understand. Now that your son is back, you must feel a sense of joy." She pulled her brows together and looked about the room. She twisted toward Cutler. "Where's your wife?"

"That's a good question," he said. "Especially since she's pregnant. I suspect she's in bed with your husband." He downed the rest of the drink he'd been holding.

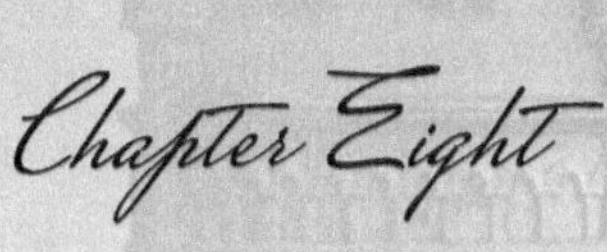

Chapter Eight

Shock rolled through Sabine. While she'd assumed Rainer and Heather had spent the day together, she hadn't considered that they'd be in bed. It wasn't that late, the sky wasn't dark, and she'd mistakenly assumed those sorts of activities didn't happen until then. Her naïveté had to be showing. The fact that Cutler had just announced it to the room made her shrink into the sofa, her face turning flaming red.

"I thought the king ended things with Heather once Princess Alina arrived?" one of the women said.

"I heard he had an agreement with the princess," someone else whispered.

"Is the child she's carrying yours?" a man asked Cutler. "You haven't been married that long, and she's showing."

Cutler pushed off the wall, coming to stand next to his father, as if for support. "The child is not mine." Defeat coated his features along with a tinge of helplessness.

"You're an honorable man to marry a woman like that, knowing her condition," one of the wives said.

It surprised Sabine that everyone was talking so openly about this.

Lady Regina placed her hand on Sabine's arm. "I'm sorry if we're being too forward around you," she said.

She didn't know how to respond to any of this.

"The truth is I've been in love with Heather for years," Cutler said as he sat in one of the vacant chairs. "King Rainer knew it. One day, he came to me and told me to marry her. I jumped at the chance. I didn't realize."

"You have to understand," Felix said, looking at Sabine as he spoke, "we all hoped King Rainer would be different from his father."

She realized they wanted her to know the sort of man she'd married and understand how others viewed him. Especially the high ranking officials in his army.

This wasn't the first time Sabine had heard sentiments such as these. She clutched her goblet, squeezing it, trying to mask her emotions so everyone here wouldn't know her thoughts until she had time to understand them herself.

"I think we're scaring our new queen," Regina said. "Let's discuss happier things. I'm glad my son is here with us." She lifted her cup in Cutler's direction.

"Yes," Felix said. "Now let's hope the king doesn't send us to war." He lifted his goblet in salute as well.

"War hardly matters with so many dying in our camps," one of the men said. "How many have been killed? Twenty-one?"

Sabine had no idea what he was talking about.

"It's definitely not an animal," Cutler said. "At least not of the four-legged variety."

"Let's not terrify the queen," Felix said.

"I don't frighten easily," Sabine replied. "I had an assassin chasing me for weeks—I've learned I can handle a lot."

"Regardless," Regina said, "this is supposed to be a

celebration. Let's change the conversation to something more pleasant."

People started talking about other things, and Cutler abruptly stood. He went over to the side of the room and began pacing. He reminded Sabine of a caged animal. It concerned her—the things he might be forced to do to escape.

Sabine awoke to a soft knock at the door. When she opened it, Drew stood there with Harper and Claire.

"Captain Drew informed me my services are no longer required," Claire said, her eyes red as if she'd been crying.

"I'm sorry," Sabine replied. "Since you're the sister to my husband's mistress, I can't have you around." Her voice was still gravelly from sleep.

"The king appointed me to serve you," Claire said, her voice wobbly, as if on the verge of crying.

"And I'm ending that appointment. You have to understand that I can neither trust you nor do I want you around."

Tears filled Claire's eyes. "I need this job."

"I'm sorry, but you're dismissed." She admitted Harper before closing the door, hating that she had to be so mean, but she needed to look out for herself. Her lady's maid should be trustworthy and someone who had her best interest at heart. She turned to Harper. "Do you have any idea what is required of you?"

"Captain Drew—your guard—spent the night training me. I'm ready to serve you." She curtseyed, her form a little off.

Sabine rubbed her face, trying to clear the sleep from her eyes. "If you're ever unsure, ask me or Captain Drew."

"I'll do my best," Harper assured her. "I have a brother in

the army. A lot of my friends have people they know or love in it as well."

Sabine raised her eyebrows. "What does any of that have to do with me?"

Harper shifted her weight from foot to foot. "You know."

No, Sabine did not know.

"Word is that you don't want to go to war."

"Where did you hear that?" Sabine asked.

She shrugged. "I don't know. That's just what people are saying. Is it not true?"

"Oh, it's true. I just didn't realize people knew that's how I feel about the matter." She eyed Harper. "Why did you take this position?" While she knew Harper didn't like being a seamstress, she didn't know why she'd agree to the job so readily.

"You're the queen," Harper said, as if that explained everything. "You don't want to go to war, you're beautiful, and I get to be in the palace."

Something about the young woman put Sabine at ease, making her believe she was being truthful and honest. "Harper, I think you and I are going to get along quite well." If Harper supported Sabine the way she thought she would, then they were going to make waves here at the palace.

Someone knocked on the door.

Harper went over, answering it. She closed the door and approached Sabine, handing her a letter. "This arrived for you."

It contained the king's seal. Sabine opened it, reading its contents. The king was throwing a ball tonight to celebrate his wife, the queen. She snorted. He must be doing damage control after flaunting Heather all over the court. While he might have been able to see a commoner while the late king still lived and Rainer was only a prince, it seemed that now that he was king and had a queen, people didn't look kindly upon his mistress—especially since he didn't have an heir yet.

"There's a ball tonight," she mused. "Harper, I must look stunning."

"I know just the right outfit." She clapped her hands together while bouncing on her feet in glee.

Sabine was starting to second-guess this plan. When she'd first concocted it with Harper, it had all seemed so easy. Now that she was wearing the dress and heading to the ballroom, she hoped she hadn't gone too far.

During her sixteenth birthday celebration, she'd wanted to dance with Harvard, the most handsome boy her age. While she'd known he was courting one of the duke's daughters, Sabine hadn't cared. She'd mistakenly assumed her position and beauty would be enough to woo him. How wrong she'd been. Harvard had flat out told her he was in love with someone else and would honor his promises to that girl. She'd been devastated at the time, going so far as to declare her birthday ruined. However, the lesson had stuck with her. A lesson in love, devotion, beauty, power. She wouldn't make the same mistake twice.

This evening, in order for her plan to work, it required her to come across as more than just the beautiful Lynk queen. She had to be sincere, loyal, and devout. She had to be one of them. Though she wasn't the same girl she'd been back when she was only sixteen, the fact of the matter remained that she was still only a young woman with little to no experience in the world. Yet, she wanted these people to believe in and follow her.

Normally, she would have gone to the king's private rooms for him to escort her to the ballroom. However, she'd been too afraid Heather would be there. If she came face to face with her husband's lover, she wouldn't have been able to go through with her plan for tonight. Her ego would have taken too big of a hit to perform the way she needed to.

Plus, Harper said a lot of servants were talking about how the king was with his mistress and ignoring his beautiful wife. It seemed people were sympathetic with Sabine—she just had to play the victim and let Rainer dig his hole even deeper.

Sabine entered the antechamber that led to the ballroom. Anton and Axel were already there, lounging on the sofas. When she closed the door, Anton glanced up, his eyes going wide and he quickly looked away.

Axel raised his eyebrows and whistled. "I take it you have an agenda for this evening."

Her eyes cut to his. The creamy white silk gown she wore loosely covered her breasts, the fabric being held in place by silver strands of diamonds that crisscrossed over her abdomen and up over her neck. Then another piece of silk loosely covered the front of her buttocks, wrapping up and over her right hip, hanging down to the floor. The left side wrapped below her hip and under her buttock, leaving her left cheek completely exposed. When she'd looked at her backside in the mirror, she'd been stunned. The straps of diamonds came up over her neck, down her back, holding the fabric in place. As she moved, the cold air caressed her skin, but the fabric remained in place. Her hair was up to show off her back. Never before had Sabine felt so bare and yet so powerful. She'd come to learn that beauty could be a weapon —and she would wield that weapon tonight.

He chuckled, shaking his head. "You're a vision. I hope you know that."

As far as Sabine was concerned, this was war—and this dress was her armor. With shaking hands, she stepped farther into the room, hoping not everyone thought she had an agenda. But by the end of tonight, she wanted every single person here at court on her side. Not that they had to denounce or even dislike Rainer. She just wanted them to sympathize with her. She'd worry about ruining Rainer's reputation later—if he didn't do that all on his own with his mistress.

When Anton caught a glimpse of the back, he cursed. "What are you doing? This isn't like you."

"She's our queen," Axel said. "Tonight, she is the epitome of what a Lynk queen should be."

"Yes, but every man will be drooling over her," Anton said.

"I think that's the point." Axel chuckled again, his eyes connecting with Sabine's. "For the record, I'm on your side."

Anton stood. "Is this because Rainer brought Heather here?"

"I don't wish to discuss my husband's mistress," she replied. "But no, nothing I do is because of that woman. Lynk is my priority."

The door swung open, and Rainer strode inside. When he spotted Sabine, he froze mid-step, his gaze slowly traveling from her head to toe and back up. He swallowed, then blinked twice.

Axel chuckled. "I believe the party has already started." He stood. "Shall we enter together or separately?"

"The two of you can go ahead," Rainer said. He cleared his throat. "I'd like a moment alone with Sabine."

She wasn't sure she wanted a moment alone with him, but she didn't protest.

Anton and Axel opened the side door, music and laughter spilling into the antechamber. Their names were announced, then the door closed, leaving Sabine alone with Rainer.

"You look exquisite," Rainer said, coming closer to her.

Another reason she wore the scantily clad outfit—to prove to everyone she was not with child. Her flat stomach was on full display for everyone to see, only decorated with the strings of diamonds. She feared Rainer would try passing off Heather's child as Sabine's, and she refused to take part in something so deceiving.

"As do you." His solid black loose pants and tunic contrasted nicely with the soft white of her dress. Sabine had always found him handsome. His husky voice, alluring manner, and good looks all pulled her in, making her want to trust him. But she'd learned it was all an act.

"I heard you fired Claire," he said.

"I did." She didn't want to have this conversation with him, at least not now, so she turned and headed toward the door. When she reached it, she glanced over her shoulder at him. "Are you coming?"

He nodded, his focus on her backside. "We, uh, need to set aside some time to talk."

"So long as we're talking and you're not lecturing, I'm more than amiable."

His eyes narrowed but he didn't respond. He came to her side, holding his arm out for her.

Just as the door swung open, she slid her hand onto his arm, and they were announced.

The people in the ballroom began cheering since this was the first time the two of them had been introduced as the king and queen of Lynk.

Similar to last time Sabine had been in this room for a ball, hundreds of candles hung from the domed ceiling, casting the room in a soft light. The archways surrounding the room remained open, the warm air breezing in. This time, thousands of flowers adorned the archways, balcony, and walls, filling the room with a sweet smell.

Rainer led Sabine to the middle of the room, then turned

to face her, their subjects forming a loose circle around them. The musicians began playing a slow tune. Rainer slid one hand into Sabine's, while his other rested lightly on her hip. They began moving to the music. At first, she feared her dress couldn't handle the dance. However, the king made sure to move slowly. She focused past him, observing those present, trying to decide who she should dance with next.

"Is it too much to ask for your focus to be on me?" Rainer mumbled close to her ear, sending a shiver along Sabine's spine.

She forced her eyes to remain on Rainer as they danced.

"Do you not have anything to say to me?" he asked.

"No, I have nothing to say that would be deemed appropriate with so many ears close by."

The corners of his lips turned up. "You can be inappropriate with me. After all, I am your husband."

How dare he try to flirt with her now. She wanted to scowl at him but kept her face pleasant. "Where's Heather?"

His hand on hers tightened. "She's not here tonight." His other hand trailed up her back, over the diamond strands. "I am trying."

"You're trying to do what?" she asked.

"Be a good husband."

She laughed. "I didn't realize you knew what the word meant."

"So you are jealous of Heather," he purred.

"No, I'm not."

"Then what's the problem? Why the attitude?"

She sucked in a breath. "Do you honestly not know?"

He shook his head.

"Your sister killed my sister. She tried to kill me."

"I've taken care of the situation. You have nothing to worry about." His voice sounded irritated, as if talking to a petulant child.

"My sister deserves justice," Sabine whispered, not wanting her hatred and anger to seep through. Not when she was trying to win over those present.

"And my sister deserves a second chance."

Sabine was about to argue when the song ended and another one began. She took an abrupt step back from Rainer, forcing him to release her.

The crowd closed in on Sabine. Several men she recognized from the various parties she'd attended asked for her hand.

Smiling sweetly, she accepted Duke Vadil's arm, and they began dancing. She spotted Rainer on the far side of the room, leaning against the wall, his arms folded, watching her. As she danced, she made sure to ask personable questions about the duke, his family, his land, and if he had any concerns she should be aware of. She assured him she was on his side. At the end of the song, he thanked her for her time.

Commander Felix was nearby, so Sabine grabbed him for the next dance. After him, she danced with several other high ranking military officers.

During a dance with a lieutenant, he told her not to worry, that they would find the person responsible for the murders. At first, she thought he meant her sister and her own attempted assassination. However, he mentioned that the murders were confined to military camps, so she knew he wasn't referring to her. Thinking back to one of the dinner parties, she recalled someone mentioning that people were turning up dead. She wondered if this was the same thing or something else entirely.

When she danced with Cutler, he didn't speak much.

After him, Anton took a turn. "How are you holding up?" he asked. "There are quite a few people here who seem to be insistent on dancing with you."

"I'm having a splendid time," she crooned. What she

really wanted to discuss with him were these murders. However, she didn't want to tip her hand that she was receiving so much information voluntarily. Anton was a smart man and would probably figure out what she was doing pretty easily.

"I suppose you should know that the League has approved Prince Evander's union with Princess Lottie."

Sabine stiffened. "Rainer is still going to marry her off?" Lottie should be in jail, not shipped off to another kingdom.

"It solves his problem."

"She can still do damage from Avoni." Lottie needed to pay for having Alina killed. It wasn't fair she got to marry Evander. Her heart felt as if it were being squeezed.

Anton leaned closer. "Is that why you're really upset?" he whispered in her ear.

"What do you mean?" He couldn't possibly know that she had feelings for Evander.

"Rainer is sending her away where she can't hurt you. What more do you want?"

"We have laws. Lottie shouldn't be above them. It isn't fair."

He nodded.

"I don't wish to discuss Lottie tonight," she whispered.

"Fair enough. You should also know that the League approved your brother's marriage to Carin."

Sabine still thought that was an odd pairing.

Anton continued, "Carin will be living in Bakley along with a dozen Avoni men serving as her guards. They have agreed to work with Bakley's army."

Anton didn't have to disclose the details of the marriage treaty but he had. Sabine filed that information away to think about later since he'd most likely told her for a reason.

Axel appeared over Anton's shoulder. "All right, brother. You've monopolized Sabine long enough. It's my turn."

Anton squeezed her hand, his eyes holding hers for a moment, as if warning her. She thought back to her time at the League's house in Nisk. Anton had revealed that he'd lied to Rainer to protect her. She didn't think he had any special affection for her, but rather he was protecting his own interests. Regardless, she gave him a slight nod.

Axel slid in front of her, a lazy smile on his face. "About time I get a turn with my sister."

Exhaustion filled her. For the past several hours, she'd smiled at her dance partners while asking questions, trying to learn their secrets and gain their trust. Suddenly it became too much, and she wanted nothing more than to crawl into bed and sleep.

"You know, the flowers are all for you," he said, waving a hand around the room.

"Are they from the townspeople?" She'd suspected as much since they were the same type of flowers they gave her when she went into town.

He nodded. "When they arrived, Rainer was furious."

"Why?"

He shrugged. "I assume because the people love you."

"All I did was go shopping." In reality, she'd wanted their trust and loyalty as well. Hopefully, this was a sign she was making progress.

Axel glanced over toward his brother. "Be careful," he murmured, close to her ear. "Rainer has been drinking, and his temper is going to snap."

"His temper?" She didn't know why he'd be the one upset. His sister was still alive, his lover was in the palace, and he seemed to get whatever he wanted. "Has he danced with anyone tonight?"

"No."

Usually the duchesses and nobles enjoyed dancing with

him. "Why not?" she asked. Maybe it had something to do with them being married now.

"People have been avoiding him."

"Why?"

He shrugged. "Given that Heather's not here, I'm guessing he's trying to do damage control.

"What do you mean?"

"Heather is only a commoner, and he has been flaunting her around the court. I think people are getting tired of his antics. You're the queen, you're perfect, and he should be with you."

She glanced about the room, searching for Rainer, but not finding him.

"I'm serious, Sabine. Go to the rooftop, visit a friend, but don't take the obvious route to your room. Even though you have guards, they can't defy the king."

Goosebumps covered her arms and the hairs on the back of her neck stood on end. She never thought Rainer would hurt her. "Why are you telling me this?"

He looked her in the eyes. "For the first time in my life, you've given me hope. I'd hate to see it destroyed." With that, he bowed and left, melting into the crowd of people.

Sabine decided she'd had enough dancing for the night. As soon as she exited the ballroom, her guards surrounded her.

"If I may, Your Majesty," Drew said as they headed along the hallway, "the stars are looking particularly bright tonight. Shall I escort you to the rooftop? I believe your lady's maid is there."

She eyed him sidelong, wondering if he knew Rainer had been drinking. "That sounds like a lovely idea," she lied. Her feet were aching and she wanted to crawl into bed.

Her guards led the way to a section of the palace she'd

never been in before. It was almost as if they were deliberately avoiding the royal wing.

At a door, Drew unlocked it, revealing a stairwell. "Harper is up there."

In other words, proof that she wasn't with another man. Sabine dragged her feet up the steps, finding her lady's maid sitting on a blanket, watching the stars.

Sabine sat next to her, thankful she had people who cared enough to watch out for her and keep her safe. She vowed to make sure they were all taken care of.

Chapter Nine

What bothered Sabine most about the palace was that it stood atop a steep mountain. It meant she couldn't go outside for a walk unless she went into town. She couldn't ride a horse, go to an archery range, or spend time running through a field. While she understood that no place would be like Bakley, she found herself feeling confined and caged in. She wanted freedom. Even in Avoni, she and Evander had traveled on the canals, and there had been a sense of peace.

Originally, she'd been told a large part of the marriage negotiations had to deal with food—mainly, Lynk needed Bakley's grain. However, she'd been in Lynk long enough to doubt that reasoning. Lynk didn't seem to lack food, neither in the palace nor in town. No one spoke of a food shortage. In fact, there was an abundance of fruit and other items that seemed to sustain them just fine. A small part of her feared Rainer had said his kingdom needed food as an excuse to get Lynk soldiers in Bakley. Yet, her father had informed her that Rainer pulled his soldiers out of the kingdom. She hoped that was the case. Because if Rainer lied about the children he'd stolen to force Bakley's hand, it made sense that he would have lied about the food as well. Knowing all of this, she needed to tread carefully.

While Sabine had purposefully avoided Rainer after the ball last night, she needed to talk to him today. Going over to the door that connected her room to the royal suite, she laid her hand on the wood, as if she could sense what was happening on the other side. Sense Rainer's mood. Sense if Heather was in there. Sabine rested her head on the wood, next to her hand. When they talked, she would pretend that Rainer was her brother. After all, she'd spent years arguing with her brothers to get her way. Taking a deep breath, she straightened and knocked.

The door swung open. Gunther, the king's steward, stood there. "Queen Sabine." He bowed.

"I wish to speak with the king."

"He's in his office." Gunther opened the door wider, admitting her.

She entered the royal suite and crossed over to Rainer's office. She found the king sitting at his desk, a map spread out before him. Instead of saying anything, she went into the room, stopping at the far side, where a wall should have been but instead, was open. Standing at the edge, she could see the pool below. The view from here was stunning.

"I'm surprised to see you," Rainer mumbled.

She shrugged, not looking his way. Silence stretched between them as she tried to decide the best way to handle the situation.

"I've been informed that Lieutenant Markis and Prince Otto left." Rainer came and stood next to Sabine, both of them pretending to focus on the view that stretched out before them.

"Yes," she replied. "My brother was eager to return home with the missing children. Since we didn't know how long you'd be gone for, he decided not to wait. I'm sure you can understand that."

"And Lieutenant Markis? I didn't think he'd leave your side."

"Now that you and I are married, he returned with my brother. I believe that was your stipulation? He could remain until we married."

"I'd hoped to get to know your brother before he left." He clasped his hands behind his back.

"I wanted him to stay longer since I miss my family so much, but he didn't think it fair to put his needs above the children's. That's how we do things in Bakley—we put our people first." It was probably an unnecessary jab, but she enjoyed taking it nonetheless.

"I'm your family now."

It felt like a punch to her stomach, but she supposed it was his own jab. Even though they were married, Sabine didn't consider Rainer her family. "If that's the case, then why bring your mistress here?"

"I wanted you to know what it felt like to watch your spouse with another person."

"You brought her here to hurt me?"

"To even the score."

"But I haven't been with another man. All you've accomplished is pushing me away."

He eyed her. "I hear you traveled alone with Prince Evander."

"I have not broken my marriage vows. I have never been intimate with another person. Can you say the same thing?" She folded her arms, not wanting him to see her shaking hands. While she had traveled alone with Evander, she didn't need to confirm it. Especially since she had remained true to Rainer.

"Your sister and I had an agreement," he reminded her.

"We knew that both of our hearts belonged to another. It's why we worked. You chose to take up your sister's mantle without consulting with me. That is not my fault, and I will not be punished for your rash decision."

"Were you going to allow Alina to be with the man she loved?" Sabine turned to face him, wondering if after she gave him an heir, if he'd release her to be with Evander. Not that Evander would want or be able to be with her since she was married. Regardless, the thought intrigued her.

"No."

It felt like the door to her cage just shut and locked. "So your arrangement was that you could be with someone you loved, but my sister couldn't? That hardly seems fair."

"She was free to write to him," Rainer admitted. "That was all, though, because there couldn't be any question as to who the father of her children was."

So Rainer could sleep with whomever he wanted while he had expected Alina to remain true to him.

"Alina knew what she was getting herself into," he said. "You can wipe the look of disgust from your face."

"I doubt she knew your sister intended to kill her."

A flash of fury flitted across his face. "Lottie didn't kill Alina."

"She hired an assassin. Same thing."

"This is never going to work if we're fighting all the time," Rainer said as he reached out and put his hands on her shoulders. "What is it you want?"

She stood there staring into his eyes, trying to determine if this was some sort of trick.

"Tell me," he insisted.

She decided to be truthful. "I want your sister to pay for killing Alina, and I don't want you to go to war with the other kingdoms." There, she'd put it all on the line.

"Finally," he said, releasing her. "It's nice to see you're capable of being honest for once."

Another jab. She swallowed her retort though the irony wasn't lost on her. Questioning him about the Bakley children and the need for food would prove him the liar, not her. However, it would get her nowhere. As to why he thought she wasn't truthful, she had no idea.

"You keep talking about war," Rainer said. "Why is that?"

"Because it looks like you're preparing for war." She tried to keep her face straight so as not to reveal every emotion and thought she had.

"I don't plan on going to war."

"Then why all the troops at the border? Why the ships off the coastline?"

He chuckled, the sound low and menacing. "Oh, I plan on taking over Carlon, Nisk, and Bakley. I just don't see them putting up a fight. My soldiers will go in and establish control. No fighting. No war."

She didn't know the state of either Carlon or Nisk's armies, but she knew Bakley's army was basically non-existent. It would be so easy for Rainer to take over. Anton's words from the ball last night came back to her. He'd said her father had agreed to have Carin come to Bakley to marry Viktor, bringing along with her ten assassins to train with their army as part of the marriage contract. Perhaps her father feared Rainer would invade. While ten assassins didn't seem like a lot, she knew how lethal and potent they could be.

"And what about the League?" she asked. "They'll never approve of you ruling over other kingdoms."

"Then it's time to dissolve the League. It has served its purpose, now it is no longer needed."

"And that's it? Your mind is made up?"

"It is."

"I came to Lynk thinking we were going to be partners," she said, her voice barely above a whisper. "While I wasn't naive enough to believe this was a love match, I at least thought you'd look to me for guidance and support. I can see now how wrong I was."

Rainer's eyes narrowed. "Partners? *I'm* the king of Lynk."

"And I'm its queen." While she understood that Rainer had grown up without a mother and queen, she thought he'd want those things. He had no idea how powerful the two of them could be if they worked together.

"In name only," he said, clearly annunciating each word. "Once you're cleared to have marital relations, you have two months to give me a child."

That sounded like a threat. "Or what?" she asked, afraid to hear the answer. "You can't take Heather's baby and pass it off as mine. It'll never work."

He went over to his desk and picked up a letter. "King Kai wrote to me. He offered his daughter, Princess Gemma, as a replacement for you."

A replacement? Surprise filled her. Evander had mentioned that Avoni had plans, but she'd had no idea it involved something like this. "Are you saying that if I'm not pregnant with a child in two months, you'll kill me and marry Gemma?" This family was even crazier than she'd thought. It felt as if her cage got smaller, pressing in on her from all sides. Sooner or later, it would kill her.

He took a few slow, menacing steps toward her. "No, I'm saying once you're cleared to have relations with me, then you have two months. I can't afford to waste any more time. I'll do whatever I have to in order to keep the royal throne." His eyes bore into hers as if trying to sear his words into her brain.

She'd seen enough from her brothers to know that sometimes it took more than a couple of tries, sometimes even a few months, to become pregnant with a child. A realization dawned on her along with the feeling of a cold snake slithering up her leg, along her back, and to her shoulder. Rainer *could* kill her. That was what happened to Alina with no consequence. This was probably why Rainer was so willing to forgive his sister—he planned on doing the same thing to Sabine.

With her hands on her hips, she started pacing. While originally thrilled she didn't have to share Rainer's bed right away, now she feared what would happen if she didn't.

"At least you seem to finally realize the stakes," Rainer said, sitting on the edge of his desk.

"I'm surprised you'd make any sort of alliance with Avoni." She noticed he hadn't said anything about invading that kingdom. She couldn't imagine King Kai sitting back and allowing Rainer to rule over Carlon, Nisk, and Bakley without putting up a fight—or a few assassinations.

"And why is that?"

"Well, for one, sending Lottie to the land of assassins seems rather dangerous when she likes to employ them. The last thing anyone needs is for her to become one herself."

He shrugged as if he couldn't care less.

"And I'm shocked you'd even consider King Kai's proposal since you killed his entire delegation." As soon as she spoke the words, she realized her mistake—no one knew Rainer had slaughtered the people on the Avoni ship.

"How do you know about that?" He stood, coming closer to her.

"My brother told me. I assume he knew from the League."

"Hmm." He didn't say anything else.

She wasn't sure the League even knew. All Rainer would have to do was ask Anton. Wanting to change the subject, she said, "I don't understand why you want to invade and take over the other kingdoms. You're the king of Lynk. Isn't that enough?"

"The real question is *why not*. The three kingdoms to our south have weak rulers and barely an army. Instead of the League having the power to make choices and laws, it'll fall to me."

"What about my parents? My brothers and their families?" She feared he planned on killing the other ruling families.

"That remains to be seen. Now, if you'll excuse me, I have matters to attend to." He went and sat at his desk. He looked at her, waiting for her to leave.

Pursing her lips, she started to walk toward the door.

"Oh, and Sabine?"

She paused and glanced over her shoulder at him.

"Stop using my money to buy things in town. That money is for my army. Not for you to waste."

She nodded and left. It was a good thing she'd already bought all those outfits.

Since Sabine's efforts in town seemed to be going so well, she decided to apply the same technique here in the palace. She spent the day wandering around, making sure to go everywhere typically deemed unnecessary for royals. Starting in the kitchen, she met the people who worked there. Then she went and spoke to the guards. Afterward, she introduced herself to those who cleaned the palace. Lastly, she met the people responsible for tending to the gardens. Now, any time she passed one of the servants, she'd smile and acknowledge that person by name.

That evening, Sabine attended Lady Karmen's event. The invite didn't say it was a party or a get-together, it simply stated it was an event that couldn't be spoken about. Having no idea what to expect, Sabine showed up and was pleasantly surprised to find tables had been set up in Karmen's suite, a different game of cards at each one. The candles burned low, alcohol flowed freely, and everyone seemed to be gossiping.

"I'm so glad you came," Karmen said with a curtsey.

"Thank you for having me." She glanced around, chuckling. "Now I understand how you always know the latest court gossip."

Karmen looped her arm with Sabine's as she led her over to one of the tables where a card game was taking place. There was a mixture of men and women here. "We don't use titles," Karmen murmured. "That way people feel safe to speak. Nothing leaves this room. Understand?"

"This is borderline scandalous," Sabine whispered. "I love it."

"I figured you would. And I thought you could benefit from a few more strategic contacts." Karmen winked.

"How often do you do this?"

"Every week." Karmen handed Sabine a glass of wine.

"Why is this the first time I've been invited?" she asked curiously.

"Not just anyone can come," Karmen explained. "It takes a level of trust and a vote of at least half of those you see here. We weren't sure which side you were on until recently. Take a seat. Join in, and have some fun." She patted Sabine on the shoulder before heading over to another table to talk to someone else.

Sabine took a seat and watched the card game unfold. Once she understood the rules, she asked to be dealt in. Unfortunately, she lost the first game. However, the conversation flowed and she found herself enjoying her time with the people around her. When a whistle sounded, the three men from each table stood and moved to an open spot. Once the vacant seats were filled, they began again.

"It's so nice we finally have a queen," the woman to Sabine's right, Ginny, said.

"Yes," another one of the women, Sarak, said. "And one who is not only stylish but exceeding all expectations by setting new trends."

"We've been in dire need of a queen for far too long," Ginny said.

"If only the queen could tame the king," Sarak said.

Sabine didn't know how to respond to those women.

The game ended, Sabine lost, and the whistle blew. The men stood and switched tables again.

When Sarak noticed Sabine watching those moving, she said, "It helps keep conversation going by making the men move."

"That makes sense," she said.

"So tell me," Ginny said, "how are you getting along with the king?"

Sabine leaned back in her chair. "We are still trying to get to know each other," she answered carefully.

"I'm sure it's hard when his mistress is hovering around all the time. You poor thing."

She felt her face warm but decided not to say anything. The point of tonight was for her to gain as much of the palace gossip as she could, not add to it by speaking negatively of her husband. He could ruin his reputation all on his own.

The new round began. The men spoke about sending reinforcements south to the army camps.

"When you say reinforcements," Sabine said, "do you mean soldiers or supplies?"

"Both," one of the men, Jemes, answered, eyeing her, as if trying to discern her intentions.

"Forgive my questions," Sabine said, trying to sound meek, "but I know so little about the army. Now that I'm queen, I wish to know more so that I may better serve you." Her gaze didn't waver.

"I appreciate that." Jemes laid down his cards, winning the round. "I am going to end on a good note," he said. "Besides, I have to run an early training session tomorrow morning. I am going to retire for the evening." He stood and bowed. "It was lovely to meet you, Your Majesty."

"No titles!" Karmen called out from across the room.

Sabine chuckled. "I'm not sure how she heard that."

"Karmen seems to hear everything." Jemes bowed again.

Ginny reached out, placing her hand on his arm. "Before you go, I heard there were more murders."

He nodded. "You heard correctly." His eyes darkened. "It's the same as the last three incidents. It happened at night, and only captains and lieutenants were targeted."

"Who do you think is doing it?" Ginny asked, her voice low.

Jemes shrugged. "I don't know. If I had to guess, I'd say an outsider. I don't think our own men are committing the murders."

Ginny nodded absently. "Thank you."

Jemes bowed again then left.

"Forgive me for asking," Sabine said, "but what murders?"

"You don't know?" Sarak said, leaning in closer and dropping her voice.

Sabine shook her head. "The king doesn't confide in me."

A new card game started.

"My husband said that everyone is scared. In the army camps, when they go to sleep, people are being murdered. It's like a ghost. No one has seen or heard anything. But only the officers are being murdered. My husband thinks it's someone who wants to prevent Lynk from going to war."

Dread filled Sabine. It didn't sound like a ghost—it sounded like an assassin.

The card game ended and the whistle blew. When the men stood to switch tables, Sabine stood as well.

"Are you leaving already?" Karmen asked as she came over to Sabine.

"I am. I have a lot to do tomorrow, and I'm exhausted. Thank you for inviting me."

"I hope you'll join us again," Karmen said, walking her to the door.

"I will."

Out in the hallway, surrounded by her guards, Sabine couldn't think straight. Instead of even trying to sort it all out, she rushed to her room and dismissed Harper for the night. Once she was finally alone with only Harta for company, she let the memories bombard her. King Kai had told her he'd sent a unit of assassins to Lynk along with the Avoni delegation. He'd also explained that though the delegation had been murdered, his assassins were still in the kingdom. Missing and possibly stuck. Then she recalled both Evander and Kai telling her that their kingdom had plans of its own and that things were already in motion. She wondered if this was it. Kai had insisted he'd stop at nothing to prevent Lynk from going to war.

Sick to her stomach, Sabine changed into her nightclothes then went out onto her balcony, gazing up at the full moon and letting the cool air caress her clammy skin. If, as she suspected, there was a group of assassins in Lynk, she wondered what their specific orders were. While Kai ruled over Avoni as its king, Evander ruled over one of the kingdom's assassin guilds. If these men belonged to Evander's guild, then he would be the one calling the shots.

She rubbed her temples, realizing she was in over her head. How she thought she could handle this on her own was beyond her.

It seemed as if there were a dozen different plots going on at the same time, and each plot had a different puppet master. Given the stakes, this was not a game she could afford to lose.

A light *thump* sounded behind her. She turned, expecting to find Harta, but a man stood there dressed in solid black. Harta began sneaking up to him from behind. Sabine reached down for the dagger she normally strapped to her thigh, only to remember she'd taken it off.

"Are you going to call off your dog so I can properly greet you?" a familiar voice asked.

A little cry escaped Sabine's mouth, and she gave the command for Harta to hold. The dog stopped advancing.

Evander pulled off the mask covering his face. It was the most beautiful sight Sabine had ever beheld. She ran at him, throwing her body against his, her arms coming around his neck.

Evander kissed her cheek, sending a jolt of warmth through her.

"You're here," she whispered, clutching onto him.

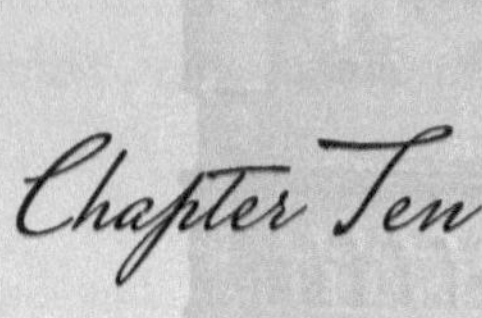

Chapter Ten

"I'm here," Evander said, one hand against Sabine's lower back and his other hand gently holding her head against his shoulder.

Sabine breathed him in. When he kissed the top of her head, she pulled back, looking at him. "What are you doing here?" Not only in Lynk, but on her balcony.

"I had to see you." His eyes roamed over her body, examining her. "Are you all right?"

"I am."

He let out a big breath. "I've been so worried about you."

She grabbed his shirt and pulled him into her bedchamber. She didn't think anyone would be able to see them out on the balcony at night, but she couldn't be sure. Since no candles had been lit, her room remained dark and it felt safer in there.

When Sabine had said goodbye to Evander in Avoni, she didn't think she'd be seeing him any time soon. "I've missed you." More than she'd thought possible.

"I've been so worried about you." He ran a hand through his hair. "Are Markis and your brother here with you?"

"No, they both went back to Bakley."

"You're all alone?" he asked.

"Not anymore, now that you're here." She had so many questions for him—like how he'd gotten into the palace. But all she could think about was touching him. She reached forward, placing her hand on his chest and breathing him in.

His hands came up to her shoulders, rubbing them. "Sabine," he whispered.

She'd always loved the way he said her name.

"You need to know that I officially arrive tomorrow."

She nodded.

"I've come to collect my bride."

She froze, the temperature feeling like it had suddenly dropped ten degrees.

"But I had to come and see you first. I need to know that you're okay."

His words felt like a knife to her heart. He reached down, placing his hand under her jaw and tilting her head up so he could see into her eyes. "You're unharmed?" he asked, his voice low and husky. "Rainer hasn't hurt you?"

"I'm fine," she revealed. "He fears you and I were intimate, so he refuses to share my bed until I've had a cycle."

"He suspects we had an affair?" Evander asked.

"I've assured him we have not been together," she said.

He took a step back, his hands going to his hips as he gazed at something behind her. "As long as he hasn't hurt you."

"There's something I should have told you before, in Avoni." She shouldn't have waited this long to tell him, especially after everything they'd been through together.

"What is it?" He reached out, his hands going to her arms. "You can tell me anything."

"Rainer and I...we haven't..." This was harder than it

should be. "We haven't consummated our marriage." She rolled her shoulders back, trying to stand tall.

Evander stilled. "Your marriage isn't consummated?"

"No."

"Does anyone else know?"

"Only my brother. He told me not to tell anyone."

Evander nodded. "Your brother's right—don't tell anyone."

"I was more concerned that I hadn't told you than as to how others would perceive the news," she admitted.

"While I personally am thrilled, I'm worried on your behalf. If your marriage isn't consummated, you can be arrested and relieved of your position here. You'd have very little protection." He ran a hand over his face again. "Now I can see why you were so adamant about us not being together."

"If I could choose who to experience my first time with, it would be you," she whispered, her heart fracturing from the admission knowing they could never be together.

He stepped closer to her, his hand coming up, cupping her cheek. "Sabine."

She closed her eyes, reveling in the feel of his hand on her face. "I've missed you."

He dropped his forehead to hers. "I need you to promise me something."

"Anything."

"If something goes wrong, if something happens to me, promise me you'll leave the palace. I want you to go to the League's house and wait there until your brother comes for you."

"What are you planning to do while you're here?" she asked, wondering if he had an assassination mission of his own.

"I can't tell you. But if things go badly, you need to get out of here."

Gazing into his green eyes, she couldn't imagine anything happening to him. "You want me to leave my subjects? Abandon my kingdom?"

"Yes. It's for your own safety."

She didn't know if she could do that. Hiding away didn't seem like it would solve anything.

"Sabine, promise me."

"I took an oath."

"But your marriage isn't consummated. The oath might not be binding. Your life might end up being in jeopardy."

She needed to know. "Is there another assassin after me?"

He didn't say anything.

"People have been turning up dead here in Lynk," she said. "Do you know anything about that?"

"The less you know, the better," he answered.

She didn't know how to respond to that. If the two of them could just be open and honest, then they could work together. But he was a prince from Avoni and she was the queen of Lynk. They had each made vows to protect their respective kingdoms.

"I wish," she said, but then thought better of it.

"What do you wish?" he probed. "Tell me."

"I wish there was a way for us to be together."

The corners of his lips pulled into a smile. "I wish that as well." He kissed her cheek. "I need to get back to my ship."

"Be safe," she whispered.

He went over to the wall beside the archway, gripped the uneven stones, and hauled himself upward. Within minutes, he was out of sight. Her assassin-pirate-prince.

Harper burst into Sabine's room, waking her. "Your Majesty," Harper said, coming to sit on the edge of the bed. "I have news."

Sabine rubbed her eyes, sitting up. "What is it?"

"A ship flying Avoni's royal flag has been spotted. The king wants you dressed for receiving guests." She pulled Sabine's covers back.

"Any word on who's here?" Sabine asked as she stood and stretched, knowing it had to be Evander.

"Not officially. But the king asked for you to wear blue. I heard him say something about it being Prince Evander coming here for Lottie." Harper dropped her voice to a whisper. "Do you think the prince is an assassin? My mother said everyone in Avoni is an assassin."

Sabine knelt and gave Harta good morning kisses. "Who knows. Maybe you can ask him when you meet him."

"Yeah right," Harper said. "I don't need an assassin coming after me. I think I'll stay away." Harper went into the closet. "You want to wear something my sister made?" she yelled.

"Yes, please," she called out. Then softer, she whispered to Harta, "You're lucky you can stay here and lounge around. That you don't have to see the man you love with another woman—especially someone as vile as Lottie."

"I have just the thing for you to wear," Harper said as she came out of the closet, carrying an outfit with her. "And it'll make you look so pretty the assassin won't even think about killing you."

Sabine stood and chuckled. While Harper was a little rough on the edges, she provided a ray of light in this otherwise dreary palace.

Once dressed, Sabine went over to the door leading to the royal suite and knocked. Gunther admitted her. She found Rainer stretched out on the sofa, his feet propped up on the low table, a glass with some sort of ale in his right hand. He had on dark blue pants and a matching tunic.

"You look nice," she said.

He tilted his head, looking her over. "And you look stunning."

She smiled. Only in Lynk would someone think her outfit *stunning*. She showed more skin than fabric. Regardless, the blue matched his clothing perfectly. The sheer material accentuated her breasts and legs, a string of pearls wrapped around her body to hold the fabric in place.

Rainer stood, setting his glass on the low table. "Sometimes I forget how beautiful you are." His hand reached out to her shoulder, trailing down her arm to her wrist.

She shivered.

"Your skin is so smooth." He gripped her wrist.

Unease filled her. His touch felt too predatory—so different from Evander's. "I was told you wanted me dressed for a visitor?" she said, hoping to remind him that they had somewhere to be. She glanced around, not seeing Gunther or any other guards on duty.

"Yes." His other hand reached for her free arm, sliding down and encircling that wrist as well.

She held still, trying not to react to his touch.

His eyes roamed over her body and he took a step closer to her, licking his lips.

She automatically took a step back, wanting to keep some space between them. Her heart beat frantically. "You said you wouldn't touch me until I bled."

He chuckled, the sound low and throaty. "No, I said I wouldn't share your bed. Two very different things."

Her brows pulled together in confusion as she tried to think of a way out of this mess.

He reached up, touching her bottom lip, causing her to

jerk slightly at his touch. "What are you doing?" she demanded.

"Hmm…so jumpy. I'm beginning to think you haven't slept with another man."

At that, she rolled her eyes. "I told you I haven't been intimate with anyone." When she'd traveled alone with Evander, they had shared a bed. While nothing untoward had happened, she wanted to make sure she was clear so she wouldn't be caught in a lie.

He leaned down, his lips nearing hers.

Instinct made her pull away. "I'm sorry." She took a step back, putting some space between them. "The thought of you kissing Heather and sharing a bed with her makes me feel dirty." Admitting this to him was difficult. Heather was Rainer's age, and she was one of the most beautiful women Sabine had ever seen. While Sabine knew Rainer didn't love her, she still wanted them to have a marriage like her parents had. She wanted him to be true to her.

His eyes flashed with anger. "What I do with Heather is none of your business—it has nothing to do with you. You're my *wife*. I can do with you as I please."

Growing up, she'd never heard her father speak about her mother in such a way. "I am your wife—not your property." Her hands started to shake as anger took root. "And the last thing your wife wants to think about is her husband with another woman."

"I had an agreement with Alina," he said, as if that made it okay.

"I'm not Alina." She pulled back farther. "How would you feel if I had a man I shared a bed with whenever I pleased?"

His eyes narrowed. "Don't forget, when I am with you for the first time, if you're not a virgin, I'll kill you myself." His words held a promise to them.

"I know." She was a virgin and had nothing to fear.

He must have seen the truth in her eyes. "Sabine." He took a step toward her.

She backed up, hitting the wall.

He released her wrist, his hands now splayed on the wall on either side of her head, trapping her in. "We're married," he said. "You will let me touch you."

She shook her head. "I'm not ready." Especially since she'd seen Evander last night and he'd stirred up emotions that she'd been trying to bury.

"You need to let me help you get ready." He leaned down, his lips pressing a kiss against the corner of her mouth, trailing down to her neck. One of his hands lowered to her waist, his calloused palm against her soft skin.

Sabine had a feeling that if she pushed him away, he'd retaliate. The last thing she wanted to do was upset him so he forced himself on her. Rainer was doing this to show her he held the power—and if she wanted to win, she needed to let him *think* he had it. Her right hand came out, laying flat against his chest as she tilted her head, giving him better access to her neck.

"Your Majesties," Gunther said. "I'm sorry to disturb you, but your guest has arrived."

Rainer pulled back, his eyes searching hers for something. "We'll finish this later," he whispered as he straightened.

Releasing the breath she'd been holding, she pushed off the wall, thankful for the timely interruption. She smoothed her dress, trying to still her shaking hands as she did so.

"Let's go," Rainer said, holding out his hand to Sabine.

She took it, and they exited the royal suite.

"Who's here?" she asked as they made their way through the palace.

"One minute," Rainer said, ignoring her question. "Gunther, have my brothers been informed?"

"They have, Your Majesty. The rest of your family should

already be there waiting for you." Gunther pulled a door open, revealing the antechamber to the throne room.

Sabine stepped inside and froze. Anton, Axel, and Lottie were there, all finely dressed, their heads bent close together as they spoke in hushed whispers.

"What's she doing here?" Sabine demanded. Lottie was supposed to be sequestered to her bedchamber, not out and about in the palace.

Rainer ignored her and went over to Lottie, placing his hand on her shoulder while whispering something in her ear.

Axel approached Sabine. "Never a dull moment. Hope you have a dagger hidden on you." He looked her over. "Though, I have no idea where you'd hide it."

She didn't bother answering him because she was too upset by Lottie's presence. Even though Evander was here to collect the princess, it didn't mean she should be given free rein of the palace.

The door opened, announcing Princess Lottie, Prince Anton, and Prince Axel. The three siblings exited the antechamber.

"Why is your sister here?" Sabine asked again.

"Now is not the time." Rainer took her hand, leading her to the doorway.

Before Sabine could argue, the herald announced, "His Majesty King Rainer Manfred, and Her Majesty Queen Sabine Manfred."

Rainer moved her hand to his arm as he led her into the throne room. The couple dozen people in attendance all bowed.

At the top of the dais, Rainer said, "Rise." His siblings all stood on the lower step, fanned out on either side of the king and queen.

"Thank you all for coming on such short notice," Rainer began. "A special guest has arrived here at the palace. I want to introduce you to him, and I have a wonderful announcement to make."

Movement at the back of the room caught Sabine's attention. Evander had arrived. He stood at the end of the aisle, a handful of Avoni guards with him. He wore a dark green silk tunic and matching pants, each embroidered with gold stitching. He also donned a sword and cape. The entire ensemble made him look like the assassin-prince he was. Sabine found it hard to breathe.

"I want to officially welcome Prince Evander Botoko of Avoni to Lynk." Rainer lifted his hand, gesturing for Evander to join him.

Everyone twisted to see the prince, bowing as they caught sight of him. He strode forward with confidence, his guards in two rows following close behind. Unlike the prince, they all wore solid black, their tunics and pants covering most of their skin, leaving little exposed to the elements. As Evander neared the dais, he didn't look Sabine's way.

Lottie glanced over her shoulder and smirked at Sabine. "Not my type, but not bad at all. I can make due with that."

Sabine wanted to rip Lottie's eyes out.

"I am pleased to announce the official betrothal of Prince Evander Botoko of Avoni to Princess Lottie Manfred of Lynk." Rainer didn't release Sabine's hand as they stood on the dais above everyone.

Lottie stepped forward to meet Evander just as he came to a stop at the bottom of the dais.

"Princess," Evander said with a bow, "it is a pleasure to meet you. You're even more beautiful than I imagined."

Lottie reached her hand forward and Evander took it, pressing his lips to the back of her hand.

Sabine wanted to tear Lottie's hand away from Evander.

"The wedding will take place next week," Rainer said.

Shock rolled through Sabine. There was no way she'd be

able to see the two of them wed. Evander was hers. And Lottie needed to be rotting in prison.

"No one is clapping," Axel murmured so low only Sabine could hear.

Rainer continued, "Tonight, my beautiful wife and I will hold a celebration for our esteemed guest. I hope to see you all there." He led Sabine from the dais to the balcony off to the side. Evander and Lottie followed close behind, Anton and Axel after them.

The throne room began to empty, leaving the royal family alone out on the balcony, the sun shining brightly overhead. A servant approached carrying a tray with goblets filled with wine.

Sabine took hers and turned away from everyone, gazing out at the view before her. As to how she was supposed to stand there and toast to Lottie—the woman responsible for killing her sister—she didn't know. And Evander...

A hand slid onto her lower back. "Darling," Rainer purred, "join us." He guided her around so she faced the group that had gathered in a small circle.

Evander and Lottie stood arm in arm across from her. She refused to raise her eyes and look at either one of them for fear everyone would see her hatred for Lottie and her love for Evander. Hopefully, this would only last a few minutes, then she could get away from them.

"Prince Evander, thank you for making the journey here," Rainer said. "You obviously know me from your last visit, and you know Anton since he's a fellow League member." Rainer gestured toward Axel. "My brother, Axel, and my beloved sister, Lottie." His hand curled around Sabine's waist. "And my darling wife, Sabine, whom you know from not only your visit here but from the League's house."

Evander raised his goblet. "Thank you for the warm welcome," he said, not bothering to acknowledge Sabine or anyone else for that matter. The prince's focus remained on Rainer, never wavering.

When Sabine had been in Avoni, she recalled Markis figuring out she had feelings for Evander after spending a couple of minutes with the two of them. He'd advised her to never be near Evander when other people were around because he said their mutual attraction was too obvious. Well, right now, standing on the balcony, Sabine wondered if Evander cared for her at all. If she hadn't seen him last night, she would assume she meant nothing to him. Sabine, on the other hand, had to force herself not to look his way.

Rainer trailed his hand up Sabine's back, making her shiver.

"I'd like to sit down with you to go over a few things," Evander said, taking another sip from his goblet. "Is now a good time?"

Rainer turned his full attention to Sabine, his lips pressing against her neck. "Darling," he murmured, "I know you *begged* me to spend the day with you in bed, but I need to take care of this. Do you think you can wait a couple of hours? I *promise* to make it worth your while."

Dread coursed through her. It took every ounce of her willpower not to look over at Evander to see his reaction. But that was what Rainer intended—to push her into revealing her feelings for the assassin-prince. She had no idea what Lottie told him about her time with Evander, but all anyone would have seen was the two of them traveling together. No one could possibly know they were friends—more than friends. Evander's family had suspected their feelings for one another went beyond friendship. Surely they wouldn't have told anyone. While they might not care about Sabine or what happened to her, they definitely cared about Evander and would protect him.

Rainer's hand slid down her back, far lower than

appropriate. This was a dangerous game. While Sabine had no problem pushing the boundaries to get what she wanted, she feared pushing this man would set her on a course she was not ready to take.

She patted his chest. "Do whatever you need to," she said, her voice low as she peered up at him through hooded eyes. "I'll be waiting for you." After setting her goblet down, she turned and strode from the balcony, not wanting to hear what anyone—especially Axel—had to say about that little performance.

She was halfway through the throne room when someone grabbed her arm and stopped her. Spinning around, she found Rainer there, his eyes searching hers. "What do you want?" she asked, glancing over his shoulder to see if anyone had followed him.

"Why are you upset?" he asked, keeping his voice low. "Is it because Evander is here?"

She rolled her eyes. "Is that what you think?"

"Something has you rattled."

He wasn't wrong. "I'm upset," she said, enunciating each word as if speaking to a child, "because the woman responsible for killing my sister is standing on the balcony, celebrating her engagement. It doesn't seem fair. She should be in jail." She needed to stay focused on Lottie so no one would suspect her feelings for Evander.

Rainer considered her. "Do you know why I agreed to this marriage?"

"To get rid of Lottie," she answered. "To solve a problem."

He nodded. "True, but there is more to it than that."

She raised her eyebrows, wondering if he'd elaborate. When he didn't say anything, Sabine replied, "Since she is free, she can arrange for an assassin to kill me. I'm scared." Though, she didn't sound scared because she was more ticked off than afraid.

Rainer chuckled and leaned toward Sabine, his lips coming to her right ear. "I know," he whispered. "Which is why I agreed to the marriage. If any assassin touches you, it will be considered a direct threat from the Avoni throne. King Kai assured me he would guarantee his assassins know that you are off limits—even if Lottie offers them an abundance of money. No one can touch you. Well, no one except for me." He straightened, watching her, observing her, as if trying to read her thoughts.

"So what you're saying is that you did this for me?" Sabine said.

"Well, I did it for me. I need you alive so you can have my child."

"I guess I should thank you," she said, wanting—*needing* —to get away from Rainer before she punched him.

"You can thank me tonight." He smirked as he took a step back. "Oh, and Sabine? Show a little gratitude next time. You don't need to act like a prissy Bakley bitch." And with that, he returned to the balcony, rejoining his siblings and Evander.

Sabine practically ran out of the throne room, her heart pounding.

Out in the corridor, she found her guards waiting for her.

"Pardon me for saying this, but you look a little rattled," Drew said as he came to walk alongside her. "Is everything all right?"

"Yes, thank you." She kept walking, thinking through everything Rainer had just revealed. He'd said that Kai had assured him *his* assassins wouldn't touch Sabine. She knew Kai wasn't in charge of any of the assassin guilds. Rainer probably had no idea how they even worked. So while the stipulation sounded good, it was an empty promise.

Entering a courtyard, Sabine ran her hand over one of the rose bushes, the soft petals caressing her skin. The thought of Evander marrying Lottie made her sick. It felt wrong. However, while she desperately wanted Lottie to pay for killing Alina, Sabine didn't want to come across as a jilted lover just wanting to stop the wedding. If she had any hope of holding Lottie accountable, she'd have to handle the matter carefully. Delicately.

She meandered over to the water fountain and sat on the bench before it. Her priorities needed to be lined up. First and foremost, she needed to stop the war. Secondly, she'd seek retribution for Lottie's crimes. Sabine needed to remember she was the queen of Lynk and was married to Rainer. Any and all thoughts of Evander had to be just that— thoughts. There was no future with the Avoni prince. If maintaining peace meant that she'd stand at Rainer's side for the rest of her life to ensure the kingdoms carried on and followed the League of Rulers, she would. Because all that mattered were her people. Her heart, her desires, were so far down on her list of priorities that she couldn't even consider them.

However, that didn't stop the pain searing through her heart. It didn't stop her eyes from filling with tears.

Chapter Eleven

"It looks like you have nothing on but diamonds," Rainer said as he joined Sabine in the sitting room. "I've never seen anything like it—you're stunning." She stood still as he walked around her, examining her from all angles. "You'll outshine everyone tonight."

That was the goal. "Shall we go?" She headed for the door, not wanting to be alone with him in the royal suite.

Rainer took her arm, escorting her out into the hallway. He wore loose black pants and an open tunic, exposing his toned chest and stomach.

Sabine assumed they'd be going to the ballroom. However, Rainer led her to the other side of the palace, stopping before a large archway covered with flowers which opened to an enormous balcony. At least two hundred guests were present, some already dancing. A group of musicians was situated off to the side. The black marble flooring reflected the stars in the night sky, creating a magical effect.

"Your outfit matches perfectly," Rainer said.

"This is breathtaking." Sabine had never been to a ball outside on a balcony before.

The herald introduced the two of them and they passed beneath the archway, striding out onto the balcony, going straight to the middle of the dancing area for their traditional first dance. Everyone stepped back to watch the two of them.

Rainer took Sabine's hand while his other one went to the small of her back. She placed her free hand on his shoulder. The music began, the song slow and inscrutable, somehow matching the mood of the night perfectly. Rainer kept his focus on Sabine, intense and unwavering. He spun her around, pulling her back to him, a little closer this time. The heat from his torso pressed against her bare stomach, feeling intimate. Scandalous. As the music slowed, coming to a close, Rainer leaned down, brushing his lips against Sabine's. Her face flushed with embarrassment. Kissing wasn't something people did in public. But she was in Lynk now so maybe it wasn't frowned upon like it was in Bakley. The music ended, and the two of them stepped back from each other, turning to face the crowd.

Rainer invited the guests of honor to dance. Evander and Lottie came forward, arm in arm.

Sabine and Rainer stood off to the side, watching the two of them move around the dance floor. They made an odd couple. While Lottie looked beautiful in a lavender dress that only covered what was necessary, exposing large amounts of skin, her dark hair in soft waves along her back, she was at odds with Evander who donned a typical Avoni outfit—long sleeves and pants, both black with red stitching along the edges, covering almost every inch of his body. The only skin visible was that on his face. His hands were even covered with gloves. As the two of them danced, neither one spoke. Lottie smiled the entire time, looking at Evander from under her lashes, but his focus seemed to be somewhere over her head.

When the song came to an end, Rainer went to dance

with his sister. After hesitating a moment, Sabine stepped forward, not sure if she should dance with Evander.

Not missing a beat, Evander strode to Sabine, holding out his hand to her. "May I please have this dance?"

Since those present were still watching the royal couples dance, she gave a single nod and slid her hand into his. Even though she couldn't feel his skin, just touching him sent a jolt of heat up her arm and to her heart. She didn't want to be so attracted to Evander, but she couldn't help it. Her body had a mind of its own. Which was crazy because when she'd first met him, she hadn't thought of him as handsome at all. It had happened slowly, over time, as she got to know him.

The music began again, another slow and emotionally moving song. They kept a respectable distance between them as they danced, though Sabine didn't dare meet his green eyes. She didn't trust her body to react appropriately.

"You look..." His voice trailed off, his lips barely moving as he spoke.

"I know it's not Avoni fashion." Like Bakley, his kingdom would consider her outfit highly inappropriate.

"No," he cleared his throat, "it most certainly is not Avoni fashion."

At that, she glanced up, making the terrible mistake of gazing into his dark green eyes. Her breath caught at the emotion she saw swirling in them. Want, appreciation, desire. Her skin felt like it was on fire. She quickly glanced away, trying to appear aloof as she focused on the people in attendance.

"You've been busy," Evander said.

"What do you mean?"

"I've only just arrived here in Lynk and I can already see everyone here loves you. You're all anyone talks about. Your kindness, beauty, how much you care about the common folk. You've won them over."

"Must be my scandalous outfits," she joked.

"Careful," he said. "You're smiling. I don't want anyone to think you're having fun with me. I'm from Avoni." His thumb rubbed circles on her palm.

"I've missed you," she whispered. Evander had such an easy way of making her feel at home.

He sighed. "Please don't lick your bottom lip like that," he mumbled. "It's hard enough to touch you without *touching* you. If you lick your lip like that again, my composure will slip, and I'm barely hanging on as it is."

Her body tensed at his words. Such simple words that evoked so many emotions. "Please don't marry Lottie." The words slipped out before she thought better of it.

"Sabine, I have to." His grip tightened ever so slightly.

"But you don't love her."

"If it keeps Rainer from declaring war against Avoni, if it saves my people, it's a small price to pay."

"She'll never make you happy."

He closed his eyes for a couple of seconds. When he opened them, he said, "I had to stand there and watch you dance with Rainer. I had to watch his eyes roam over your body, as if he's entitled to it. When his lips caressed yours…"

"I haven't shared a bed with him."

"But you will." When she went to protest, he shook his head. "My point is simply that I know what it feels like, so you don't need to tell me. I understand. It hurts."

"I don't want to share his bed. Ever." The words came out barely a whisper.

"I know you. You'll share his bed if it means saving your subjects." He raised his brows, daring her to tell him he was wrong.

"For once I'd like to do what I want," she mumbled.

"We could, you know."

"What do you mean?" Her heart began to pound,

demanding to know if there was a way for them to be together.

"Just say the word, and I'll get you out of here. We can run away together."

Her feet froze, and she stood there staring at him. "You'd do that?" He'd run away with her knowing it would put Avoni at risk—his family, his subjects, his assassin guild?

He nodded.

The song ended.

"The question is, would you?" He bowed then turned, going over to Lottie and taking her hand. The crowd descended upon them, consuming the dance floor, as a lively tune began playing.

Sabine remained standing there, dumbfounded. Evander would run away with her, but she couldn't even consider the possibility. As much as she wanted to, she wouldn't abandon her people. If she did, then Alina's death would have been for nothing. She needed to stay and fight.

"Queen Sabine," Commander Felix said, bowing before her. "A dance?"

She nodded and took Felix's hand. He spoke of unassuming topics, none of which held her interest because she couldn't stop thinking about Evander.

At the end of the song, he whispered, "The report you requested is in your room. I put it under your mattress. Please let me know if you need anything else." He bowed.

Axel stepped in front of her, requesting the next dance. "I'm not sure where to put my hands," he said. "You look practically naked. I'm afraid to touch something I shouldn't."

She rolled her eyes. All necessary parts were covered with skin colored fabric.

"If I move one of these strands of diamonds, will they all fall off?" He cocked his head to the side.

Sabine chose to ignore that comment. Instead, she asked,

"Why isn't Rainer dancing?" He stood off to the side, his arms folded, not even talking with anyone.

"People are upset with Rainer." His eyes sparkled with mischief.

"Because he wants to go to war with other kingdoms?" If that was the case, maybe she could convince him to stand down. Maybe Felix could even talk with Rainer.

He shook his head. "You honestly don't know?"

Annoyance filled her. "If I knew, we obviously wouldn't be having this conversation."

"Well, my dear Sabine, it seems the people of Lynk love you. They're upset with Rainer for flaunting his mistress around court. Haven't you noticed she's not here tonight? Normally, she'd be at an event like this."

It hadn't crossed her mind to even look for the woman—she'd been too distracted by Evander.

"Whatever you're doing," Axel continued, "keep doing it. Right now, Rainer is attempting to rectify his reputation. You must understand, Lynk hasn't had a queen in quite some time." He pushed her back, holding her at arm's length. "And right now, you're the most beautiful queen our kingdom has ever had." Axel twirled her around before pulling her back into his arms. "What's even more impressive is that you seem innocent, but I think you know exactly what you're doing. When you first arrived here, I didn't think you'd survive Rainer. Now, I don't think he's going to survive you."

The song ended.

Axel winked then turned to find another partner.

Off to the side, Sabine spotted Lottie leaning against the railing, talking to Anton. Without overthinking it, she headed that way. Since she'd returned to the palace, she'd made it clear Lottie should be locked up. If she allowed this evening to pass without making a small scene, then people might think she was okay with Lottie now that the princess was leaving the kingdom, and that was far from the case.

When neither noticed her approach, she cleared her throat.

Anton glanced over his shoulder and upon seeing Sabine, he straightened and turned to face her. "Your Majesty." He nudged his sister in the ribs.

Lottie slowly turned around, eyeing Sabine.

"Do you need something?" Anton asked.

"I just came over to see what the protocols are for Lottie," Sabine replied. "I assumed she'd have a guard and would return to her room once her dance with Evander was over."

"I believe she is no longer confined to her room." Anton shifted uncomfortably.

"Are you saying she will not be punished for the part she played in Alina's death?"

Lottie smirked. "What bothers you more? That I'm not in the dungeon or that I'm marrying the man you're in love with?"

Sabine's eyes widened in shock. "What did you say?" There was no way Lottie could know Sabine had feelings for Evander.

Lottie took a step closer to Sabine. "I knew you'd traveled with him," she said, her voice low and containing a threat rumbling through it. "Enough people saw the two of you. What I didn't know was that you'd fallen for him."

"I have no idea what you're talking about." Sabine's body prickled with heat.

Lottie took another step closer. "You're young and innocent. Prince Evander probably didn't even have to lure you to his bed. You probably offered yourself willingly. Pathetic."

Fury filled Sabine. "You are out of line." Her hands balled into fists.

"You're only upset because I speak the truth."

"The truth?" Sabine sneered, trying to keep her temper in check so she wouldn't say something she'd end up regretting later. "The truth is you're responsible for Alina's death. You tried to have me killed. You want your brother's throne."

"Keep your voices down," Anton said, moving to stand between the two women.

"You're just jealous I'm marrying Evander," Lottie said, leaning around Anton to look Sabine in the eyes. "When you're in bed with Rainer, do you imagine he's Evander?"

Sabine wanted to hit her.

"That's enough," Anton said, twisting to face Lottie. "Like it or not, Sabine is your queen. You will treat her with respect."

"She's just jealous," Lottie mumbled.

"Is there a problem?" Rainer asked as he joined them, looking at Sabine.

Sabine didn't know what to say.

Rainer gently gripped her elbow. "Tell me what's wrong."

"Nothing." She forced a smile on her lips. "It's just—"

"Are you all right?" Evander asked as he came to stand next to Sabine.

"This is ridiculous," Lottie snapped. "She's a grown woman and can take care of herself. She doesn't need to be doted on by every male in the vicinity. Unless..." Her eyes focused on Evander.

"You're wrong," Anton said, garnering everyone's attention. "Sabine is our queen. Everyone's focus should be on her—including you, sister."

"Whatever," Lottie mumbled.

Sabine rolled her shoulders back, trying to regain her composure. "I'm sorry to have caused a scene at this lovely ball," she said, her focus on Rainer as she spoke. "However, you know how I feel about the woman responsible for my sister's death. I am finding it difficult to be around her."

Evander reached a gloved hand out to Lottie. "Let's have one last dance. Then I'll escort you to your room for the night."

"I'd love that," Lottie cooed. "Then we can spend some time together. Alone. It'll help us get to know one another better." Her eyes darkened as she took Evander's arm, leading him over to the dance area.

"If you'll excuse me," Anton said before hurrying away.

Taking a deep breath, Sabine leaned against the railing, gazing out at the stars without really seeing them. "I'm sorry. I should have ignored Lottie."

"She'll be gone soon," he assured her, tucking her hair behind her ear.

Sabine had to force herself not to flinch from the touch. "I still don't understand why she doesn't face the same laws as every other Lynk citizen."

"She's my sister," he said, as if that explained everything.

"And Alina was mine." Why didn't he understand that simple fact?

"Let me ask you this," Rainer said as he came to lean on the railing next to her. "If the tables were reversed, could you condemn one of your brothers to die? Or would you find a solution that worked for everyone involved?"

"None of my brothers would hire an assassin to kill someone."

"Are you sure about that?"

She was sure. "Let's flip that. What if one of my brothers killed your sister? Would you be content to let it go if I found an easy solution that didn't hold him accountable? Could you live with that?"

He considered her.

Movement caught Sabine's attention, and she gazed past Rainer to Heather standing on his other side. She stiffened.

"What?" He followed her line of sight. "Heather, I asked you to stay in your room tonight."

"I went for a walk," she said, stepping even closer to him. "Then I saw the party. I came in to dance with my husband."

Heather was impeccably dressed for a supposed walk. And, come to think of it, Sabine didn't remember seeing Cutler this evening.

"It's late," Rainer said. "I'll walk you back to your room. You and the baby need rest." The two of them left.

Sabine stood there, dumbfounded. He hadn't even bothered to say goodnight. Maybe he'd forgotten she was there. Well, she'd certainly had enough of this farce of a party. There was nothing to celebrate.

She made her way past the dancers and to the balcony's exit. Her guards joined her, and she headed through the palace. At one of the intersections, she spotted Evander coming her way.

"Your Majesty," he said as he approached. "Can I accompany you somewhere?"

"Where's Princess Lottie?"

"In her room."

She wished she was back in Avoni with Evander. Traveling in a boat on one of the canals.

"Sabine?"

"I'm just retiring for the night. It has been a long day."

"Excellent, I'll escort you."

Instead of arguing with him in the middle of the corridor, with her guards mere feet away, she simply nodded, and they began walking.

Evander slid his hands in his pockets. "Is there somewhere we can go to talk?" he whispered, peering back at her guards.

"I don't think that's a wise idea."

"Even though Rainer just left with that other woman?"

"He's escorting her to her room." Wherever that may be.

"And she's pregnant with Rainer's child?"

"I can't do this right now," Sabine said, coming to a stop, her hands on her hips.

"Then leave with me," he whispered. "Tonight. Right now. Let's go."

She wanted to, she really did, but she couldn't. "I have to stop Rainer from going to war."

"I told you my family has plans in place." Plans as in multiple, not singular.

However, she couldn't count on the Avoni king and queen. She could only count on herself. "I can't leave."

"Sabine." He took a step closer. "Please leave with me. Trust me. Please."

Drew cleared his throat, garnering Sabine's attention. When she realized how close the two of them were, she abruptly took a step away from Evander, putting some space between them, just as Rainer rounded the corner, Heather on his arm. Drew's warning had been impeccably timed.

"What's going on?" Rainer demanded.

Evander, hands still casually in his pockets, turned to face Rainer. "I just walked Princess Lottie to her room. Somehow, I got turned around and ran into Queen Sabine. She was just giving me directions back to the guest wing."

"Really?" Rainer asked, coming closer, Heather still clutching his arm. "I find it hard to believe that you, of all people, would get turned around."

He had a point, but Sabine remained silent.

Evander shrugged. "Everything looks the same around here. And quite honestly, I wasn't really paying attention to my whereabouts when I walked with Lottie. I had other things on my mind."

Rainer looked at Sabine, his brows raised.

Since she didn't know where the guest wing was, it would be difficult for her to give directions. "I told him one of my guards could direct him." She observed Heather. "However, now that you're here, perhaps you can escort Prince Evander to the guest wing."

"Oh, I'm not—" Heather began.

Rainer squeezed her arm, silencing her. He opened his mouth to speak, but Sabine beat him to it.

"Unless you're not staying in the guest wing because you're too busy sharing my husband's bed. If that's the case, I can escort Evander myself." Not wanting to hear either of their replies, she spun on her heel and stalked back the way she'd come from.

"Sabine," Rainer called out after her.

She didn't stop.

"I can show you to the guest wing," Rainer said to Evander.

"I don't need your help," Evander replied. "I'll figure it out."

Sabine rounded the first corner she came to and leaned against the wall, squeezing her eyes shut.

Chapter Twelve

"That husband of yours is a piece of work," Evander said.

Sabine's eyes flew open to find Evander standing before her.

He nodded his head to the right. "Let's go somewhere more private to talk before that idiot comes after you." Without waiting for her to respond, he headed down the hallway.

Not wanting to overthink it, she followed him, her guards trailing her.

"Captain Drew," Evander said, waving him forward and surprising Sabine that he knew her guard's name. "I'm thinking of going to the library. Will that afford us some privacy?"

"I think that's a wise decision at this hour," Drew replied, stepping back to rejoin the rest of her guards.

No one spoke as they made their way to the other side of the palace where the library was located. When they got there, the room was dark, lit only by the moonlight filtering in from the tall window at the far end.

"I recommend keeping the oil lamps unlit," Drew stated as he remained near the doorway. "With the ball still going on, people may pass by. Since privacy is what you desire, lights would only attract unwanted attention and make it easier to see inside."

"I agree," Sabine said as she stepped into the room.

"I'll remain here by the entrance with one other guard," Drew said. "The rest will stay nearby out of sight."

"Thank you." Sabine headed over to the window.

"I forgot how much I despise Lynk," Evander whispered. "Its climate, its king, and this confining palace."

Sabine glanced over her shoulder as Evander headed deeper into the library and out of sight.

A few minutes later, he returned, sitting on one of the chairs at the table in front of the window. "I just wanted to make sure no one else was in here. We're alone. Talk to me."

"What's there to say?" The last thing she wanted to do was discuss Rainer and his mistress.

As if reading her thoughts, Evander changed the subject and said, "I've been informed that your brother, Viktor, is marrying my sister, Carin."

She still thought it an odd pairing. "Why Viktor?" Otto would have been a better option.

"I have no idea why my father picked Viktor, but I'm sure he has his reasons."

Aligning Bakley and Avoni was a smart move. However, she wished it would have taken place months ago, then maybe all this nonsense with Lynk wouldn't have happened. Maybe, just maybe, she could have married Evander to align their two kingdoms. Fate could be so cruel. Leaning her head against the glass, she kept her back to Evander.

"Do you plan on standing over there all night?"

If she turned and faced Evander, if she stared into his

green eyes, she was afraid she'd do something stupid, like kiss him.

"Sabine?"

She loved the way he said her name. Having him here, with her, was harder than she'd expected. While she'd missed him, being this close to him made her realize she didn't want to be without him. If he married Lottie, it would kill her. Lottie had already taken Sabine's sister, she couldn't have Evander too. It wasn't fair.

"Please talk to me." His voice was gentle and kind. "I'm not used to you being so quiet. You're starting to scare me."

"I can't," she whispered, tears filling her eyes.

He came and stood next to her, his fingers brushing hers. It reminded her of that time on the bridge at the Avoni palace.

"He doesn't deserve you," Evander whispered. "Leave with me."

His words felt like a warm blanket on a rainy day. She wanted to wrap them around her forever. However, she couldn't. "I have to stay. If Lynk invades Bakley, my family will need me to ensure their safety."

His fingers brushed hers again. "Why is it your job to take care of your family when they sent you here?"

Of all people, Evander had to understand the predicament she was in. He was the youngest of four and knew about duty and obligation. "I can't do this with you right now." A tear slid down her cheek.

"You won't even consider leaving with me?"

"If we ran away together, the consequences would be severe. Rainer would seek retribution. I have no idea what your family would do, and I'd rather not find out given you're from a kingdom of assassins."

He sighed. "I'm tired of being a pawn."

So was she. "That's just it—I've been a pawn, but now I'm a queen with the power to change things."

"As long as it doesn't change you." His pinkie finger hooked around hers. "I like you the way you are."

It felt as if he'd hugged her soul. While she didn't want to change, she had to in order to do what needed to be done. She'd already changed so much just to survive this place.

"Let me ask you this," Evander continued, "if Heather is pregnant with Rainer's child, why does he need you? Doesn't that child provide him with the heir he needs to keep his throne?"

"The child must be of royal blood, and Heather is a commoner. Therefore, the child doesn't meet the requirement." But what had been nagging Sabine was this: if the law stated Rainer's child had to be of royal blood, he had to follow the rule. However, when it came to Lottie, why could Rainer choose to ignore the law? It made no sense. Unless Sabine forced him to follow the rules.

"What?" Evander asked. "I can tell you're thinking of something in that beautiful head of yours."

She'd considered it before and had planned on throwing Lottie in the dungeon and having her tried for treason. The problem was that once Lottie was found guilty, then Rainer, Anton, and Axel would be killed as well. The law was harsh about certain situations. The point of the blood law was to deter people from committing acts of treason by threatening their relations through blood.

If Sabine invoked the law, she'd be the one left standing and in control of Lynk. While she didn't want to be the sole ruler, if it meant getting rid of Rainer and preventing a war, it would be worth it. The part she found hard to live with was sacrificing Anton and Axel. However, they were only half-siblings, so maybe they'd be spared. And if she acted quickly, she might be able to stop Evander from marrying Lottie.

"What is it?" he asked.

"You'll see," she replied, not wanting him to know about her plan. If he knew, he might try to stop her.

"Do you want my help?"

"I can do it."

"I know you can, but you don't have to do it alone."

"I should get going." It was getting late, and she didn't want to be seen returning to her room so long after having left the ball.

"Will you spend the day with me tomorrow?" he asked.

"I don't think that's a wise idea." Rainer would be furious if he found out the two of them were spending time together. She needed to convince the king there was nothing going on between her and the Avoni prince, not fuel the fire.

"We'll go somewhere away from here. I'll take care of everything so the king won't find out. I need to get out of this palace for a few hours."

Truth be told, she could use a day out of this palace as well. Allowing herself to finally turn and look at Evander, she whispered, "Yes."

The corners of his lips rose. "I was hoping you'd say that."

Sabine entered her room and flopped onto her bed, exhausted. Harta jumped up, joining her, licking her face. This silly dog always made her feel better.

"You're back, uh, Your Majesty," Harper said. "Sorry I keep forgetting your title."

"Don't worry about it," Sabine said.

"How was the ball?" Harper came over and sat on the edge of the bed, petting Harta's back.

"Eventful." She didn't feel like talking about it.

"I heard the king's mistress showed up." Harper folded her arms, raising a single eyebrow, looking like she was personally offended.

Sabine propped herself up on her elbows. "Harper, I'm glad that you're here." It was nice having someone she not only felt comfortable around but could talk to as well.

"Me too. I hated working at my aunt's shop." She started pushing her cuticles back.

"Does the king ever ask you anything about me?" Sabine had no idea if Rainer was checking up on her through her lady's maid.

"No," Harper said with a snort. "And I wouldn't talk to him if he did. I work for you, not him. Besides, Drew already told me how he is. I know to be careful."

That was not how she thought Harper would answer. First, she was thankful to have the woman's loyalty. Second, it warmed her to know that Drew had thought to put Harper on guard.

Sabine needed to word this carefully and clearly. "Do you believe the king can override me?"

"What do you mean?"

"If he asked you something about me, and you refused to tell him, he is still your king and you must answer to him." Now she waited to hear how Harper responded before she decided what to do next.

She shrugged. "He can claim he's my king all he wants. But I am your lady's maid. Drew said the law protects me as long as I protect you."

Sabine smiled. "Excellent. I need your help—but it requires your utmost discretion and complete secrecy."

"I'm all in."

Sabine started the day like any other. She got up, dressed, then ate her breakfast. After, she declared she was headed into town to go shopping. Shortly thereafter, she left the palace with Harper, Drew, and a handful of guards. Though Sabine was nervous since she didn't know the details of the plan, Harper kept patting her arm, telling her not to worry about a thing. Apparently Harper and Drew had spent the night planning everything.

"Okay," Sabine said, "we're in the middle of town, now what?"

"Just keep walking." Harper smiled as she led Sabine along the road.

At the seamstress's store, Harper led Sabine into the back room where she was given commoner clothing to put on.

After changing, Sabine came out and found that Harper and her guards were all dressed similarly in nondescript outfits befitting a commoner.

"From here on," Drew said, "we'll be in groups of two. No names or titles will be used once you step foot out the door. Make sure everyone stays spaced out so we don't attract unwanted attention."

Two men exited the back door. Sabine and Harper waited a minute before leaving. The two women walked arm-in-arm, laughing and chatting as they made their way along the back road. They passed a few people but no one paid them any heed.

Sabine knew the rest of her guards followed in groups of two, but she made sure not to look back at them.

Harper chatted about the fabric her aunt had received, a recipe for bread she wanted to try, and about the family party for her niece's birthday that would be held in a couple of days.

After about a mile, they turned and began to descend the mountain on a steep, dirt path.

"Two of your guards will remain in town to keep an eye on things," Harper explained. "We want to make sure no one else comes this way or tries to follow you."

It took nearly an hour to reach the bottom, and by the time they did, Sabine was hot and her legs ached from the descent.

"Another two guards will remain here," Harper whispered.

The two of them continued on, following a narrow path into the jungle. At a large boulder, Harper stopped and whistled a bird call. A matching whistle sounded back.

"This is as far as I go," Harper said. "Continue on straight ahead. Follow the trail. I'll be here with Drew and Erikin. We'll see you in a few hours."

"You're not coming with me?" Sabine asked.

"Nope. It's safer this way if none of us see what you're doing or who you're doing it with."

She squeezed Harper's hand, then headed along the narrow trail. After about a hundred feet, the path curved to the left. Up ahead, Evander stood leaning against a tree trunk.

Even though she didn't see anyone, she knew he could have guards hidden nearby. "Are we alone?"

He pushed off the trunk. "I am. And it appears you are too. When Harper and Drew told me their plan, I was impressed at how well thought out it was."

They stood facing one another. "So," she said, wondering what they were going to do. Maybe they'd just sit and talk for a bit.

The corners of his lips pulled into a grin. "Shall we?" He gestured to the dirt path ahead of them.

"Where are we going?" She had no idea where this trail led.

"You'll see." He smirked.

"How is it you know where we are and what's around here?"

He tapped his head. "Assassin, remember? Before I came here the first time, I memorized over a dozen maps of the area and the terrain." He left the trail, heading deeper into the jungle, past lush vegetation.

"This is quite different from Avoni," Sabine said. The humidity was so thick it was almost hard to breathe.

"That it is." After a moment of silence, he glanced over his shoulder at her. "How come you didn't tell me you hadn't consummated your marriage?"

"In the beginning, I didn't know you. Otto insisted I keep it a secret." She stepped over a skinny tree that had been uprooted. "Then I was afraid."

"Afraid?"

There had to be a way to explain it so he understood. "I was afraid that if we were together, then Rainer would know."

"I hadn't thought about that part." He scratched the side of his neck.

The trees abruptly ended revealing a crescent shaped beach spread out before them. The white sand met crystal clear water. The waves were small, only a foot or so.

"This is beautiful," Sabine said. "How did you find this place?"

He eyed her sidelong. "Seriously?"

She rolled her eyes. "Forget I asked. Of course you know every beach along this coastline, oh mighty assassin who knows all. We should all be so lucky to have your knowledge."

He nudged his shoulder against hers. "These past few weeks have been so peaceful without your sarcastic comments."

"You missed my sarcastic mouth," she said, teasing him, glad for the light mood and bantering.

"You have no idea how much I missed your mouth," he mumbled, sending a jolt of warmth through her, making her toes curl.

Peering up at him, she examined his lips, remembering the feel of them against hers.

"Don't look at me like that," he said. "I'll end up doing something that will get us in trouble." He plopped on the sand, stretching his legs out and folding his hands behind his head. Lying there, he focused on the light blue sky.

Sabine sat next to him, watching the waves curl before crashing onto the beach, the sound calm and peaceful. They didn't have beaches like this in Bakley. There, the water was frigid and the coastline covered with rocks and cliffs.

Evander closed his eyes. "I do enjoy the sun on occasion, and this is one of those occasions."

Sabine wrapped her arms around her bent legs. "Thank you for bringing me here. I needed this." Not only did she appreciate being outside, but she was glad to be away from the palace and the people there. Today, she could just be herself. It felt like a holiday.

"You know," Evander said, his voice softer than before, "since your marriage isn't consummated, it's not binding."

"I know. Which is why no one can find out." It would ruin everything. Then there would be no one to stop Rainer from going to war. She reached out, splaying her hand on the ground, digging her fingers into the warm sand. Lifting her hand, she watched the sand slide off.

"I wish I'd known sooner. It changes things."

She didn't know how it changed anything. Besides, next week, her monthly course would come. Then she'd consummate her marriage. Her face flushed from what Lottie had said to her earlier—about her pretending Rainer was

Evander when being intimate. Would she have to do that to get through it? She had no idea.

"What are you thinking about?" Evander asked, watching her.

"Nothing worth mentioning." Her face turned even redder. She was forced to think about how her marriage gave her the chance to stop a war. That had to be her focus—not her own wants and desires. "Let's not talk about Rainer." Today was supposed to be a break from all that.

"Your wish is my command." Evander twisted to his side, his arm propping his head up as he faced her. "Are you in the mood for something adventurous?"

"What do you have in mind?"

"Something dangerous."

"I've had enough danger to last a lifetime."

"Something thrilling."

She cocked an eyebrow. "I'm intrigued."

"Is that a yes?"

"Yes." She could use a little adventure and something thrilling right about now.

Evander smirked as he jumped to his feet and reached down for her hand, pulling her up. "There's a cliff not far from here. If we climb to the top, we can jump into the water."

"You want to jump off a cliff?" she asked incredulously, a smile spreading across her face. That sounded amazing.

"It's a thirty foot drop," he said, leading the way back into the jungle, his voice laced with excitement. "It feeds into a lagoon."

She was about to ask him how he'd found the cliff but thought better of it. "Do you like to do these sorts of things?"

"I do. I assume you do as well." His face was lit with excitement.

"You assume correctly. But how'd you figure that out?" In Avoni, they hadn't done anything like this.

He shrugged. "The way you readily agreed to sail the boat, how adept you were at climbing that tree, the way your eyes lit up in the tavern."

It always amazed her how well he seemed to know and understand her even though they'd only known each other for a short amount of time.

They traversed between the trees until they came to a rock wall, part of it covered with vines.

"There's enough places to put your hands and feet for leverage," Evander said as he began to climb.

Mimicking him, Sabine followed him up, easily able to navigate the rock wall since there were so many divots and grooves to latch onto. When she reached the top, she found Evander a few feet away, peering over the ledge. She joined him, gazing below into the small, black lagoon. "Is it safe?" She couldn't see the bottom. For all she knew, it might only be a couple of feet deep.

"I checked it out and it's deep enough. You just have to make sure to aim for the center."

The lagoon was about twenty feet in diameter. "Great. You go first." Then, once he survived, she'd take her turn.

He chuckled. "Nope. We're going together." Evander clutched her hand and stood with his toes over the edge, waiting for her to position her body alongside his.

She stood next to him, her toes also hanging over the edge. "All right," she said, squeezing his hand. "I'm ready."

"Are you a screamer?" he asked, a wicked gleam to his green eyes.

She laughed. "I don't know. I guess we'll find out."

"On the count of three. One...two...three!"

They jumped.

Sabine clung to Evander's hand as they flew through the

air, the wind rushing past them. It felt as if she'd left her stomach on top of the cliff. It was exhilarating—the freedom, the loss of control.

Evander whooped, joy radiating from him. He released her hand when they hit the water.

Sabine crashed into the water, darkness filling her vision. After a moment, she saw a faint light so she kicked, heading toward what she assumed was the surface. A moment later, her head came above the water and she sucked in a big breath. A laugh burst from her. "That was fantastic!"

Evander surfaced next to her, shaking his head, his hair spraying water in her face. "Your smile is infectious."

It had been far too long since she'd let loose and had fun like this.

"Want to go again?" Evander asked as he headed to the side and climbed out.

"What kind of silly question is that? Of course I do." She lost count of how many times she jumped from the cliff that day.

After reluctantly parting ways with Evander, Sabine turned the corner and found Harper, Drew, and Erikin waiting for her right where they were supposed to be. They made their way back up the mountain, the rest of her guards gradually joining them. Evander had chosen to return to the palace via another route.

At the seamstress's store, everyone changed back into their clothing. When Sabine emerged from the dressing room, Harper stood there with her hands full.

"My aunt made these for you," Harper said. "And someone brought you a loaf of bread. And there are flowers from some kids."

At least it would look like they'd been shopping all day.

Sabine's guards gathered the items, and they exited the seamstress's shop just before sunset. They made their way back through town using the main road. The bridge was already lowered so they went across it.

The second the bridge closed behind them, Captain Lithane approached, handing Drew a sealed letter. "The king requests your presence immediately. I'll escort the queen to her room."

After handing the items he'd been carrying to another guard, Drew left.

"This way, Your Majesty," Lithane said.

Given her activities today and Drew being called away, unease filled her. She joined Lithane, and they began making her way toward the wing of the palace that her room was located in.

"Tell me, Captain Lithane, is everything all right?" Sabine asked, fearing Drew was in some sort of trouble for what she'd done today. If Rainer found out, he'd execute Drew.

"It's nothing to concern yourself with, Your Majesty," Lithane responded, his voice curt.

"That wasn't my question." She stopped walking. "I am your queen, and you will answer me when I ask you a question." She lifted her chin in the air and looked down her nose at Lithane.

Clasping his hands behind his back, he said, "Forgive me, Your Majesty. I've been informed that the king wishes to increase security at the palace. Since Captain Drew is in charge of your royal guard, the king wishes to speak with him on that matter, especially considering who we have visiting us."

This was about having assassins staying in the palace. Even though they were officially Evander's royal guards,

Sabine knew the men who'd accompanied him had to be skilled in the art of killing. Rainer was right to be concerned.

Sabine resumed walking, not bothering to make small talk with Lithane since she didn't care for him. When she reached the door to her room, she dismissed him and entered, her guards coming in with her to set the gifted items down in her room. Once they went back out into the hallway, Sabine closed her door and looked around for Harta, not seeing her dog anywhere.

"Harper," she called out.

"Yes, my queen?" she said, coming out of the bathing room.

"Please find out where Harta is."

Harper nodded. "Absolutely." She went to the door and paused. "Your bath is ready. Do you need me to help you with anything else before I leave?"

"No, thank you. I'm just worried that Harta isn't here."

"I promise to find her." With that, she left.

Sabine hoped everything was all right.

Feeling gross from trekking up that mountain in this heat, she stripped and stepped into her sunken bathtub. After washing, she leaned her head back against the edge of the tub, letting the hot water soothe her muscles. Closing her eyes, she remembered jumping from the cliff with Evander. They'd jumped countless times today. She hadn't had that much fun in a long time. Whenever he'd had the chance, he'd touch her hand, tickle her side, or twist a strand of her hair.

Warm hands touched Sabine's cheeks. Her eyes flew open —and her pulse spiked when she saw Rainer kneeling behind her.

"You look so peaceful," he said.

She tried not to shake—he could twist and snap her neck so easily from his position.

He leaned down, placing a kiss on her forehead. "Where have you been all day?" he murmured against her skin.

"I went shopping in town." It surprised her that he'd noticed she was gone. She slid under the water, forcing him to release her. She surfaced in the middle of the round tub, where Rainer couldn't reach her. She kept her legs bent so her chest remained under the water. "What are you doing here?" Given that he'd asked to see Drew and now he was here in her personal space, she feared he'd discovered she'd spent the day with Evander. She needed to tread carefully.

Rainer stood, reaching his hand out to her. "We need to talk."

As if she'd let him pull her out of the tub naked. "My towel is behind you." She pointed to the bench against the wall.

He turned and grabbed the towel, holding it open for her. She noticed he was wearing casual clothing—loose cream colored pants and a v-neck top, the sleeves rolled up. His hair was wet. Like Sabine, he must have just bathed.

"Your Majesty!" Harper called out from the other room, followed by the sound of a door slamming.

Harta came barreling into the bathing room. The dog stuck her paws on the first step in the tub, trying to get to Sabine. Sabine laughed and went to Harta, keeping her body under the water so Rainer wouldn't see anything. Harta started licking her face.

"Oh, I'm sorry, Your Majesty," Harper said as she came into the bathing room. "I didn't mean to interrupt. Harta was out on a walk, so I brought her back for you." She glanced between Sabine and Rainer. "Do you need anything? Should I take Harta on another walk?" She began fidgeting with her hands.

Sabine looked at her lady's maid then darted her eyes

toward the towel. It took several times before Harper caught on.

"Oh." Harper jumped then grabbed the towel from Rainer. Turning her back to the king, she blocked him from view as she hovered at the top of the steps to the tub.

Sabine quickly stood, wrapping the towel around her. "Thank you, Harper. Please get my robe."

Harper left the bathing room.

Rainer stood there with his hands on his hips, his lips pursed. "She's rather informal," he muttered. "She didn't address me once."

Sabine didn't care—all she cared about was that Harper had arrived just in time to help her out of the tub. As far as she was concerned, Harper was the perfect lady's maid.

Harper returned, placing the robe on Sabine's shoulders. Sabine tied it before removing the towel.

"Leave us," Rainer said, waving Harper away.

Harper looked at Sabine. "Do you need anything else, Your High—Majesty?"

"No, that will be all. Thank you." She reached out and squeezed Harper's hand in thanks.

Harper nodded before leaving.

The king rubbed his face and headed into Sabine's bedchamber.

After towel drying her hair, she followed him. "You said you wanted to talk?" Going over to her vanity, she sat and began combing her hair, trying to act as calm and casual as possible. She kept her focus on the mirror while carefully watching Rainer's reflection as he meandered around her room. He examined her packages before turning his attention to her.

The robe slid off her shoulder. She quickly pulled it up, covering herself.

"Sometimes I forget how young you are," Rainer

mumbled. "How inexperienced." He came up behind her, looking at her in the mirror. His eyes darkened as he slid his hands over her shoulders, gently rubbing them.

Sabine froze, not knowing what to expect from him.

"Did you have a good day?"

He'd never asked her that sort of question before. It implied he cared about her on some level—which she was certain he did not. "My day was fine."

Rainer slid the robe from her shoulders, leaving her skin exposed.

Sabine quickly grabbed the fabric, holding it against her chest, making sure it didn't slide down any farther. "What are you doing?"

"You look tense," he murmured, rubbing her bare shoulders while watching her in the mirror.

She set the comb down and stood, moving out of his grasp. "I'm not tense." She pulled her robe back up on her shoulders. "I just don't want you touching me."

"I'm your husband."

"And you're sharing someone else's bed."

He stepped closer to her, trapping her against her vanity. His hands came to her hips while he lowered his head, looking her in the eyes. "You expect me to only share your bed?"

That was the way it was with her parents. "Yes."

"And you will only share my bed?" His eyes searched hers, as if looking for something.

"That's what a marriage is," Sabine ground out. "We are supposed to only be with one another." This was not what she wanted to be talking about right now. Today had been wonderful. Now, dealing with Rainer made her want to poke her eyes out.

He reached forward and tugged the tie at her waist, releasing it.

Sabine held the robe closed. For all her flirting back home, she thought she'd be ready for something like this. But she wasn't, especcially not with Rainer.

He slid his hand inside her robe, trailing his fingers across her abdomen, around her hip, and to her lower back. "If you let me," he said, his voice low and soft, brushing against her ear, "I can show you so many things." His fingers hovered right above her buttocks.

"Please don't touch me." She shoved his arm away.

Rainer chuckled, the sound deep and rumbly. He tucked a strand of Sabine's hair behind her ear. "You're not ready. I understand." He took a step back.

Sabine tied her robe closed, her hands shaking. She should have been better prepared for something like this. They were married. It was only a matter of time until they slept together.

"Come," Rainer said, holding out his hand to her. "Let's go to my sitting room where we can talk for a bit."

She didn't want to go anywhere with him, but he'd respected her request and had stopped touching her when she asked him to. There had to be some concession on her part, so she didn't push him over the edge.

He led her over to the door to the royal suite, ushering her inside. "Have a seat."

Sabine went and sat on the sofa, curling her legs up under her, making sure her robe covered everything. At least no one else was here to see her dressed like this.

"Oh good, you're here," Rainer said.

Sabine followed his line of sight to the far side of the room where Evander stepped out of the shadows.

Chapter Thirteen

"I got a message you want to talk," Evander said as he came farther into the sitting room, folding his arms across his chest, not once glancing Sabine's way.

Rainer pushed his sleeves up higher then raked a hand through his wet hair, as if combing it.

Horror filled Sabine. It looked as if she and Rainer had just bathed together, among other things. This was a set-up—she was sure of it. Anger coursed through her at how easily she'd played right into Rainer's hands.

The king sat on the sofa next to her, his arm going around her shoulders. "Have a seat, prince." Rainer motioned to the sofa across from them.

Since she'd sat in the corner of the sofa, she couldn't scoot away from Rainer. However, she wouldn't even if she could. Not only was Rainer going to stake his claim to her in front of Evander, but he was testing her as well. To pass, she needed to pretend as if she felt nothing for the handsome Avoni prince. As if his mere presence here didn't affect her.

Evander scratched the side of his neck before sitting

across from Rainer and finally peering at Sabine. "Your Majesty," he said, a slight bow to his head.

"I'm sorry I'm so informally dressed," she said. "I didn't realize we had a visitor."

"You traveled together," Rainer said, motioning between the two of them. "I'm sure the prince has seen you dressed *casually* before." He squeezed her shoulder, the gesture part assurance and part threat.

Her skin prickled with unease. Clasping her hands together, she took a deep breath, trying to calm her nerves so Rainer wouldn't know how uncomfortable she was right now.

"I have three older sisters," Evander said. "I'm used to women running around in robes. And since the queen and I did travel together, and I'll be marrying Princess Lottie soon, I consider Sabine like family. My fourth sister." The corners of his lips curled into a slight smile.

Her face warmed with humiliation. *A sister.* When she'd first realized Evander wasn't the horrible assassin she thought him to be, and that they actually got along quite well, she considered him as a sibling of sorts. But then their friendship grew, and she realized he was neither sibling nor friend. He was so much more.

Rainer stroked the side of her face, the act possessive. "Are any of your sisters this beautiful?"

Evander chuckled, resting his arms on his legs and leaning slightly forward. "I learned early on to never compare women's beauty as they are all beautiful in their own right."

"Smart man," Rainer said. "Lottie is lucky to be marrying you."

"I feel like I'm the lucky one," Evander replied smoothly.

Wanting to change the subject, Sabine asked, "Why is the prince here?"

"We have some business to discuss," Rainer said, his face

turning somber. "Sabine, darling, why don't you go to bed. I'll be along shortly."

His words made her cringe. He wanted Evander to think they shared a bed, that the king owned her body. But he didn't. Evander had to see through this act. He had to know that after the day they shared together, she wouldn't give herself to another man—even if that man was her husband. At least not yet. Not tonight.

"Yes," Evander said, a slight drawl to his voice, his eyes not looking her way. "Run along. Let the men discuss important kingdom matters." His voice held a sharp edge to it. Sabine knew he had to be joking because there was no way he agreed with the way Rainer treated her, excluding her from crucial matters. If she were married to Evander, it would be an equal partnership.

She stood, wanting to say something snarky, but not wanting to upset Rainer and have him take it out on her later. Instead, she bid them both goodnight and went to her room, locking the door from her side.

A soft knock sounded on her outer door. She went over, cracking it an inch, revealing Harper and Drew standing there. "Is everything all right?" she asked.

Drew shook his head. "We need to talk."

Dread filled her. Not wanting to have an important conversation with Rainer so close, she quickly dressed before joining them out in the corridor. They silently headed to the nearby turret. Her guards remained in the stairwell with Harper, while Drew and Sabine went onto the rooftop, going over to the railing, as far away from the stairwell as possible so no one could overhear them.

"You're scaring me," Sabine whispered. "What's going on?"

"Earlier, the king called me into his office and informed

me that there have been a slew of murders in our military camps across Lynk."

Sabine had heard about these murders first at Felix's gathering, then again at Karmen's.

"So far, the victims have been mostly high ranking military officials," he continued. "No one knows who's responsible or who will be next. It's causing panic across the kingdom."

"This is why the king spoke to you?"

"Yes."

Then it had nothing to do with her activities today. She needed to talk to Evander about these murders to see if he knew who was committing them. King Kai had informed her that a group of Avoni assassins were stuck in Lynk. Though, she suspected *stuck* was a bit of a stretch. Even though Rainer had burned and sunk the Avoni ship the assassins were supposed to leave on, the group had to be resourceful enough to find another way out of Lynk. After all, Evander had managed to do so without issue.

"The king said he was going to question Prince Evander about the murders," Drew said.

"When and where did the most recent murders take place?"

"Last night, about ten miles from here." He leaned on the railing.

That explained why the king wanted to meet with Evander. "Obviously the prince isn't committing these crimes." She rubbed her forehead, realizing he wouldn't be able to reveal his alibi for today since it was her. If these murders were tied to Avoni, Evander would be in grave danger.

"If it's not the prince, it could be one of the prince's men."

Since Drew didn't seem to know about the missing Avoni

assassins, Rainer must not either. That being the case, the most likely person to pin this on would be Evander or one of his personal guards which explained why Rainer was questioning him. "Thank you for telling me this."

"Of course, Your Majesty. You should also know that Rainer has increased security around both the town and the palace. You'll need to be more careful with your daily trips."

She nodded, hoping no one had seen her today and reported her movements to Rainer.

"I should escort you back to your room."

"Before we go, I want to thank you for your kindness and loyalty."

"Of course, Your Majesty." He bowed.

"Can I ask you why?" She wanted to know if it had something to do with her, an oath he'd taken, or if he had his own personal reasons.

"I believe you're what's best for Lynk," he answered honestly. "At the end of this, if only one monarch is left standing, I want it to be you."

Sabine didn't sleep at all that night. After going over various scenarios in her mind, she determined the easiest way to stop the war would be to get rid of Rainer. The easiest way to do that was to accuse his sister of treason and have him executed right alongside her. It was a bold move and one she hoped would work. Thousands of lives would be saved.

Sabine and Harper utilized the quiet hours of the night to write letters to everyone of importance not only in the palace, but in the nearby town as well. When they finished, Harper took the letters and hid them. Once Lottie was arrested, Harper would see that the letters were delivered.

The plan was for Rainer to not know what was happening

until it was too late to stop it. Once he figured out what she'd done, he'd probably want to kill her himself.

Not wanting to second-guess herself, she dressed and had her guards escort her to the military compound. When she arrived, she found Commander Felix training with a group of men and asked him for his assistance. After he appointed someone to lead the drill in his place, he joined her. The two of them stood off to the side, far enough from her guards and the other soldiers so no one would overhear their conversation.

"Your Majesty, is everything all right?" Felix asked.

Fiddling with her hands, she tried to keep her uncertainty from showing. "Commander," she said, wanting him to know she was there on official business. "I personally overheard Princess Lottie speaking to an assassin about killing me. I also heard them discuss my sister's death. Therefore, I intend to have Princess Lottie arrested and tried for treason."

He nodded, folding his arms. "How can I assist you?"

"Who do I speak with about having her arrested?" She didn't think Felix would handle this sort of thing, but she wasn't sure.

"I'm assuming you already discussed the matter with King Rainer?"

"I have."

"And he isn't pursuing the correct course of legal action?" he prompted.

"No, he is not."

His face remained passive, not showing a hint of emotion. "And is Captain Drew in charge of your security?"

"He is."

He nodded, rubbing his chin. "Then I'd have Captain Drew make the official arrest. He'll work with Captain Lithane since he is in charge of all security matters at the palace."

She hated asking Drew to get involved in this matter. However, if this was the correct chain of command, she would take it. "Thank you." She took a step back, about to turn and leave when Felix held up his hand, taking a step closer to her.

"A word of advice, be careful. The king just learned some of his orders with regards to his army have been altered." Felix looked pointedly at her. "The king is upset. When you have his sister arrested, be prepared for his temper. You haven't seen it yet. You need to know that he can be wild and unpredictable."

This wasn't the first time she'd been warned of the king's temper. Reaching out, she took his hand, squeezing it. "Thank you. Your council is much appreciated and won't be forgotten."

He bowed before returning to the group of men he'd been training with.

When Sabine rejoined her guards, Drew asked, "Back to the palace?"

She hadn't informed Drew of her plan yet. Before she returned to the palace and set it into motion, she needed to make sure he was okay with his role in this. She didn't want to put him in a compromising situation, especially if Drew had a family Rainer could use against him. "Is there somewhere we can talk for a moment?"

"Just the two of us?"

"Yes. Somewhere private if possible."

At the entrance to one of the narrow corridors jutting off from the main cavern, Drew ordered her guards to remain there. Then he led her down the corridor, past dozens of closed doors.

"What's in these rooms?" she asked.

"Some are offices, others contain supplies. The kennels are down there." He pointed to a hallway that went to the left. After another thirty feet, he stopped before a door and knocked. When no one answered, he pushed it open. "Wait here." He went inside and lit an oil lamp. "Please come in, Your Majesty."

Sabine stepped inside the small office, closing the door behind her. There was a single desk and not much else, so she remained standing.

"If this is about the murders, I haven't learned any additional details," Drew said.

"It's not." Sabine pursed her lips, trying to think of the best way to approach this. "I'm going to be blunt, and I want you to be honest with me."

"Okay."

"I want you to officially arrest Princess Lottie so she can be tried before the nobles."

He whistled and sat on the edge of the desk. "What do you want her formally arraigned on? Treason?"

"Yes. If the king won't hold her accountable, I will."

"Why are you discussing this with me instead of just giving me a direct order?" he asked.

"I would hate to ask you to do something you don't agree with or that might cause harm to you or your family. If this is something you don't want to do, please tell me, and I'll go to Captain Lithane."

He rubbed along his jawline. "Do you fully understand what this means?"

"I do. Once Princess Lottie is found guilty, her family by blood will be executed alongside her."

"That includes the *king* of Lynk."

"Yes, it does." Until this moment, she hadn't realized how much Drew's opinion meant to her. If he didn't agree with her, then most of the people in Lynk wouldn't either. She held her breath, waiting for his response.

He nodded, his focus on the floor and not on her. "I think

it's the right thing to do, and I'm on board with arresting Lottie. However, I just want to make sure you understand that this will cause an uproar in the palace." His gaze finally met hers.

"I took an oath to uphold Lynk's laws. What kind of queen would I be if royalty are not held to the same standards as our subjects?"

He stood and went around the desk, opening one of its drawers and pulling out several daggers, which he set on top. "These are poison-tipped daggers." He withdrew several sheathes, sliding a dagger into each one.

A chill passed over her body. "Poison?"

"Yes. A nick will cause the person to sleep for at least an hour. It comes in handy when dealing with situations such as this one." He took three of the sheathed daggers, sliding one up each sleeve and tucking one into his boot. Then he handed the last one to Sabine. "Keep this on you at all times. Just in case."

"Thank you." She took it, not sure where to put it on her body with such limited fabric. "Do you have family nearby?" While he'd said she was doing the right thing, he hadn't addressed any sort of retaliation issues.

"No. My parents live far from here, and I'm not married." His face reddened.

Over the past couple of days, Sabine had wondered if there might be something brewing between Drew and Harper. While she wanted to ask him, it was neither the time nor place. Maybe she'd ask Harper when the opportunity presented itself.

"How do we proceed from here?" she asked.

"I'll escort you back to the palace. Erikin will take over as the head of your royal guard. I will speak with Captain Lithane since he is in charge of palace security, and the two of us will make the arrest together. From there, things will happen very quickly."

The one issue that had been bothering her about this entire ordeal was Anton and Axel. She had no idea if the blood law included them or not since they were only Lottie's half-siblings."What about the twins?"

His eyes met hers. "They'll face the same fate as the king." His voice sounded grim. "Do you still wish to proceed?"

"Laws are laws, and as the queen, I need to enforce them." The thought of sending both Anton and Axel to their deaths was a stab to her heart. Neither deserved to die. However, she'd already decided ahead of time that if their deaths saved hundreds or even thousands of lives, it was worth it.

Drew came closer and placed his hand on her shoulder. "I know you outrank me, but I have a few years on you, so I'd like to offer you some advice if you want it?"

All her life, she'd been raised as a princess, not as someone who'd be a queen one day. There had been several times she felt ill-prepared for this role. Any and all advice was much appreciated. "Please, whatever you can offer, I'll take."

"You're doing the right thing." He squeezed her shoulder before releasing it. "Rainer must be stopped. You've only seen a sliver of him."

Which implied he was more of a monster than she'd imagined. Cold terror filled her. This plan of hers would force some sort of reaction out of him.

"I know this may not be my place," he said, "but know the king will use anyone you're close to or care about to get back at you."

Which was why she'd come to Drew in the first place.

"So, if there is someone else here in the palace you care

for," he looked pointedly at her, "that *person* probably deserves some sort of warning about what you're going to do."

Her face flushed. While Drew might not know the details of her relationship with Evander, he knew something was going on since he'd planned that outing yesterday.

"Consider this," Drew continued, "if Rainer punched *someone* you care for right in front of you, how would you react?"

If Rainer punched Evander, she'd probably react without meaning to. It would be instinctual.

Reading the emotions playing across her face, Drew said gently, "That's all Rainer has to do. Threaten *someone*, you react, he has you. You'll be arrested for treason. This is what you're up against."

Now she understood why he'd brought this up. Rainer would be watching her every move. If she did anything that questioned her loyalty to the king, he'd have her arrested. It would be a tit for tat so to speak. In order to survive the next few days, she'd have to push Evander away.

"I want Lottie arrested directly after supper this evening." That way, she had time to warn Evander and he, in turn, had time to make his own plans and arrangements.

"Consider it done, Your Majesty."

Chapter Fourteen

Sabine entered the royal family's private dining room. Since she was the first to arrive, she headed out onto the balcony. A light breeze blew, caressing her skin and offering a reprieve from the excessive heat. Leaning on the railing, she thought over everything she needed to do once Lottie was arrested in a few short hours. If something went wrong, she'd need a back-up plan. If there was one thing she'd learned from Evander, it was that nothing ever went according to plan, so she had to be prepared.

"I'm graced with a moment alone with you," Axel said as he sauntered onto the balcony.

Sabine twisted around to face him.

He stopped before her, blinking several times. "That's another *magnificent* outfit." He pulled the collar of his shirt away from his neck.

This was one of the more subdued dresses she'd had made. The pale pink fabric clung to her with thin straps over her shoulders, widening to cover her breasts before falling in a straight, graceful line. Slits on either side revealed long stretches of her legs. A strand of silver wrapped around her waist, holding the fabric in place.

"It seems that no matter what you wear, whether it's Lynk fashion or a new trend you're setting, you're lovely. Exquisite even."

"You're such a tease." She laughed, shoving Axel's shoulder.

He rolled his eyes. "I'm serious. You light up a room."

Her eyes narrowed, considering him. He couldn't possibly know what she had planned for after supper. "Why the sudden compliments?" If he knew she'd ordered Lottie's arrest thereby condemning him, he might be trying to get in her good graces.

He shrugged. "I think the entire situation is rather ironic. You didn't want to dress in Lynk fashion, but Rainer forced it on you. Now, you're the epitome of Lynk. You're everything he wished for and more."

"I'm not sure that constitutes irony."

He took a step closer to her, lowering his voice. "If you weren't our queen, if you weren't married to Rainer, every man in this palace would be vying for your affection, myself included."

"I doubt that," she replied, wanting to lighten the mood. She wasn't used to Axel being like this with her. "Have you been drinking?"

He laughed. "Oh Sabine, you have no idea."

She stopped paying attention to him when she noticed Anton enter the room.

Anton went over to the side table, pouring himself a drink before coming out on the balcony and joining them. "There's a League meeting tomorrow. As soon as supper is over, I'm leaving." He took a large gulp from his glass.

"Why is there a League meeting?" Sabine asked.

Anton stood a few feet away, his gaze going from Axel to

Sabine before saying, "The League has a few matters to discuss." He took another sip.

That was vague. "Is Evander going with you?"

"Evander?" Axel said. "Isn't that Prince Evander to you?" His eyes narrowed.

Sabine felt her face warm—she'd need to be more careful with how she spoke about and addressed the Avoni prince so others wouldn't question her relationship with the man.

"He is," Anton said, taking another sip.

"How long will you be gone for?" she asked.

"I expect to be back in two or three days."

Evander entered the dining room, heading straight out onto the balcony. "My queen," he said, lifting Sabine's hand to his lips. His mouth lingered against her skin, his eyes holding hers with a heat that made it hard to breathe.

She wanted to melt into him.

He turned to Anton. "I'm ready to leave when you are."

Anton gave a curt nod. "As soon as this is over, we'll take off." He took another sip.

"Where's the king?" Evander asked, releasing Sabine's hand.

"Who the hell knows," Axel said. "He'll be here when he's done doing whatever or *whomever* he's doing."

Sabine's face flushed from the embarrassment of having Rainer's affair so casually flaunted before other people, especially Evander.

"Your kingdom is very different from mine," Evander said, sliding his hands in his pockets. He came and stood beside Sabine, mimicking her position. His shoulder brushed hers. "In Avoni, when we marry, we only are intimate with our partner. I don't understand why you'd marry someone only to be with another."

Anton snorted. "You have an arranged marriage to Lottie.

You can't tell me you plan on being monogamous with someone you don't even know."

Evander tilted his head to the side. "In Avoni, when we marry, we make a vow to that person to be true. In my kingdom, we honor our vows."

"Huh." Anton took a sip from his cup. "What if you hate the person you're married to?"

Evander considered him. "Why would that change anything?"

"If you don't like that person, and that's the only person you can be with—"

"Then that's the only person I'll be with. I don't understand why that's so hard for you to grasp. Let's say, for example, that I married Sabine. If I married her, made a vow to her, I would never lie to her, I would never cheat on her, and I would *never* forsake her." He glanced sidelong at her. "What's it like in Bakley?"

She licked her lips. "It's the same in Bakley. We do not take lovers outside of our marriage."

"Really?" Anton said. "I find this fascinating. I can see if you married someone you love, but an arranged marriage? A marriage for political reasons? That seems far-fetched. I can't imagine being forced to marry someone, then only sleeping with that one person the rest of my life—especially if I didn't like that person."

Axel chuckled. "Evander, you might change your mind after spending some time with Lottie."

"I will be true to my wife until the day one of us dies," Evander said.

Axel slapped Evander on the back. "That explains it—if your wife is annoying, you'll just kill her."

Evander held up a hand, a smile sliding over his face. "While I believe in not cheating on my spouse," Evander mused, "I have no qualms about killing one."

Sabine laughed, knowing Evander was joking. He was an assassin, in charge of a ruthless assassin guild, but he would never kill someone on a whim. Having spent so much time with him, she knew his heart.

Rainer chose that moment to enter, Lottie at his side.

Sabine's laughter died in her throat. "Why is *she* here?"

"*She* is Evander's fiancée." Anton took another sip of his drink, finishing it off. "At least he didn't bring Heather."

"Probably because of Prince Evander," Axel mumbled. "He's afraid he'll push Sabine straight to the prince's bed if he keeps flaunting her around."

Sabine looked at him, considering his words. "Is that true? Is that why she hasn't been around as much?"

Axel shrugged. "If I were in Rainer's position, and I had a beautiful woman I'd just married and a rival prince showed up, I'd tread very carefully. You've played your cards well, Sabine." He winked then headed inside, welcoming his brother.

"Shall we?" Evander asked, holding out his arm to escort her.

"I'm sorry about last night," she whispered. "Nothing happened between Rainer and me." She slid her hand on his arm, reveling in the warmth and feel of him.

"Oh, I know." He chuckled. "The entire thing felt like a setup. I could tell he wanted a reaction out of me—or you." He led her toward the dining room. His free hand came up, covering her hand on his arm. "Though it would be well within your rights since you're married to the man."

"Evander." She didn't want to make light of the situation.

"Of course, if he took advantage of you, I'd either go insane or kill the man with my bare hands." Evander released her as they stepped into the dining room. He went over toward Lottie, taking her hand and bowing over it.

Smug satisfaction filled her when she noticed he didn't

kiss Lottie's hand like he'd kissed hers. She went and took her place at the head of the table, opposite Rainer. Evander and Lottie sat on one side, Anton and Axel on the other. Once they were all seated, the servants brought in dishes of fish, rice, and vegetables.

"Prince Evander," Lottie said as she scooped food onto her plate, "why don't you tell me about Avoni. I would like to know about the kingdom I'll be living in."

"It's the opposite of Lynk," he replied. "It's cloudy, cold, and it rains all the time." He waved his hand at her. "You'll need to dress differently there, not only warmer, but more reserved to suit Avoni fashion."

"Oh." Lottie pouted her lip. "I *adore* the fashion here in Lynk."

"Our own queen has become quite the trendsetter," Axel said, a wicked glean to his eyes. "Queen Sabine truly is the epitome of what a Lynk queen should be. We are lucky to have her." He raised his glass, saluting her.

"When I was training with your men," Evander said, "the sentiment was shared by many. Almost every soldier commented on Queen Sabine's beauty—many saying it's unmatched."

"I've also heard many talk about her kindness," Axel added.

Sabine didn't know what Axel was trying to do, but she wished he wouldn't push Rainer.

"It has been a long time since we've had a queen on our throne," Anton commented before he, too, saluted Sabine with his glass of wine.

Not knowing how to respond to these unnecessary compliments, Sabine simply raised her glass in thanks, taking a sip of the heady wine.

Lottie's eyes narrowed as she looked between Anton, Axel, and Evander. Reaching out, she set a hand on Evander's arm, garnering his attention. "What's the queen of Avoni like?"

"Queen Serilda has been trained in the art of assassination, as most women in Avoni are," Evander said. "My mother and father live in one of our more centrally located palaces. My sister, the heir, lives with her family in another palace."

"Which palace will we live in?" Lottie asked. Her smile had gotten larger at the mention of multiple palaces.

Evander shrugged. "We'll probably live in mine. It's the smallest of the palaces since I'm the youngest. It's a simple four-room structure. It's pretty secluded, so it's safe. But there's always a risk an assassin will come for me. I'm not home often since I'm out on missions most days. I'll try to find someone who can live at the house to help you, though I'm not sure where that person will sleep." He scratched the back of his head. "You need to understand that our palaces are nothing like yours. They're small and humble. For us, it's all about safety from the warring assassin guilds."

Lottie's face had gone white about half-way through Evander's speech. She turned to her brother. "Are you marrying me off to Avoni so I can end up dead?"

Sabine had to keep her focus on her food so she wouldn't start laughing. Lottie would hate Avoni.

"Don't be dramatic," Rainer replied. "No one there will know who you are, so no one will want to kill you. Unless you open your mouth and annoy them. From what Evander has told me, you'll be fairly secluded, so the chance of that happening is slim."

Sabine coughed to mask her snicker.

"Avoni doesn't have an army," Evander said. "Just five warring assassin guilds. But my family has control. At least for now, so we should be fine." He picked up his fork and began eating.

Lottie started picking at her food—she seemed no longer in the mood to talk.

After supper, Rainer excused himself to walk Lottie back to her room. Anton and Evander left to pack their bags in order to depart immediately for the League meeting being held tomorrow. Axel mentioned something about needing to visit a woman and a bed being involved.

In the few moments Sabine had with Evander before supper, she hadn't been able to warn him about having Lottie arrested. However, since he was going to be out of the palace for a couple of days, that might work in her favor. Rainer couldn't take his frustration out on Evander if he wasn't here. Hopefully he wouldn't come after Sabine.

The candles flickered, a soft wind cascading into the room.

Drew stepped inside. "Your Majesty," he said. "It's time."

She stood and faced him. "You're going with Captain Lithane now?"

"Yes. Erikin is taking over for me. I suggest you not be in your room. Go somewhere the king can't find you, but make sure someone is with you so you have an alibi."

Sabine took a deep breath, letting it out slowly. "Okay. Good luck."

"Once we have her in the dungeon, Captain Lithane and I will remain guarding her until she's brought before the court tomorrow. Expect an announcement to be made either later tonight or first thing tomorrow morning."

"Thank you."

He bowed then left.

Out in the hallway, Sabine found Erikin and her guards waiting. They headed through the palace. As she walked by one of the courtyards, she spotted Karmen with a handful of women at her side.

"Good evening, ladies," Sabine said as she passed Karmen and the others.

They all curtseyed and smiled.

"Your Majesty," Karmen called after her, "a moment please."

Sabine turned around and faced the group. "Of course." She folded her hands together.

"We are having a disagreement," Karmen said. "Perhaps you can settle it for us?"

"I'm not sure how much help I can be," Sabine replied.

Up ahead, a handful of guards ran past heading toward the royal wing. It had to be something involving Lottie. Unease took root. The guards were probably escorting the princess to the dungeon at this moment. Hopefully they would use the inner hallways instead of going through one of the populated courtyards, such as this one.

"We need to know which lord is more handsome," Karmen said. "Lord Garnet or Lord Henly?"

Sabine forced herself to laugh so no one would realize how uneasy she was at the moment. "I'm sorry, but I'm not familiar with either gentleman, so I can't give you an answer."

"Lord Garnet is on the upper level to your left," Karmen said. "He's the one in green."

Sabine peered in that direction. "Oh, he is good looking." He had blond hair, appeared to be in his thirties, and his skin was golden.

"Lord Henly is over there, to the right. The one in blue."

"Hmm," Sabine said. Henly looked to be in his late twenties with dark hair similar to Rainer's. "I think I prefer Lord Garnet."

"I knew it!" Karmen said, slapping her leg. "And we have a winner."

The ladies all laughed.

Another group of guards ran by.

"Does anyone know what's going on?" Karmen asked in a soft voice, her focus directed at Sabine.

Given that word would spread soon enough, Sabine decided to tell them. "Princess Lottie has been arrested." There was a collective gasp. "As some of you may have heard, the princess hired an assassin to kill my sister, Princess Alina. She also hired an assassin to kill me. The king chose to do nothing since she's his sister. However, the law doesn't work that way, so I intervened."

The women's eyes widened, and no one spoke.

Sabine faced Karmen. Sweat prickled along her arms and neck. These were the people who'd determine Lottie's fate. If Karmen wasn't on her side, no one else would be either.

"Good for you, honey," Karmen said. "It's about time someone respects our laws here in Lynk." She moved closer to Sabine, wrapping an arm around the queen's shoulders. "Since you're new to Lynk, do you know that this means the king and the princes will be arrested as well?"

"I know that when Lottie is found guilty, they'll face the same fate as her, but I didn't realize they'd be arrested as well." Drew hadn't mentioned anything about arresting the king and princes.

Karmen nodded. "They'll be arrested and thrown in the dungeon so they can't run. That's how the law works."

Dread filled Sabine. She didn't know Rainer would be arrested tonight. But at least that meant he couldn't hurt her. However, Drew had warned her to watch out for Rainer's temper and to remain out of his reach for the evening. With Rainer in the dungeon, there was no need for Sabine to worry about him coming after her.

Another group of guards ran by.

Karmen shook her head. "Something's not right. Let's get the queen out of here." She looped her arm around Sabine's, leading her from the courtyard, the other ladies following close behind, Sabine's guards trailing after the group.

They were twenty feet from the closest archway when Rainer came storming out, a hoard of guards behind him.

When he spotted Sabine, his face contorted with malicious rage. "What have you done?" he demanded, his voice filled with fury.

Sabine took a step back, fear taking over.

Chapter Fifteen

aving grown up with four older brothers, Sabine could read men's moods and intentions fairly accurately. She knew when to push and when she needed to back off. With Rainer heading straight for her, his eyes dark, hands balled into fists, and arms shaking, she knew he was angry and planned on directing that rage at her. Taking another step back, she swiftly turned and headed toward another archway, wanting to get out of the courtyard as quickly as possible. She just needed to find some place she could hide.

"Stop her!" Rainer roared.

Knowing she couldn't outrun the king and that it would be better to face him here in public, she stopped. Her guards hovered nearby. "Don't let him take me anywhere," Sabine said to Erikin, afraid that if Rainer got her alone, he'd hurt her.

Erikin gave a curt nod.

In order to deal with Rainer in his current state, she needed to be calm and not antagonize him further. Just as she turned to face him, his hand came up, encircling her neck and squeezing. He lifted her off the ground. She kicked ferociously, clawing at his arms as she gasped for air. The irony was that Rainer had been the one to teach her what to do in this situation, yet all rational thought eluded her.

Her guards withdrew their swords.

"Stand down," Rainer ordered.

A collective gasp resounded through the courtyard as everyone watched the king and queen.

Tears streamed from Sabine's eyes as pain radiated from her neck to her chest. This was it—she was going to die. Her sister's face flashed before her and ignited a burst of energy. She couldn't die here, not like this. Too many lives depended on her and she'd sworn to avenge Alina's death.

A guard neared, saying something to the king and pointing behind him.

Sabine noticed several people talking, but she couldn't hear a single word with the blood rushing in her ears.

Rainer glanced over his shoulder, realizing they had an audience. He set Sabine on the ground, releasing his hold on her neck.

Unable to support herself, she collapsed to her knees, falling forward on her hands. She heaved in a gasp of air. It felt like knives were being shoved down her throat. The pain was excruciating. Black clouds hovered in her peripheral vision. She feared she'd pass out.

"No one is allowed to help her," Rainer ordered, his hands on his hips, his shoulders rising and falling.

"Your Majesty, she is our queen," one of the guards said.

"And I am your king. I outrank her."

Rainer's boots came into Sabine's line of sight, but she refused to look up into his eyes.

After a moment, he said, "Don't be so dramatic. Get up. Now. You're causing a scene."

Not wanting to make him angrier, Sabine pushed off the

ground and stood, her entire body shaking. Her lungs burned, her throat felt like it was on fire, and she couldn't speak.

Rainer grabbed her arm, squeezing harder than necessary as he dragged her toward the archway that led out of the courtyard.

Her mind screamed *no*, but she couldn't voice the word. Her body was too weak to protest or fight back.

"Your Majesty," Erikin said, blocking their path. "The queen is my responsibility. I took an oath, and I cannot allow harm to come to her. Please release her so I can take her to a healer."

In one swift move, Rainer withdrew a dagger from his waist, plunging it into Erikin's stomach. "You're relieved of your responsibility and oath," Rainer spat.

Sabine's vision swam. This could not be happening.

Rainer wrenched his dagger free.

Erikin collapsed to the ground, blood pooling from his wound as life drained from his body.

Frozen in shock, Sabine tried to figure out what to do so no one else died. She caught sight of Captain Cutler on the other side of the courtyard, but he turned and ran the opposite direction. There was no one to help her. None of the nobles present could stand up to the king. Her poor guards couldn't do a thing.

Rainer tightened his grip on Sabine's arm, dragging her around Erikin's body and through the archway. To the right, Sabine spotted Harper, her eyes wide in fear. Harper clasped a hand over her mouth and ran the other away.

Sabine tripped on her own two feet, but Rainer's hold on her was so tight, he kept her upright. "Where are we going?" she croaked, pain lacing though her throat.

He slammed her against the wall. "Where are we going?" he snarled into her face, his eyes wild with rage. "I should take you to the dungeon. After all, that's where you think I—your husband and king—belong." He bashed his free hand against the wall beside her head, making her flinch. "I told you to leave my sister alone. I don't know what game you're playing, but you lose. I win."

"This isn't a game," she whispered, tears sliding down her cheeks. "You just killed my guard." Erikin was dead because of her.

Pressing his arm against her throat, Rainer said, "And I'm debating whether I should kill you as well." His eyes focused on hers, and Sabine could see the truth of his words. It wouldn't take much for him to end her.

"Your Majesty," an urgent voice shouted. "There's an emergency. You're needed immediately." Commander Felix came running into view, his chest heaving, indicating he'd just ran there.

Rainer let go of Sabine as if she were on fire.

She leaned against the wall, afraid to move.

"What's the problem?" Rainer asked, facing Felix.

"A message just came in from Hillard."

Rainer reached out. "Hand it to me."

"I, uh, left it at my office. I'm sorry, Your Majesty. I was in such a hurry to reach you, I forgot it."

Rainer's eyes narrowed. "That's unlike you." He folded his arms.

Felix glanced at Sabine before focusing back on Rainer. "We should hurry—the message was marked *urgent*. I'll escort you there." He gestured toward the hallway, away from Sabine.

Rainer turned toward the guards present. "Take the queen to the dungeon."

"I've committed no crimes," Sabine wheezed, panic filling her.

The king started to walk away.

Sabine tried again. "The law must be followed," she rasped. "Princess Lottie has been arrested for treason." Hopefully the princess was already in the dungeon. If Rainer had gotten wind of it ahead of time, he may have thwarted Sabine's plans. "That means Prince Axel, Prince Anton, and you, King Rainer, are to join her since you are her blood relatives. Not me. I am not related by blood." He started to walk away. Raising her voice, she cried out, "Just because you don't like the law, doesn't mean you can throw the one enforcing it into the dungeon. It doesn't work like that."

He froze, then slowly turned to face her. "Don't you dare tell me how Lynk's laws work," he said, his voice menacing. Then to the guards, "Take her to the dungeon. I'll visit her there once I'm done with this urgent matter." Lowering his voice so only Sabine could hear, he whispered, "In the dungeon, there will be no one to hear you scream." Grinning, he left with Felix.

The guard to her left cleared his throat. "Your Majesty."

Still leaning against the wall, her entire body violently shook.

"Are you able to walk unassisted?" he asked, his hand going to her elbow.

She forced herself to stand upright. "Yes, thank you. I can walk." Her voice didn't even sound like it belonged to her.

Near the archway to the courtyard, a handful of people were watching.

Lady Karmen pushed past several of the people and came to Sabine, eyeing her neck. "Are you all right, Your Majesty? You have a nasty bruise forming."

"I am," she replied, her voice raspy. It felt as if her throat were on fire every time she spoke.

Several guards were kneeling next to Erikin.

"Is he truly dead?" she asked.

"He is, Your Majesty," one of the men replied.

While Sabine wanted to cover her face and mourn Erikin's death, she had to be strong. Dozens of people were nearby watching her.

"Do we take the queen to the dungeon?" one of the guards asked no one in particular.

"You cannot arrest me for no reason," Sabine said. It hurt too badly to speak, but she needed to make sure everyone knew what really happened. "Princess Lottie has been arrested for treason. The king found out, and he is furious with me. I'm sorry you all had to witness that spectacle."

"The king just tried to kill the queen," Karmen said, addressing everyone present. "That's treason."

Duke Vadil came forward. "The king ordered the queen to be taken to the dungeon," he reiterated. "Do we know what she's been charged with?"

The guards looked at one another, no one knowing.

"When is the princess facing trial?" he asked.

"Tomorrow," Sabine answered. "You should all be receiving details shortly."

Duke Vadil put his hand on Sabine's shoulder. "Then I suggest everyone retire for the evening. If the king isn't going to the dungeon, then neither is the queen. It looks like we're going to have quite the day ahead of us tomorrow as all of this gets sorted out." When no one moved, the duke started motioning for everyone to leave.

If Sabine went to her room, Rainer would find her. And if he found her, she didn't know if she'd make it to tomorrow. His volatile behavior and aggressive anger frightened her. She'd been terrified when she faced the assassin back in Avoni, but at least she'd known who and what she was dealing with. Rainer, on the other hand, pretended to be one thing when he was another. There was something deeply disturbing and frightening about that.

Everyone left except for Sabine's personal guards.

"Your Majesty," one of the men said. "Shall we escort you to your room? Or a healer?"

The healer was probably the right place to go. However, Rainer would look for her there.

She didn't know what to do. Tears filled her eyes—her neck hurt.

Lady Regina rounded the corner. "My queen." She curtseyed. "May I please have a word in private?"

She nodded, unable to speak.

The guards moved a respectable distance away.

"I wish to offer you my rooms for the night," Regina said. "We need to hide you."

We. Sabine wondered if that included Felix and Cutler.

"Is that acceptable to you?" Regina asked.

Sabine nodded, tears streaking down her cheeks. When she turned toward her guards to inform them of her destination, Regina shook her head. "I'll take care of it. Don't try to talk." Regina wrapped her arm around Sabine. "Guards, this way."

For the first time in weeks, Sabine felt as if she had a mother taking care of her. She hadn't realized how much she needed this comfort right now. She relaxed and let the older woman guide her through the palace, taking corridors and passageways she hadn't been in before. Some of them were so narrow and dark she wondered if they were in the servants' passageways.

They entered Lady Regina's rooms from a hidden door. Regina ushered the guards inside as well. Then Cutler stepped forward and ordered the men to guard every door and entryway. Regina took Sabine into a small bedchamber, sitting her on the bed.

"My dog," Sabine whispered, worrying about Harta's safety.

"I already sent Harper to your room to take care of the

dog and a few other things. She's the one who came and got me. But right now, I need to take care of you." She went over to the side table and pulled out a box. "I'm going to put something on your neck to help with the swelling. It'll take the edge off the pain as well. You'll still be sore, but you'll be able to talk in a few hours."

Sabine absently nodded as Regina administered the ointment to her skin. "How do you know this will work?"

"I used to help the previous queen with situations such as this all the time."

Her words felt heavy, like lead.

This was not a life Sabine would allow herself to live. If things didn't go her way tomorrow, she would flee the palace. She'd find another way to make sure Rainer didn't go to war. It was a good thing Evander wasn't here. If he were, Rainer would be dead and she'd have a diplomatic crisis on her hands.

"Was there really an emergency?" Sabine whispered, wondering about Felix's timely interruption.

"Cutler came and got him," Regina revealed. "But I do believe a letter of importance arrived—it just wasn't an emergency."

Who knew Cutler would turn out to be someone who helped her? "When Rainer doesn't find me in the dungeon, he'll start looking for me."

Regina capped the ointment and returned it to the box. "Tonight, you'll be safe here. Tomorrow, we'll have a plan to get you to the throne room." She moved to the door.

"Regina," Sabine said, her voice still raspy. "Thank you."

"Of course, my queen."

Mumbling sounds came from the other side of the door, waking Sabine. She peeled her eyelids open, and memories of last night came flooding back. When she swallowed, it hurt, but it wasn't nearly as bad as last night. She slid out of bed and padded over to the mirror. A gasp escaped her lips. While the swelling had gone down, a bruise the shape of a hand had formed on her neck. Glancing at her arm, it also bore a bruise in the shape of fingers. Anyone who saw her would know someone had attacked her.

She shoved away all thoughts of Erikin being murdered. If she allowed herself to think about him, she wouldn't make it through the day. A chill spread over her as the image of an angry Rainer grabbed her neck, squeezing, wanting her dead. She could almost feel his fingers on her skin. Shaking, she went over to the door and opened it, needing a distraction.

Lady Regina and Commander Felix were in the sitting room, deep in conversation.

"Queen Sabine," Regina said as she stood and curtseyed. "I hope you slept well. Harper delivered an outfit for you." She gestured to a dress draped over the chair. "And I have breakfast on the table for whenever you're ready to eat." She sat back down, folding her hands together.

Felix ran a hand over his chin, his focus on something far away.

"Commander, is something the matter?" Sabine asked. She slid her hand onto his shoulder, squeezing.

He sighed. "Oh, child. I am so sorry for last night." He patted her hand as he looked at her, shaking his head when he caught sight of her bruises. "I'm sorry for the death of your guard and for the way the king treated you." He stood and faced her.

"Thank you." She stared at her feet, not wanting to talk about it right now. She needed to prepare for the day, and that required getting her confidence up to be able to face the nobles in the palace.

"There's something you need to know," he said, leading her over to the sofa.

Sabine took a seat, instinctively knowing bad news was coming.

"There's no easy way to say this."

"Just tell her, Felix," Regina said.

"Yesterday, a letter arrived. I'd assumed it was to inform the king of another murder. However, I was wrong. It carried news of a prisoner. This man is believed to be the one responsible for killing so many of our soldiers. He arrived here at the palace last night and was placed in the dungeon."

"That's good news, isn't it?" Sabine asked, her body relaxing.

"Yes, it's good that this man has been caught. However, since he is dangerous and in our dungeon, Princess Lottie was moved back to her room. I was also told Prince Axel is in his room as well, and Prince Anton isn't in the palace at the moment."

"Then I assume the king is in his room. How convenient." She folded her arms, trying to hold herself together. "Will Lottie's trial even take place today?" Or would the powers that be deem it too risky.

"It will."

That was all that concerned Sabine at the moment. Taking care of Lottie fulfilled Sabine's promise to her sister, and it would take care of Rainer by getting him out of the way. She'd be able to stop the war before it even started. Right now, that was all that mattered.

"Who decided all of this? Shouldn't it have been me?"

"The king determined everything. I'm so sorry."

Of course he did.

"Go and dress," Regina said. "Once you're ready, the

commander will escort you to the throne room for today's proceedings."

Sabine returned to the guest room, considering everything Felix had said. A man had been brought in late last night—the same night Evander left. King Kai had indicated a handful of Avoni assassins were in Lynk carrying out a mission. If a single man was brought in for murder, it didn't necessarily mean he was one of the Avoni assassins. However, she couldn't dismiss the possibility.

Felix didn't want to escort Sabine to the antechamber in case Rainer was there, so he led her directly to the throne room's main entrance. When they arrived, Sabine found the room so packed she couldn't even see the dais from the back of the room. Her guards shifted around her and moved forward, clearing a walkway for her. As she made her way toward the dais, people began to notice her. Within seconds, the room fell silent, and every face turned in her direction.

The outfit she wore made no attempt to cover the bruises on her neck and arm. If anything, the light pink fabric highlighted the marks on her body. Since enough people had seen Rainer hurt her in the courtyard last night, word would spread. Everyone would know what the king had done.

Halfway down the aisle, she spotted Rainer seated on his throne on the dais, with Lottie and Axel standing on the steps before him. Since Sabine had never been to a trial before, she wasn't certain what would happen or what the protocol was. However, she made sure to keep her head high and at least act as if she knew what to do.

The herald officially announced her, and everyone dropped into a low bow or curtsey. When she reached the dais, she stood at the top and turned to face her people, telling them to rise.

Drew entered the room, joining the ranks of her personal guards.

"Thank you all for coming," Sabine said. "It is with a solemn heart that I am here addressing you today." She made a point to meet as many eyes as she could, willing them to see her sincerity. "I came to Lynk, taking my sister's place, for several reasons. My family needed an alliance with Lynk. They desired Lynk's protection. Lynk needed Bakley's food, and my old kingdom had more than enough. King Rainer needs a child of royal blood in order to maintain his throne, and I am of royal blood and able to provide him with that child. It seemed that by coming here, two kingdoms benefitted."

She folded her hands. "Of course, I only came because my sister was murdered. It took a great deal of courage to fill Princess Alina's shoes. Since being here, I have discovered the person responsible for her death. Naturally, I want that person punished. However, what I want is of no consequence. I married King Rainer, I was crowned queen, and I took a vow. I promised to uphold Lynk's laws."

She took a deep breath and continued. "The night of the masquerade, I saw Princess Lottie speaking with a man. I heard her order him to kill me. During their conversation, he implied he'd killed my sister, Alina. Therefore, Princess Lottie is guilty of treason."

A hushed murmur went through the room.

"I told King Rainer and asked him to have Princess Lottie arrested, but he refused. I then learned that for a crime such as this, the perpetrator's entire bloodline will suffer the same fate. Which means King Rainer, Prince Axel, and Prince Anton will receive the same punishment as Princess Lottie. I assume that's why the king chose to ignore the law and refused to act. I do not wish to see the king suffer the same consequences as Lottie. However, the law is the law. We can't pick and choose which laws we do or do not follow based upon how convenient they are. Therefore, I believe Princess Lottie should be stripped of her title and executed. As the law states, her bloodline will face the same fate." Sabine remained standing there, letting everyone soak in what she'd said.

Rainer pushed to his feet. "My dear people of Lynk," he said, coming to stand beside Sabine. "I understand that this is a lot to take in. Our dear queen is still grieving the loss of her sister and perhaps isn't seeing things clearly. No matter what she says, she desires revenge." He paced a few steps before continuing. "To charge someone with a serious crime requires proof. In this particular case, Queen Sabine doesn't have any proof—it is simply her word against my sister's. I have known my sister all my life and trust her. I haven't known the queen for very long. You all know Princess Lottie. There is no reason for her to want the queen dead, and the princess doesn't want my throne."

Rainer folded his arms, as if contemplating his next words. "I do not believe it wise to kill the entire royal family —except the queen—on one person's word. Especially when the queen is the one bringing the charges forward. It's almost as if the queen wants to get rid of me. Not only that, but we are facing war. The other kingdoms are restless. We have someone in our kingdom committing murders. People have been showing up dead since Princess Alina's death. Perhaps these murders are tied to the late princess's murder. Thankfully, word came last night that a foreigner has been apprehended. He was caught trying to murder one of my military officials. He was brought here to the palace and is in the dungeon. I need to question him to get to the bottom of this."

People began talking to one another.

Sabine wanted to scream. Rainer spoke half-truths to make her look bad.

The king held up his hand, getting everyone's attention. "If we look at the situation objectively, Queen Sabine has more motive to kill me than my own sister does. But let's put that aside and focus on Princess Lottie. She is engaged to Prince Evander of Avoni. She is leaving our kingdom once the marriage takes place. She won't be any threat to me—if she was ever a threat at all." He moved back a few steps so he was now in the center of the dais, behind Sabine.

"I believe Princess Lottie should proceed with her marriage to Prince Evander. The wedding will take place in five days. Then Prince Evander will take Princess Lottie to Avoni where she will live with him, posing no threat to Lynk. I will get back to work and focus on our prisoner and find out why he's been committing these murders. I will ensure he is punished according to our laws."

People began talking again, more enthusiastic this time.

Tears filled Sabine's eyes. She'd come here to bury Lottie, but Rainer had just taken a hammer and pounded Sabine into the ground. Of course the people would side with the king after that eloquent speech. Plus, they knew him and the royal family better than Sabine. She'd been naive to think she could have outsmarted him.

A soldier ran into the throne room, heading straight for Rainer. When he reached the king, the soldier held out a letter to him.

Rainer took it, tearing it open. He cursed. "This trial is over. All guards to the front of the palace." The king handed Axel the letter then took off running down the aisle.

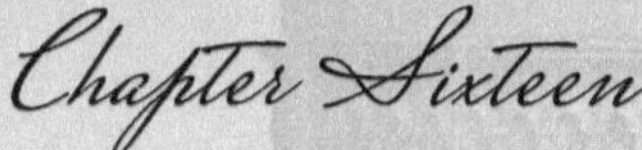

Chapter Sixteen

Chaos erupted in the throne room. "Let me see that letter," Sabine said as she rushed to Axel's side.

After reading it, he folded it and looked at her. "Never a dull moment with you around." He tucked the letter into his pocket.

"If you won't let me read it, at least tell me what it says." Axel had to be upset with her for having him arrested even though he hadn't gone to the dungeon.

"It seems you've caused my dear brother a most troublesome problem he needs to deal with." He turned and strode over to one of the dukes, striking up a conversation with him.

Sabine had no idea what he was talking about. Glancing around the room, she saw most people stood in groups discussing what had just transpired.

Lottie approached Sabine.

The queen's guards immediately surrounded them.

"It's a shame you went through all this trouble for nothing." Lottie smirked.

"You deserve to be in the dungeon."

"But I'm not." Lottie took a step closer to Sabine, a smile curving her lips. "And in five days, I'll be in Evander's bed." She stared at the queen, a challenge in her eyes.

Sabine knew Lottie wanted a reaction—probably to have evidence to claim that Sabine had committed treason by being with another man. Forcing her face to remain frozen and not show any emotion, she simply shrugged as if the thought of Lottie and Evander sharing a bed meant nothing to her.

Lottie took a step back. "I'm going to go and pack for my journey to Avoni." She left the room.

"We need to get you out of here," Drew said from her side. He ushered her to the antechamber off the throne room. When the door closed, he dropped to one knee. "Queen Sabine, I must apologize."

"What for?" she asked.

"Last night."

"If anything, I should be the one apologizing." She still couldn't believe Rainer had killed Erikin so callously.

He peered up at her. "I wasn't there when you were attacked." He stood.

"If you had been, you'd be the one dead, not Erikin."

"I spent the night outside Lottie's bedchamber making sure she didn't escape. I didn't hear about what happened to you until this morning."

The door opened and a soldier entered. "The queen is to be immediately taken to the keep."

"What's going on?" Drew demanded.

"There's a riot. The people in town are up in arms. They're all saying the king tried to kill the queen. They're demanding the king be hanged."

Sabine rubbed her temples. "How did they find out?" She'd assumed only those in the palace would have known what happened.

"My guess would be the servants from the palace. Many live in the town and go home at night," Drew explained.

Rainer would use this as another piece of evidence claiming Sabine wanted his throne.

"Let's get you to the keep," Drew said, heading for the door.

"Where is it located?" In all her time here in the palace, she'd never heard anyone mention there being a keep on the premises.

"It's near the dungeon."

Sabine didn't want to be locked up or anywhere near the dungeon. "I have a better idea."

Standing at the top of the turret, Sabine observed the scene before her. The main street that cut through town was filled shoulder-to-shoulder with angry people shouting. From where she stood, she couldn't hear what they were saying. "There has to be over a thousand people," she mused. It looked like everyone who lived in town had come out for this. "What's the standard procedure for a riot?" She'd never seen anything like this in Bakley.

"No idea," Drew answered. "We've never had something like this happen before."

The bridge was lowered. Approximately fifty soldiers marched out of the palace, Rainer leading them. They crossed the bridge and headed straight into town.

The angry crowd rushed toward the king like a storm of bees.

"Let's get you inside," Drew said. "This isn't going to end well."

She considered what he said. "If these people are truly upset with the king because he hurt me, I should address them to de-escalate the situation." No one else needed to be hurt defending her. She was already responsible for one death.

"It's not safe for you to do that." He turned his gaze toward the mob again. "Besides, do you really want to help the king after what he did to you?"

That was a good question. "No, I don't. But I do want to help my subjects." She couldn't stand there and let Rainer kill his own citizens—because that was exactly what he'd do. He'd force his soldiers to kill everyone if he had to. These people didn't deserve to die for defending their queen. And, honestly, she didn't want any harm to come to the soldiers. It wasn't fair to make them kill their own families and countrymen. "It may be our only option to save lives." Her own words solidified her resolve. She ran down the stairs, heading toward the front of the palace, wanting to stop this before it became a bloodbath.

"Think this through, Your Majesty," Drew said, running after her.

"Don't try to talk me out of it. I'm doing this."

"Okay, but at least have a plan. Where do you want to address the people from so that they can hear and see you?"

She didn't know. "Does anyone have any ideas where I can address the people from?" she asked her guards.

One of them said, "My father owns a tall building about two blocks south on the main street. If we can get you there, you'd have access to the roof."

"That's worth a shot." Since it looked like most of the people were gathered on the main street, if Sabine and her guards went west a few blocks before cutting south, they might be able to make it there unnoticed. They just had to make it across the bridge before Rainer spotted them.

She ran.

When Sabine was eight years old, she had been out riding with Viktor when he'd started teasing her about being a girl and having to ride sidesaddle. She was so mad, she rode closer to him. When she had the chance, she shoved his shoulder. It had only been meant as a warning, but he'd fallen and broken his leg. She'd had to ride home, alone, to get her mother and father and tell them what she'd done. Even though she hadn't meant to hurt Viktor, he'd broken his leg because of her. The entire ride home, she'd been fearful of what her parents would say and do to her. A small part of her knew that she could run away and escape their wrath. However, the right thing to do was confront it head on.

As Sabine ran across the bridge, toward the chaos, this reminded her of that childhood memory.

The second she stepped off the bridge, she veered right, her guards surrounding her, hoping no one noticed her amongst them. Since most everyone was on the main road, they were able to make it two blocks west before they turned and headed south. They passed a few people here and there, but no one bothered to look at the woman in the middle of the group.

They stopped before the back door to a tall, nondescript building. One of her guards pulled out a key, unlocking it. The door opened, and Sabine ran up three flights of stairs. At the top, she pushed open another door, bursting onto the rooftop.

Sabine instructed her guards to wait near the door so the crowd's attention would be on her. If they saw palace sentries, the people might become even angrier at Rainer. Nearing the edge, she silently cursed that it didn't have a railing. Thankfully, it wasn't that windy out. The key was to not think about how high up she was.

Peering over the side at the mayhem below, she saw people throwing rocks and rotten fruit toward the soldiers who had set up a barricade at the northern end of the main street, just before the bridge. Rainer stood safely behind his soldiers, his sword in hand, as he shouted instructions. Several citizens near the barricade laid on the ground, blood pooling around their bodies.

"Are you sure you want to go through with this?" Drew asked from behind her. He was kneeling on the rooftop, out of sight, but within reach of Sabine should she need him.

Nodding, she took a step closer to the edge. "People of Lynk!" she shouted, trying to gain their attention. However, her voice hadn't fully recovered from last night, so no one heard her. Not having time to waste, she removed one of her bracelets and tossed it over the side, hitting a man on the shoulder. He glanced up and spotted her. She waved at him. He turned to those around him, pointing at her. Within minutes, a hush descended over the crowd and everyone now faced Sabine.

A loud bang came from behind her. She glanced over her shoulder and saw her guards struggling to hold the door shut. Rainer had probably sent his soldiers to acquire her. Her purpose here was now two-fold—she needed to not only stop this riot and save these people's lives, but she needed to calm Rainer down so she could save her guards as well.

"My fellow citizens of Lynk," she shouted, ignoring the pain in her throat. "One of my greatest joys is coming into town and visiting your stores, businesses, and you, my dear people. Please know that as your queen, I serve you." She gestured to her subjects. "I understand you're upset. I'm upset as well. However, this is not the way to solve our problems." She looked to where Rainer stood, his hands on his hips, staring at her.

"Did the king try to kill you?" someone shouted.

"It looks like it!" another yelled.

The dress she wore showed both the bruise on her neck and the one on her arm. "Yes, there was an incident last night. As you can see, I am okay. It is nice to know that you all care enough to be out here, fighting for me. Please know that I will continue to fight for you in any way I can."

More banging came from the door to the rooftop, her guards grunting as they held it shut.

"It is time for this violence to stop," she said. "I don't want anyone else to die today. I am going to come down and return to the palace with King Rainer. Now that the king has seen how faithful our subjects are, I am certain no harm will come to me. Otherwise, the outcome would be severe. The army is loyal to the king because he serves his subjects. Should he harm his own queen or make a move against his own citizens, I am certain the army would rise up against him, as it would be their right to do so." She hoped her threat was enough to keep her and her guards safe.

She motioned for her guards to release the door. It flung open and a handful of soldiers stormed onto the rooftop. "You will escort me to the king." She headed toward the stairwell, the expectation of her command being followed clear. Her guards surrounded her, making sure the soldiers didn't touch her.

The group of them made their way down through the building and to the main street. Citizens parted, allowing Sabine and her guards to walk along the road, toward the barricade. As she passed her subjects, she reached out, squeezing hands, greeting and thanking as many people as she could. She smiled to show her sincerity. Many expressed how upset they were over her bruises. Again and again she repeated that the situation had been very scary, but it was over now and she was certain it wouldn't happen again. Children started handing her flowers. She took them, tears in her eyes, grateful for everything these people had done for her.

At the barricade, Rainer gave the order to let her pass.

"Actually," Sabine said, taking control of the situation, "I want the barricade removed. Everyone back to the barracks or your stations."

The soldiers immediately did as she said.

Sabine turned to address the citizens nearby. "Thank you all for coming out today. I'd like everyone to return home." She stood next to Rainer and whispered to him, "The two of us need to walk amicably across this bridge and into the palace."

Without a word, he sheathed his sword and did as she said. If he ordered her to be taken to the dungeon, everyone would know and he'd have another riot on his hands. In order to maintain control, he needed to keep her safe. She didn't think he'd lock her in her room either because she needed to continue to make appearances in town.

They entered the palace. "We need to talk," Sabine said.

"Yes, we do," he ground out.

Claire approached. Sabine hadn't seen her in days—not since she'd told the woman she didn't want her as her lady's maid any longer.

"King Rainer," Claire curtseyed. "You're needed."

"Is everything all right?" Sabine asked, wondering what the king was needed for.

Claire ignored her and instead, turned, leading the king away, their heads bent together in conversation. Since Claire was Heather's sister, Sabine assumed it had something to do with Heather.

With Rainer currently occupied, she could address those

at the palace without his interference. Wanting to take advantage of the situation, she headed to the throne room, telling everyone she passed to spread the word to meet there in fifteen minutes.

Standing on the dais, Sabine observed the packed room before her. It seemed like everyone in the palace—both nobles and servants—was in attendance. When she was about to speak, a messenger arrived, handing her a letter.

She broke the seal and read the contents. It was from Axel and stated that while Rainer was handling the riot, everyone inside the palace voted on the matter regarding Lottie. She was found innocent and all charges had been dropped. Sabine crumpled the letter. It felt as if her heart had turned to stone and dropped in her stomach.

"Your Majesty?" Drew said. "Is everything all right?"

Snapping out of her spiraling thoughts, she smiled. "Yes, thank you." Taking a deep breath, she looked at her subjects. After thanking them for coming, she quickly told them about the riot in town, Rainer's response, and what she'd done to de-escalate the situation. She assured her subjects all was well.

"I was also just informed that Princess Lottie has been found innocent. Thank you all for taking your time to be here today to help with these matters." She took a step back, about to retreat to the antechamber, when someone spoke.

"Why are you addressing us alone?" Lady Regina asked, glancing around the room. "Where is the king?"

"King Rainer is currently with his pregnant lover. However, I am here and will deal with what needs to be done." She didn't even know where Axel or Lottie were.

After assuring everyone that they were safe and everything was okay, people began to leave.

Commander Felix asked to speak with her alone in the antechamber. She joined him there.

"People in town are concerned," he said. "My men are assuring everyone you'll either make an appearance tomorrow or send Harper in your stead."

"Good idea." Sabine began pacing, biting on her thumbnail. "I really thought I had him. I thought my plan was going to work." She'd failed and made a mess of things.

"I'm sorry it didn't work out the way you'd intended," he said.

That made two of them. "I'll let you get back to work. I'm sure you have a lot to deal with."

"I do, especially with the new prisoner."

She'd forgotten about that. "The assassin?"

"Yes."

"Is he from Avoni?"

"I haven't had a chance to interrogate him yet. From the initial reports, we can't tell where he's from. He's being difficult."

A trained assassin would never reveal any pertinent information. "Can I see him?"

"No offense, Your Majesty, but I'm not sure that's wise. Let those experienced with this sort of thing handle it."

While she understood why he'd said that, something in Sabine's gut told her this prisoner was an Avoni assassin who'd come with the delegation all those weeks ago. She thought if she could see him, she might be able to know for certain. If she had to guess, she'd say this man was sent by King Kai to kill strategic military personnel in order to prevent a war. "I'd like to see him. Please."

"Very well. Let's head there before the king knows what you're doing and stops you."

Trailed by her guards, Felix led Sabine through the palace and to a corridor she hadn't been in before. They went to the end, stopping before a solid metal door guarded by two soldiers. Felix withdrew a key, opening the door and ushering Sabine and her guards inside.

The smell of mildew hit her, making her hesitate. A dimly lit corridor stretched out before her, unwelcoming, illuminated by torches spaced every twenty feet.

The door shut behind them. Felix locked it from the inside then joined her. "Do not leave my side. Understood?"

She nodded. Having never been in a dungeon before, she didn't know what to expect.

They went down four flights of stairs, each level getting colder. They had to be inside the mountain. Sabine shivered.

"Did they bring this man in through the palace?" she asked. It didn't seem prudent to bring prisoners in that way. Not only because the king and queen lived here, but with all the people around, it didn't seem safe. Plus, allowing prisoners to see the palace, the format, and structure was unwise.

"No. He was brought in through the training center. Then he was transported here." They turned a corner. "This is actually a small dungeon. We have several holding facilities throughout the kingdom."

"Why have one here at all?" she asked.

"For situations like this," Felix explained. "This man was arrested, held in a dungeon, then brought here to face the king. Normally, the king would go wherever the prisoner is being held. However, given the state of things, the king didn't want to leave the palace, so we had the prisoner transported here. No one has ever escaped from this dungeon. You have nothing to worry about."

Sabine didn't mention that there was a first for

everything. "How many prisoners are in here?" She tried to imagine Lottie rotting down here where she belonged.

"Three."

When Felix didn't elaborate, Sabine decided not to ask. She probably didn't want to know. They came to another metal door guarded by two soldiers. Again, Felix used his key to unlock it. Sabine entered a darker hallway, accompanied only by Drew and Felix, since the rest of her guards were not permitted to go any farther. The metal door was closed and locked. A single torch lit this hallway, casting long shadows on the walls and floor. Five metal doors were on either side of the hallway, all of them closed. A dripping sound echoed in the distance.

"Do you still want to do this?" Felix whispered.

"Yes." Her answer sounded loud in this dank place.

Felix headed to the end of the hallway, stopping before the last door on the left. "There are two rooms in there," he explained. "An outer room and the cell with the prisoner."

Sabine nodded, trying to envision what she was about to walk into. She'd assumed she would only be able to peer through some sort of window at the prisoner.

"This door only opens from the outside—this side," Felix explained. "Once you and I are in there, we can't get out unless Captain Drew—who's going to remain here in this hallway—lets us out. Do you understand?"

"Yes." She assumed this was some sort of safety precaution.

"Commander," Drew said, "is this safe?"

"I'll be in there with her," Felix said. He withdrew his longsword and set it on the floor. Then he withdrew a dagger from his boot, tucking it into the back of his pants. He looked at Sabine. "Do not get close to the bars. Stay out of arm's reach."

"Can I talk to him?" she asked.

"You can try, but he hasn't spoken a single word since being arrested." He reached for the door. "Are you ready?"

She nodded.

He pulled the door open, peering inside. Satisfied with what he saw, he gestured for her to follow him.

They entered a small room, about fifteen feet wide, lit by a single torch. Three of the walls were made from solid stone. The third wall, straight ahead, was made of stone blocks on the lower half, while evenly spaced metal bars formed the upper half. Sabine followed Felix to the middle of the room.

She faced the bars, looking past them and into the second room. It was roughly the same size and contained a chamber pot, a bed of hay, and a person sitting in the middle of the space. The man sat cross-legged, his hands folded together, facing Sabine as if he'd been expecting her.

A chill slid through her. She cleared her throat. "Who are you?" Her voice was barely a whisper.

He tilted his head to the side. "Hello, Queen Sabine Manfred of Lynk. It looks like someone tried to kill you. Sloppy and unsuccessful. Pity."

"And you are?" she asked, scanning his wrists for the tattoo marking him as an assassin from Avoni. Unfortunately, his long sleeves went down to his hands, covering his skin.

The man's lips curled into a smile. "Interesting," he said. "Very interesting." In a lithe move, he slowly stood, coming to the bars, curling his fingers around them as he observed Sabine.

If he knew she'd been looking at his wrists for the assassin guild mark, then he had to be from Avoni. Sabine kept her feet firmly rooted in place, far out of the man's reach.

"I must confess, I expected to be arrested weeks ago." The man's attention never wavered from Sabine. He didn't spare

Felix a single glance. "What took your incompetent soldiers so long?"

While she assumed he had predetermined military targets to assassinate, the thought of him being captured on purpose had never occurred to her. She wanted to glance at Felix to see if he'd caught that, but she couldn't take her eyes off the assassin. Not even for a second. He was too dangerous.

"You could have come to see me last night instead of making me wait," he continued. "But I guess if someone..." His eyes scanned her from head to toe before settling on her eyes again. "King Rainer, perhaps? If he tried killing you last night, then you were busy and couldn't greet me properly. I forgive you."

Sabine could feel Felix's attention on her, silently asking if she knew this man. This assassin. The guy certainly acted as if he knew her.

The man chuckled, the sound echoing in the room. "This is going to be fun. A little more challenging than my usual assignment."

So then he was here on King Kai's orders.

"You'll want to be careful, little queen," he purred. "You never know what might be lurking in the shadows or under your bed."

Terror gripped her as she stood there staring into the eyes of this assassin. However, that was what he wanted. It was time to flip the table on him. "Or maybe I do." She took a deliberate step toward him but was careful to remain out of reach. "Since my bed is on the floor in Avoni fashion, I welcome the shadows where *I* can hide. Having been trained by Evander myself," she purposely mentioned his name, hoping it provided her with some form of protection, "I think I've learned a thing or two." She took another step closer, almost within range. "And yes, it'll be fun to finally have a challenge. Ex was far too easy a kill."

At the mention of the notorious assassin Ex, the man's eyes widened ever so slightly. She would have missed it had she not been paying attention.

The man slowly slid his hands farther up the bars, smiling. "Challenge accepted." His sleeves slid down his arms just enough to reveal the smallest hint of a red tattoo on his wrist—the tattoo of the Crimson Cloaks. Evander's guild. He winked.

He'd revealed the tattoo on purpose; Sabine was sure of it. Probably because she'd mentioned Evander.

"If we're done here," the man said, "you should get back to your pretty little palace in the sky. Sweet dreams. Think of me when you sleep."

The man's warning coated her skin like a blanket.

"We're done," Sabine said, taking a step away, then another. Not wanting to turn her back on him.

Felix knocked on the door. Drew immediately opened it. Sabine went through first, stepping into the hallway and taking a deep breath.

Felix joined her, closing the door behind him. "We need to talk."

She nodded. "Not here."

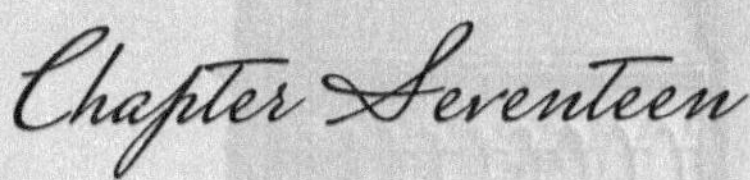

Back in the main section of the palace, Sabine felt like she could finally breathe. She never wanted to step foot in the dungeon again. As she traversed through the palace, her hands shook from the encounter with the assassin.

"We can talk in my room," she murmured to Commander Felix. Not only did she want the privacy her room afforded for this conversation, but she wanted to check on Harta to make sure she was okay.

When they reached the door to her bedchamber, Felix instructed her guards to wait in the hallway. He closed her door then quickly checked the room to ensure they were alone.

Harta was lounging on the sofa on the balcony. Sabine went over, kissing and petting her dog's head.

"I see your bed isn't actually on the floor," Felix said as he joined her on the balcony.

"No, it's not." She sat on the sofa next to Harta.

Felix rubbed his jaw. "I have to ask, do you know that man in the dungeon?"

She'd known that question was coming. It was one of the reasons she'd wanted to talk to Felix. "No, I don't."

He squatted so they were eye level. "The prisoner didn't speak a word to my soldiers. Not when he was arrested, not during his transportation, not during his interrogation, and not since being in that cell. But he spoke to you." He raised his eyebrows in an unspoken question.

Sabine had been trying to figure it out. "I think he was taunting me."

"Why?"

Shrugging, she replied, "Who knows how the mind of an assassin works." Thoughts of Evander surfaced. Even though she'd only spent a short amount of time with the Avoni prince, she felt like she knew him, and he seemed normal— not at all like the man she'd met in the dungeon. That man had goaded her and had reveled in it. "I honestly think he wanted to scare me in order to make his assignment more exciting for him."

"Assignment?"

"He's clearly a trained assassin." Felix had to know that.

The commander stood and folded his arms. "How do *you* know he's an assassin?" Felix asked. "I mean, I agree with you. He's killed dozens of my soldiers. But how do you know? Are you guessing or is there more to it that you're not telling me?"

Even though Felix had been loyal to her, helped her, and kept her alive, it felt wrong to tell him about the Avoni assassin guilds' tattoos. "It's just a feeling," she lied. "I don't have any proof."

He nodded. "At least he's in the dungeon where he can't kill anyone else."

"About that," Sabine said. Based on what the man had said, there was only one possible reason why an assassin of that skill level had been captured in the first place. "I think he wanted to be arrested and brought here." They'd been stupid to bring an Avoni assassin into the palace, even if he was locked in the dungeon.

"That may be the case, but he can't get out of his cell." He began to pace.

Sabine wasn't so sure about that. While the dungeon had seemed secure, Avoni assassins were well trained. "I think we should increase security in the dungeon. Just in case."

The door to Sabine's room opened, and Rainer strode inside. "Commander Felix," he said by way of greeting. "I didn't know you were here. With the queen." He stopped under the arch to the balcony, his focus on his commander.

"Your Majesty," Felix said. "I was debriefing the queen. Now that I'm done, shall I debrief her guards as well? Or do you want to have Captain Lithane handle that?"

"Why do you feel the queen needs to be debriefed about something she was at?" Rainer asked.

"Forgive me, Your Majesty," Felix replied. "I was explaining to the queen that Princess Lottie has been found innocent and that the trial is over. The paperwork has been completed but requires the queen's signature since she brought forth the charges."

Sabine had to force herself to remain calm. Rainer had outsmarted and outplayed her. "I'll come by to sign everything."

Felix gave a quick bow before leaving the room without so much as a backward glance. Sabine couldn't believe how smoothly he'd just lied.

Drew stepped inside her room, standing next to the door. His presence gave her a measure of security, though she knew there wasn't much he could do to protect her from Rainer. She had to trust the threat of another riot would be enough to taper the king's temper.

"I often forget that you're still a child," Rainer said.

"You're only eighteen and have no knowledge or experience of the world. Especially given your pampered upbringing."

The comment stung. However, she would play along if it kept her safe and Rainer's temper in check.

He clasped his hands behind his back as he came out onto the balcony, heading over to the railing and gazing out at the mountains. "Your actions have caused me a lot of trouble." When she didn't respond, he turned to face her, leaning against the railing. "You have a job," he went on. "You're my wife. While you are the queen of Lynk, that is a title, a name, and not a position which requires you to do anything. You will remain here, in this palace. You will not leave it. You will have my child so I can maintain my throne. Once I have an heir, then we will discuss your situation."

So many parts of what he said grated on her nerves. He couldn't expect her to remain in the palace, never leaving it, just so she wouldn't cause him any trouble. It was preposterous. Knowing she couldn't question him about any of that right now, she honed in on the last thing he'd said. "My situation?"

"Yes, your situation. That is, if you'll remain here in Lynk or return to live with your parents."

She hadn't even considered the possibility. "And what of our child?" If they had a child together, she wouldn't be able to abandon him or her.

"Our child—*my* heir—will remain here with me. You and I will be married in name only. Unless things change between us, which I don't see happening."

Now that Rainer wasn't going to be executed for Lottie's crimes, Sabine needed another plan to stop the war. She never should have let herself hope because now that spark was dead. The obstacles ahead of her seemed insurmountable. "If you start a war against the other kingdoms, I might not have a home to return to." She sat there, petting Harta.

"Your family will remain safe. I promised you their safety, and I honor my promises."

That statement almost made her laugh. However, she kept her face neutral, not wanting her true feelings to show. "Thank you." It was all she could muster. If she failed to stop the war, she prayed Rainer wouldn't end her family. They didn't deserve to die for her failures.

He pushed off the railing, coming to stand before her. "You will join me for supper this evening. You need to apologize to Axel and Lottie for having them arrested last night."

The mere thought of apologizing to Lottie irritated Sabine. She didn't know if she could physically do it.

Rainer watched her for another minute before he reached out toward her neck. She jerked backward, not wanting him to touch her. "You bruise easily," he said, as if that explained the marks on her neck. He turned and let himself out, not bothering to apologize for trying to strangle her.

Sabine stroked Harta. "Well, girl, we have an assassin in the dungeon. I think he's here to kill Rainer. And probably me along with the entire royal family. At the end of this, Evander might end up sitting on Lynk's throne."

And that was the thought she'd been trying to avoid—Evander's involvement in all of this. She had no idea how much of his father's plan he knew and if he was actively involved in it. Evander had warned her several times that his family had something in the works. There were things that Evander—even if he didn't agree with it—might not be able to stop. Maybe that was why he'd been trying to get her to leave this palace and run away with him.

When Sabine awoke the next day, Harta was gone. Harper told her that Drew had been instructed to retrieve the dog and return it to the kennels for additional training. For some reason, Sabine felt like Rainer had ordered her dog to be taken away out of spite. Or to prove a point that the gift he gave her for companionship and protection could easily be taken away. She suddenly felt very alone.

Growing up with five older siblings, Sabine had learned at a young age that when they bothered her, not to let it show. If she did, it would only encourage that behavior in the future. As hard as it was not to demand Rainer return her dog, she forced herself to let it go. If Harta wasn't back in a few days, she'd go to the kennels herself. Under no circumstances would she breathe a word of this to Rainer. She couldn't let him know how much the dog meant to her.

Needing to calm herself down, she decided to do a workout. Once changed into comfortable clothes, her guards led her to the training center. While Rainer had said she was required to stay in the palace, she considered this an extension of it, especially since she could access it from the tunnel in the palace.

When she entered the cavern, Cutler spotted her. He immediately came over to see how she was doing after the events of the past two days.

"I have a request," she said, her voice low so it wouldn't carry to other ears. "I have some basic defense skills, but I want to learn how to handle a situation like I faced the other day."

He raised his eyebrows. "You mean when someone much larger than you tries to kill you?"

"Yes." But it was more than just that. "I need to know what to do when it's unexpected. When I think I'm safe, then someone turns on me."

"Meaning you don't have time to prepare or analyze the situation, when your behavior must be automatic?"

"Exactly."

Cutler nodded. "I think that's a good idea." He led her over to a group of a dozen people, both men and women, stretching. "You can train with us. We're going to work on hand-to-hand combat without weapons." Then closer to her so only she'd hear, he said, "I'll do what I can today, but next time I'll tailor it more specificity to your needs."

Sabine pulled her hair back and joined the group, her guards off to the side watching.

Cutler ran them through various drills. He'd paired himself with Sabine, making sure to give her additional techniques the others either already knew or didn't need. After an hour, she was sweaty but felt great. Not only had she learned some new skills, but she'd been able to burn off a lot of her anger.

"I'll accompany you back to the palace," Cutler said, wiping his face with a towel.

Her guards were more than capable of escorting her, so she assumed Cutler had something he wanted to discuss with her.

As they made their way through the tunnel, Sabine thanked him for his help the other day. Instead of acknowledging the part he'd played in keeping her safe, Cutler lowered his voice and said, "Heather isn't doing well."

This was the first time Sabine was hearing about it. Then she remembered Claire coming to get the king yesterday. "Is her sister tending to her?"

"She is. Claire has been a great help. The pregnancy hasn't been easy on Heather. She got sick about a week ago and isn't getting better. I'm worried."

"I'm sorry to hear that," Sabine replied. "Is there anything I can do to help?"

He eyed her sidelong. "You want to help the woman your husband is having an affair with?"

"No. I want to help *you*, who I consider my friend. Heather is your wife. If there is anything I can do, please let me know."

Nodding, he replied, "Thank you. I appreciate that. But there is nothing you can do. I am telling you this so you may understand that the king is a bit more temperamental than usual."

Regardless of the circumstances, there was no excuse for Rainer's behavior. Attempting to kill another person just because you were upset doesn't justify the action.

A scream echoed through the palace. Cutler picked up the pace. At the intersection, a handful of guards ran by.

"Does anyone know what's going on?" Sabine asked.

Neither Cutler nor her guards knew.

"Guard the queen," Drew ordered. Instead of following her, her guards surrounded her and Cutler, acting as a barricade.

They began making their way through the palace. They passed another group of guards running by, weapons drawn.

"I'm going to see if anyone needs help," Cutler said, taking off after the men.

He'd taken two steps when a palace sentry approached them. "Captain Cutler," the man said. "You're needed. It's your father."

Cutler took off running.

"What happened?" Sabine demanded before the sentry could leave.

"This morning, Commander Felix was found dead in his room."

Sabine froze. "Was he murdered?" If so, the Avoni assassin had to be responsible. After all, he'd been arrested for killing high ranking military officials.

"I don't know," the sentry replied before bowing and running after Cutler.

Sabine followed them. She'd just spoken to Commander Felix. The thought of him being dead was hard to fathom. He wanted to retire, live at his manor, and spend time with his family. He looked forward to having grandchildren. And Lady Regina had to be devastated.

Guards filled the corridor. Sabine shoved past them and entered the commander's suite where she found a handful of soldiers. She walked past them to the bedchamber where Rainer was speaking with someone next to a bed with a body in it. She looked away, not wanting to see a dead man. Lady Regina stood off to the side, her eyes wide and her skin white. Cutler was shaking his mother's shoulders, not getting a response.

Sabine rushed over to Regina, wrapping her arm around the woman. "I've got her," she told Cutler. "Let me take care of her while you focus on your father." She led Regina from the room and out into the hallway, wanting to get her away from the chaos. Since the royal wing was on the other side of the palace, Sabine took her to the royal dining room. Pulling out a chair, she told Regina to sit.

"What can I do to help?" Drew asked.

"I know this isn't your job, but please find someone to bring her some tea. And get word to Cutler about where she is so he won't worry."

"Consider it done."

When he left the room, Sabine went over and sat next to Regina, taking her hand. "I'm so sorry," she whispered. "What happened?"

Regina shook her head. "He didn't wake up."

For some reason, those words gave Sabine hope. Maybe Felix had died from natural causes.

"I got up this morning," Regina continued, her voice

barely above a whisper. "I dressed and had breakfast prepared. When I realized Felix was still sleeping, I went in and shook him. His body was cold."

By all means, it seemed as if Felix had died in his sleep. However, this sounded eerily similar to how Alina was found. They'd only discovered she'd been murdered because there was leftover poison at the corner of her mouth.

Drew entered, carrying a cup of tea.

Sabine jumped up and took the cup from him. She whispered, "I want to know if the prisoner is still in the dungeon. I want visual confirmation."

His brows rose, understanding what she was implying without voicing it. "Yes, Your Majesty."

She returned to Regina, setting the cup of tea in front of her. They sat in silence. Regina gazed outside, lost in thought.

Cutler found them an hour later. His hair was standing up as if he'd been pulling on it, his shirt disheveled. He plopped on the chair next to his mother, not looking at her.

"What is it?" Sabine asked.

He shook his head.

Regina slowly turned toward her son. "I didn't see any blood," she began, "so I don't think he was stabbed."

"He wasn't," Cutler said.

"Did he die of natural causes?" Sabine asked.

The corners of Cutler's mouth turned down. "He had a white substance in his mouth."

"My husband was murdered?" Regina asked.

Cutler gave a single nod. He placed his elbows on the table, his hands gripping his hair.

Rainer entered, his eyes scanning the three of them as he went over to the side table, pouring two drinks. He handed one to Cutler before taking a seat.

The commander of the Lynk army was dead. Murdered right here in the palace. Sabine couldn't help but think that this had something to do with the prisoner in the dungeon. The Avoni assassin. And no one was safe.

Chapter Eighteen

The official word circulating the palace was that Commander Felix had died in his sleep. Funeral preparations were already underway to honor the great man. Lady Regina had announced that she would return home to her country estate as soon as the funeral was held.

Sabine meandered through one of the many palace courtyards, reveling in the feel of the sun on her skin. Unable to leave the palace, she tried to be outdoors as much as possible. Since Drew had assured her the assassin was in his cell—he'd seen him with his own eyes—she didn't think the man had killed Felix. King Kai said he had a unit of assassins in Lynk, so maybe one of the others had snuck into the palace to do the job.

Lady Karmen entered the courtyard, heading straight for Sabine. She curtseyed. "I just came from Lady Regina's. Terrible to lose one's husband."

Sabine agreed, looping her arm with Karmen's. "Terrible indeed. I can't even imagine."

After a few minutes of silence, Karmen asked, "How are you doing?"

"I'm fine."

"Liar." Karmen eyed Sabine's neck. "I've been wondering if the commander's death is meant to distract everyone from what the king did to you, Lottie's trial, and the town riot."

Sabine hadn't considered that angle. "Are you implying that the king ordered his own commander's death?"

"I'm not implying anything," Karmen said. "I'm simply stating facts. The timing is awfully convenient." She glanced back at Sabine's guards, far enough away to not overhear their conversation. "Let's not forget, Commander Felix is the one whose impeccable timing stopped Rainer from killing you."

"Do you think the king knows Felix stepped in to help me?" And if so, would Rainer kill his own commander for that? After what she saw of him the other night, she wouldn't put it past him.

"I don't know what the king does or doesn't know. All I'm doing is stating facts. Speaking of the man."

Rainer crossed the courtyard, heading straight toward Sabine.

Karmen released her, taking a step back to put some space between them. Sabine's guards moved a little closer, their hands going to the hilts of their swords.

"My queen," Rainer said, stopping a few feet away, his voice taking on a mocking tone. "There's been a change of plans for this evening. We are now hosting a private party for a few select guests. It's being held in the solarium at seven. I will meet you there. You can apologize to the prince and princess on your own time." He turned and left without waiting for her to respond.

"Guess that means I'm not invited," Karmen mused.

"We have a solarium?" Sabine asked.

"Yes, it's on the east side, top level," Karmen said as she took Sabine's arm again. "I wonder what the point of the private party is. Maybe he's going to announce the new commander."

"It's a little soon for that, don't you think?" They hadn't even had the funeral yet.

"An army needs a commander."

Sabine sighed. Especially an army preparing for war.

"Does he really expect you to apologize to his siblings?" Karmen asked.

"He does." Sabine had decided she would never apologize to Lottie.

After putting on a golden dress, Sabine headed to the solarium, her crown atop her head. At the doorway, her guards were instructed to remain outside.

Sabine entered alone, observing the stunning room. The white marble floor complemented the glass walls. Potted palms and brightly colored flowers had been placed throughout the space. In the center of the room, a shallow pool was situated, several curved sofas around it. Delicate candles hung from wires giving the illusion of stars. One woman played a stringed instrument near the door.

Rainer approached Sabine, bowing. "My queen." He held out his arm. She took it, and he led her to one of the sofas, sitting next to her.

The guests immediately sat on the other sofas. Most had a drink in hand. Rainer introduced the six couples. Each man had the title of a high ranking military officer. Sabine didn't recognize any of them and wondered if they'd been stationed outside the nearby town.

The conversation quickly turned to military matters.

About ten minutes later, when Sabine was about to fall asleep from boredom, Axel came strolling into the room with a woman draped on his arm. While Sabine had seen him with plenty of women, he'd never arrived at one of these events with one.

"Sorry I'm late," Axel drawled, "but we were busy." He winked and sat on the other side of Sabine, the woman squeezing in next to him. He didn't bother to introduce her. Maybe everyone already knew who she was.

"As I was saying," Rainer interjected, "I need to appoint a new commander."

Karmen had been right about the purpose of this event. These men must be the candidates to replace Felix.

A servant walked by, handing Sabine a drink. She thanked the woman and was about to take a sip when Axel bumped her arm, causing her to spill half of it on her own lap.

"Sorry," he said, drying her leg with his sleeve.

Sabine shoved him away, not wanting him to touch her skin like that in front of these people. It implied an intimacy which they did not have.

Rainer ignored her and continued speaking about needing someone strong and commanding who could effectively lead his men.

Axel leaned toward her, giving her a napkin and murmuring, "Don't drink it."

She stared at him, her brows pulling together in question.

He leaned back, holding his own cup. However, he made no attempt to drink from it.

Sabine's mind reeled. Axel couldn't possibly be the murderer, and he wouldn't have been so bold as to poison every person here, especially since Rainer had a glass in hand and was drinking. If Axel knew something, he should say it. Regardless, she decided to heed his warning.

Each man took a turn speaking, droning on and on about

what qualities they possessed and what traits they had that would make them a good commander. Most looked to be in their late thirties or early forties. It didn't seem like Axel was paying attention as he sat there with his arm draped around the woman he'd brought, whispering in her ear while she giggled.

None of the wives spoke. They all diligently sat there in silent support of their husbands.

"What do you think, Prince Axel?" Rainer said, garnering his brother's attention.

Axel straightened, shoving the woman away from him. "Captain Gruttek, Captain Liam, and Captain Tristten don't have enough experience and should remain in the positions they are currently in. However, each deserves a pay raise for the job they are doing. Captain Dregger and Captain Keen are both good candidates and have the necessary experience. However, Captain Neron exceeds both. He has proven time and time again that he is loyal and competent. I'd give it to him." He raised his glass to Captain Neron in salute.

Sabine narrowed her eyes, and Axel winked at her. While he'd sat there pretending not to listen, acting aloof, she'd written him off just as every man here probably had done. However, he'd been listening the entire time and had clearly done his research.

"I agree," Rainer said, standing. "Captain Neron, thank you for your service. If you're willing, I'd like to promote you to the position of commander." Rainer raised his glass.

"It would be my honor to serve you, Your Majesty," Neron said.

Everyone began congratulating him and his wife.

Sabine sat there, watching everything, wondering what sort of person Neron was. Would he eagerly lead their troops into war? Unable to stop herself, she said, "I wish to offer you my heartfelt congratulations, Captain Neron."

Everyone's attention suddenly went to her. "I hope you plan to serve the great kingdom of Lynk well. We all want peace and prosperity. I hope you don't lead us to war." She looked pointedly at him.

Rainer cleared his throat. "To Neron," he said, taking everyone's attention away from her and back to him.

People began milling about, so Sabine headed over to one of the glass walls, looking outside into the night. The soft light of the solarium reflected on the glass, allowing her to see Axel approaching from behind her.

"You could have been a tad more subtle," he said.

"Why?" She was from Bakley and known for being blunt.

He chuckled. "Well, for one, it would upset Rainer a little less."

She shrugged, not caring at all about Rainer.

"To play the game," Axel murmured, "you need to watch your back."

That was the second warning he'd given her tonight. "What's with the drinks?"

Axel still held his, though it didn't look like he'd drunk any of it. "My brother has been known to slip something in drinks at events such as this."

"Why?" Not for the first time, she wondered if Rainer had been the one to poison Felix.

"He likes to loosen people up so they speak without reservation and reveal their secrets." Axel poured his drink into one of the potted plants.

"Are these drinks laced with what you speak of?"

"I have no idea," he answered. "But I'm not taking any chances. I know my brother well enough to not to drink what he serves."

Commotion came from the arched entrance. Sabine glanced that way in time to see Anton striding into the room. Her breath caught. If Anton was here, that meant Evander had to be here as well. She peeked into the hallway, not seeing the Avoni prince anywhere.

Axel chuckled. "Easy, tiger."

"What's that supposed to mean?"

"It means you need to be more subtle if you don't want my brother to know you're in love with Prince Evander."

She faced Axel. "Why do you think I'm in love with him?"

He raised his eyebrows. "Because it's written all over your face."

Sabine entered her room and closed the door, relieved to finally be away from Rainer. Normally, she'd curl up on her bed with Harta. However, since the dog wasn't there, she was truly alone. Instead of dwelling on that fact, she went out on her balcony and began pacing. She needed to find out more about Neron. His wife hadn't seemed friendly, and Sabine didn't know if they were even staying at the palace. Regardless, she'd extend an invitation to the couple.

It dawned on her that Axel was well aware she wanted to prevent Lynk from going to war. Perhaps he'd recommended Neron to replace Felix because the man's beliefs were more closely aligned with hers rather than Rainer's. The problem was that she didn't trust Axel because he always seemed to have an ulterior motive.

The candles inside Sabine's room simultaneously went out, casting her bedchamber in darkness. She froze. If an assassin was in her room, he might not have seen her. The last thing she wanted to do was bring attention to herself out on the balcony. With nowhere to hide, she started to slowly move to the side, wanting to blend in with the shadows cast by the palace wall.

A figure dressed in black pants, a black shirt, and a

knitted hat appeared in the archway. "Sabine, it's me," Evander whispered.

Relief coursed through her. "You're back." She ran to him, throwing her arms around his neck and hugging him tightly.

After a minute, he kissed her temple then held her at arm's length, flinching when he noticed her neck. "What happened?" he demanded. Then he lifted her arm, spotting the bruise there as well. His eyes darkened, transforming his face into someone she didn't recognize—someone terrifying.

If she told him Rainer did this to her, that the king had almost strangled her, Evander would kill him. "There's been a murder in the palace," she said, trying to change the subject. "It happened yesterday. And we have an Avoni assassin in the dungeon. I think he's from your guild."

"What happened?" he said again, annunciating each word slowly.

"It has been handled."

"Sabine, answer the question right now before I lose it."

Sliding her hands to his shoulders, she squeezed him and said, "Rainer got upset with me, but Commander Felix stepped in and diffused the situation. Unfortunately, the commander was found dead yesterday. They're saying he died in his sleep, but I know he was poisoned."

Evander pulled the cap off his head, running his hand through his thick, red hair. "And you believe Rainer had him killed?"

She shrugged. "It's a possibility." It would make sense if the king ordered the commander's assassination, but it also seems reasonable that it was an Avoni assassin since there have been a string of military officers murdered.

"Has a healer looked at your neck?" His fingers gently touched her skin.

"No, but Lady Regina tended to me. It will heal."

"Why didn't you fight him?" he asked. "I told you to have a weapon on you at all times."

Most of her outfits didn't accommodate a dagger. However, after the incident, she would make sure to always have something on her. "It all happened so quickly," she said. "I'm not trained like you. It's not second nature to whip out a knife and stab someone."

He closed his eyes, taking in a deep breath. When he opened them, they'd cleared, the anger gone. "I'm sorry this happened and that I wasn't here to help you. Will you at least consider leaving with me? I can get you out of here tonight."

"I can't." If she left, no one would stand up to Rainer and try to stop the war.

Evander nodded, as if he expected that answer. "I have something for you." He pulled out a letter, handing it to her. "This is from Otto."

She took the letter, seeing her family seal intact, thankful for this distraction and that Evander didn't storm off to kill Rainer. She tore the letter open and read it. "It's from my mother. She implores me to visit Bakley." Folding it back up, she contemplated her mother's words.

"What's the matter? Is someone sick?"

The letter hadn't been written in code, but Sabine felt there was a hidden message. "Everyone is fine," she said. "My mother writes that the Lynk soldiers have all withdrawn from Bakley, the children have been returned to their families, and that my brother, Viktor, is getting married and wishes for me to be there." She turned it over, making sure nothing was written on the back.

"When does she want you to visit?"

"Immediately."

"What are you going to do?" he asked.

"I don't know." She wanted to go but didn't think Rainer

would let her. Not only that, but there was too much going on here for her to just take off and leave again.

"You should go. Right now."

She eyed him. "Is this because Rainer hurt me? Or is there something else you're not telling me." If his family planned on assassinating the Lynk royal family to stop the war, and that included Sabine, Evander needed to tell her. Hinting that she should leave wasn't enough.

"Sabine." Evander clutched her hands. "Go and visit your family. I know you miss them."

"I do." She squeezed his hands. "I'll think about it."

He leaned his forehead against hers. "I should go."

She stood there, reveling in his warmth and the steadfastness of him. "How was your trip?"

"Productive. We signed off on my sister's marriage to your brother." He righted himself. "We also decided what to do if Rainer proceeds with attacking other kingdoms."

"How does that work with Anton there?" It didn't seem prudent to have the prince of the kingdom causing all the problems there hearing what the other kingdoms planned to do to stop it.

"Anton is involved in making decisions. We all are. He knows what's at stake. He has a role to play, and I hope he can do it."

When he didn't elaborate, she realized he wouldn't be telling her any more than that. It grated on her nerves only knowing bits and pieces of everything.

A soft breeze floated into the room.

"Where's your dog?" Evander asked.

"Rainer sent her back to the kennels for some additional training." At least that was the reason she was given. In reality, she knew it was a punishment. He'd taken away her safety and companionship because she'd had Lottie arrested and tried for treason.

"Can I ask you something?" Evander said, pulling her farther into the room. He sat on the edge of her bed, so she did the same.

"You can ask me anything."

"We're friends?"

She nodded, wondering where this was going.

"Do you like me more than a friend?"

Smiling, she said, "Yes."

"But you are loyal to King Rainer? You wish to stay married to him and be faithful to him?"

They'd gone over this in Avoni. "Yes. You know I want to keep the peace among our kingdoms. If that means I need to be here with Rainer, then so be it."

"Let's say he didn't plan on invading the other kingdoms. Would you still want to be here at his side? Be loyal to him? Or are you only here out of obligation?"

She understood what he was implying and why. "I can't think about hypotheticals." She could only look at the facts and decide accordingly.

He slid his cap from his pocket and put it back on, covering his hair. "Sometimes I wonder what would have happened if you hadn't married Rainer."

"If my sister were still alive, if I hadn't taken her place, I'd like to think the two of us would have found each other." It was wishful thinking, a dream. There was no place in her life for what-ifs and dreams.

He nodded, not meeting her eyes. "I have to marry Lottie in a couple of days."

Hearing those words sent a jolt of panic through her. She'd secretly hoped that Lottie would have been found guilty before her marriage to Evander took place so their marriage contract would have been severed. But that plan was slashed to pieces.

"And unlike your situation, I don't have a legitimate reason to put off sharing her bed."

His words felt like a boulder had been dropped on her head. Her stomach twisted with nausea at the mere thought of Evander sharing a bed with Lottie. She stood, wrapping her arms around her body, unable to face the man she'd fallen in love with but could never have.

Soft rustling sounded behind her.

"I've done a lot of things I haven't wanted to," Evander whispered, his voice right behind her.

She closed her eyes, feeling the warmth of his body next to hers.

"The one thing I want more than anything, I can't have. And that kills me." He trailed his fingers up her bare arm. "I've had no choice in so many things." His body pressed against her back, his breath caressing her ear.

"Please don't ask me for something you know I can't give," she whispered.

"I'm not. I won't." His hands slid to her hips. "I just don't think it's fair. We take care of everyone else, but not ourselves. How can such sacrifices be asked of us?"

She didn't know. She pressed her body against his, and his arms wrapped around her waist, his face nuzzling her neck.

"I just wish I could make love to the one person I love."

Tears filled her eyes because she wished for the same thing.

"I want my first time to be with you," he mumbled.

Shock filled her. She hadn't realized he hadn't been with a woman.

His right hand splayed across her stomach, the feel of his callouses pressing into her soft skin.

"Sabine," he whispered into her ear. He kissed her neck.

Each touch sent a jolt of fire into her body. She wanted to

cave in, give herself to him, but she couldn't. She twisted to face him, her hand cupping his cheek.

"He doesn't love you," Evander said. "He's probably with another woman right now."

Her heart hurt because he was right.

"Why deny yourself this?" he asked.

"Because it's the right thing to do."

"I wish I could argue with you, but I understand—especially if your parents are anything like mine. And, honestly, I probably wouldn't love you as much as I do if you weren't so loyal." He kissed her cheek. "Just know, I wish it was you. I'll always wish it was you." He kissed her forehead and took a step back.

She had a strange sense that he was saying goodbye.

Chapter Nineteen

"Wake up," Harper hissed.

Sabine's eyes flew open and she found her lady's maid standing over her.

"Sorry, Your Majesty, but you need to get up." Harper glanced over her shoulder at the door. "Hurry."

"What's the matter?" Sabine rubbed her eyes, sitting up. A heavy fog coated the land outside, hiding everything beyond her balcony.

"There's all kinds of commotion in the palace. Drew went to find out what's going on, but he said to get you up and dressed in case he needs to take you somewhere." Harper yanked Sabine's covers back.

She got out of bed and hurried to her closet, putting on the first outfit she came across. A few minutes later, someone banged on her door.

"Captain Drew is here," Harper said as she admitted Drew and two additional guards into the bedchamber.

"What's wrong?" Sabine asked.

"There's been another death," Drew said through clenched teeth. "Captain—I mean Commander Neron."

Dread filled Sabine. That was the man chosen to replace Felix. "This can't be a coincidence." This second death in the palace indicated that they had an Avoni assassin in their midst rather than Rainer ordering the deaths. "How was he killed?"

"I don't have the details," Drew said. "But a targeted assassination in the palace is madness."

"Does the king know?"

"Someone just went to find him," Drew said.

Sabine wanted to talk to Evander but knew she couldn't seek him out. "I wish to see my dog." Not only did she want the comfort of something she loved, but she needed to get out of her room. The walls felt like they were moving toward her. If she stayed here, she'd be crushed.

Harper stayed behind to try to find out more details about the assassination. Drew and the rest of Sabine's guards escorted her to the military cavern. When they reached the corridor where the kennels were located, her guards remained there while Drew escorted her down the hallway, stopping before a door. He opened it, revealing a long, rectangular room with at least three dozen cages along one side, a dog in each one.

"There are more kennels through there," Drew said, pointing to one of three doors at the end of the row.

Sabine didn't say anything as she walked past cage after cage, looking for Harta. Each kennel had a bowl of water and food. Some even had chew toys. The dogs all looked well kept and healthy. When she reached the end of the row, she spotted Harta wagging her tail in the last kennel.

Kneeling on the ground, Sabine let Harta lick her through the bars. Joy filled her and she laughed. "I'm sorry you're stuck back in here," she whispered. Other than Rainer wanting to punish Sabine, she didn't know what other possible reason he had for taking the dog away from her.

While she'd considered bringing Harta back to her room with her, she'd decided against it. Since there had been another murder in the palace, it wasn't safe for Sabine to spend the night in her room. She'd have to find somewhere else to sleep—somewhere the assassin wouldn't be able to find her in case he came for her. While the dog could offer a level of protection by warning her if someone was approaching, she wanted to have the freedom and flexibility of moving swiftly and quickly without having to worry about Harta.

Drew unlocked the kennel door, opening it. Harta jumped on Sabine, licking her face.

"There's a room where you can play with her," Drew said, indicating the door on the right.

Sabine went into the kennel and snatched Harta's ball. "You want to play?"

Harta wagged her tail, running circles around Sabine.

Drew opened one of the three doors at the end of the hallway, revealing a large room filled with agility equipment for the dogs. Harta ran into the room, eager for Sabine to throw the ball.

Smiling, and feeling lighter than she had in days, she was about to enter the room when she paused. "If there's another kennel through the door on the left, and this is a training room, then what's beyond that last door?"

Drew hesitated. "I'm not sure. Why don't you open it and see?"

Perhaps he wasn't allowed to tell her and this was a way around that order. She moved to the door in the middle and opened it, peering inside. A tube stretched out before her, the ceiling low. About fifteen feet away, another tube intersected this one. Only that tube had water in it, reminding Sabine of the time the Lynk soldiers had taken her and Markis in the boat through the mountain's lava tube.

"Where does this go?" she asked.

"I don't know."

Off to the side, dozens of boats were stacked. There were also empty bowls and dozens of leashes. These boats had to be used for transporting the dogs. The water in the lava tube smelled salty. "Is this water coming from the ocean?"

Drew shrugged before peering over his shoulder. The hallway behind him remained empty. "We should go."

Sabine exited and shut the door. She'd have to think about this more later. Entering the agility room, she found Harta in the middle, eagerly waiting for her to throw the ball. She chucked it and the dog sprinted after the ball, jumping over the small walls and logs that were in her way. Sabine spent the next thirty minutes tossing the ball, smiling as Harta bounded after it again and again.

When her stomach growled from hunger, she finally took Harta back to her kennel, locking her inside and promising to visit again. Drew led her out of the kennels and through the corridor to the main training room.

As she skirted along the edge with her guards in tow, she spotted a man training with two other men. Her feet stopped of their own accord and she stood there, watching the one guy. Shirtless, sweat covering his torso, he sparred with two opponents at once. He jabbed at one, ducked a strike from the other, then swiped his leg out, taking one down. He grappled on the floor, his back muscles moving.

The second opponent jumped on top of his back. He flipped him off, twisted, and put him in a headlock while flinging his legs around the other, squeezing the man's neck. The sight made her inhale sharply.

Evander had both his opponents tapping out.

"Your Majesty?" Drew said from behind her.

Unable to make herself move, she remained there, staring at Evander.

As if sensing her, the prince stood and turned to face her, their eyes locking on one another.

"Queen Sabine?" Drew said, coming to stand at her side. "Is everything all right?"

"Yes. I was just thinking I need to train." Not a lie.

Even though Evander wasn't nearly as large as Rainer, his lean frame was all lithe muscle. Her face warmed thinking about their time together in Avoni when he'd been stabbed and she'd had to clean and sew his wound.

Evander excused himself from the two men he'd been training with and came over to her, bowing. "Queen Sabine," he said by way of greeting.

Her face warmed as she imagined running her hands over his chest, him pushing her against the wall, pressing himself into her. It took an enormous amount of effort to focus on his face instead of ogling him as she said, "Did you hear there was another murder?"

He lifted a single eyebrow, as if he knew what she'd been thinking about. "I did."

If she kissed him right now, he'd probably taste salty from sweating. She licked her lips, about to ask him what he knew about the murder, when Rainer exited from the corridor twenty feet to her left, Anton and Axel close behind him. Immediately spotting her, Rainer's eyes narrowed as he looked between Sabine and Evander.

The two men Evander had been sparring with came over, flanking him. One handed him his shirt. Evander took it, wiping off his face before putting it on.

When Rainer was close enough for Sabine to hear him without him raising his voice, he asked, "Why are you here?"

She pointed behind her. "I came to visit Harta."

He nodded before sliding his hand on her waist and kissing her jaw. His lips moved to her ear. "Return to the palace." Rainer pinched her side hard enough to make her yelp in pain. Leaning back, he looked her in the eyes. "Now."

Instead of responding, Sabine glanced over at Evander. His hands were balled into fists.

Rainer rolled his shoulders and tilted his head to the side, cracking his neck. "Let's go." He turned and headed to the right.

Anton immediately followed Rainer.

Axel slowly strolled past, smirking at Sabine. "Never a dull moment."

"We'll talk later," Evander mumbled before he, too, hurried after Rainer, his own two men going with him.

"Any idea what that's about?" she asked Drew.

"My only guess would be that it has something to do with the murder."

The mention of the murder reminded Sabine of the assassin in the dungeon. Since Rainer was here in the cavern, that meant he wasn't in the palace. It was time to go and pay the Avoni prisoner a visit.

"I can't let you do this," Drew said. "It's not safe."

"How is it not safe if the man's locked in the dungeon?" Sabine asked, folding her arms across her chest. "I've been down there before." As the queen, Drew had to do what she said. He shouldn't be questioning her like this.

His hand went to the hilt of his sword, clutching it. "Commander Felix was in charge last time."

And now he was dead. "If you're worried about getting in trouble, don't be. I'm your queen, and I'm ordering you to move aside so I can go down there." Now more than ever, it was imperative for her to question the prisoner. While she understood Drew's concern, he couldn't become paranoid with her safety to the point of being unreasonable. Yes, there had been murders. In fact, a murder was what brought her to Lynk in the first place. What they needed to be doing was solving these crimes, not hiding away.

"You don't have the key," he pointed out.

She'd forgotten about that. "Don't you?"

"No."

The head of her guard should have access to the dungeon. Although, the more she thought about it, she didn't see a reason for her guards to have a key to the dungeon. If there was an issue, Captain Lithane would work with them to handle it. The less people who had access, the better. Regardless, that didn't help her right now. An idea came to her.

Without another word, Sabine turned and headed to see Lady Regina. Not having much time until Rainer returned, she hoped Regina would have her husband's keys. Sabine was just about to knock on the door when Cutler exited the suite.

"My queen," he said. "If you're here to visit my mother, she just fell asleep."

Sabine didn't want to wake Regina, since she'd had a rough few days. "I'm actually here for another reason," she admitted. "I am hoping your father's keys are in your suite." She nodded behind Cutler.

"Keys for what?" His eyes narrowed.

"The dungeon." There was no point lying or hiding her intentions.

He raised his eyebrows. "What do you want to go down there for?"

"I wish to question the prisoner."

He shook his head. "That's not a good idea. The man is dangerous."

Cutler sounded like Drew. "Your father took me down there. He let me talk with the prisoner." And she'd been the only one he'd spoken to. She'd probably gleaned more information than anyone had.

Cutler rubbed his jaw. "Walk with me," he finally said as he headed down the hallway. Sabine hurried to join him. "I am on my way to see Heather. She's still ill. I only left her to come here to check on my mother."

"I'm sorry she's not improving," Sabine said. "Where is she staying?" She hadn't seen Heather in Rainer's room and she hadn't seen her in Regina's suite either.

He shook his head. "I can't get into it with you right now. The situation is...well...you're a queen, so I don't want to curse in front of you."

Sabine appreciated him being so forthright with her. "I hope your mother is doing better."

"She is, but she's worried. And tired. She leaves in a couple of days. I'm trying to get the king to agree to let me leave with her."

"Surely he'd let you accompany your mother to her estate."

He clasped his hands behind his back. "I want to leave with my wife."

Ah, that was the problem. Rainer didn't want to let his lover go. It shouldn't have surprised Sabine, yet it did.

"Why do you want to see the assassin?" Cutler asked.

"I want to make sure he's still locked up and hasn't gotten out." She shivered, imagining him sneaking out of the dungeon at night to kill people.

"You can't believe he murdered Neron."

"I think he did. And I think he killed your father." She didn't know how, but she'd seen enough Avoni assassins to know it was possible.

They walked in silence for a few minutes.

"Queen Sabine, I can personally assure you that the prisoner is in the dungeon. As for my father's keys, the king took them, and I don't have my own key to enter the dungeon."

Irritation filled her. "Then how can you be so sure the man is still locked in the dungeon?"

He rubbed his shoulder. "I interrogated him," he said quietly.

Cutler had the title of a captain. For some reason, it never occurred to her what or who he was in charge of. She'd assumed he was similar to Drew in his station and rank. To hear that he'd interrogated someone, and that someone was an Avoni prisoner, meant he had to be in charge of that sort of thing. Instead of questioning him about it, she said, "What did you learn?"

"Nothing. He refused to speak even when dubious means were used."

"You hurt him?" she asked.

"I tried to encourage him to answer the questions. He didn't, no matter what I did."

"Were there other soldiers with you?"

"Yes. Why all the questions?"

She didn't know if she should tell him about her conversation with the assassin. Grabbing Cutler's sleeve, she yanked him into an alcove. "When did you question him?" she demanded.

"Earlier today. The king took me into the dungeon. He told me what he wanted to know."

"Which was?" she prodded.

Cutler sighed. "He needed to know if the assassin had help. In other words, if he was working alone or had a partner." He ran his hands over his face. "The king is afraid we've arrested one assassin but still have a second on the loose. He's afraid the second is coming to free the first one."

"Who does the king think is responsible for the two murders in the palace?"

Cutler looked her in the eyes. "He's questioning Prince Evander as we speak."

Dread filled her. "Surely he doesn't think Evander killed those men? He wasn't even in the palace when your father died."

"Evander?" Cutler said. "That's rather informal of you."

Sabine chose to ignore him.

When she didn't respond, he continued, "You need to stay out of the investigation. Don't go near the dungeon—you don't want people questioning your motives."

"I understand." She might not agree with it, but she understood what he was saying. "Thank you for your time."

He nodded then left.

Sabine leaned against the wall considering everything. Her sister had been killed by an Avoni assassin with poison similar to what was used on Felix. That couldn't be a coincidence. She needed to find out how Neron was killed. She pushed off the wall and continued along the hallway. While Sabine didn't think Lottie had anything to do with the current murders, she had to at least consider it. Lottie had hired the assassin who killed Alina and tried killing Sabine. While there were some similarities, she knew that King Kai had sent that unit of assassins here. The man in the dungeon had to be a part of that unit.

Except that King Kai wasn't in charge of the assassins.

Evander was.

Chapter Twenty

That evening at supper, Sabine sat at the table, picking at her food, unable to eat. She'd been trying to ignore Rainer and Evander's conversation at the other end of the table. Pretending it wasn't happening. The last thing she wanted to hear was Evander planning his wedding to Lottie.

"Will we spend the wedding night here?" Lottie asked. "Or on the ship?"

"You should spend it here," Rainer answered. "Then you two can leave in the morning."

"Yes," Evander said. "I think that's wise. Do you have someone to verify the marriage has been consummated?"

Sabine thought she was going to be ill.

Anton reached out, touching Sabine's hand and garnering her attention. "Everything all right?" he mumbled.

She nodded, not looking him in the eyes.

"It appears a lot happened while the prince and I were gone," he said.

At that, she peered up at him. "I'm sorry," she whispered. Anton had to be upset with her for what she'd done. If he'd been here, he would have been arrested as well. That was the one part of her plan that had grated on her nerves—that Anton and Axel would meet the same fate as Lottie. They didn't deserve it.

"You're sorry?" He pulled his hand back. "I'm not the one with a bruise around my neck."

Reaching up, she covered the mark with her hand, wishing she could hide it. The constant reminder of what Rainer had done, of what he was capable of, scared her.

Anton resumed eating. "If you need anything or want to talk, I'm available."

The offer warmed her. "Thank you." He had no reason to be kind to her, yet he was.

Feeling someone watching her, she glanced up. Directly across the table from her, Rainer took a sip of his wine, his eyes meeting hers over the rim of his goblet.

"Is something the matter, dear?" Rainer asked, setting his goblet down. "You don't seem to be in your usual chirpy mood this evening."

"Two people died in this palace. Not only is that a tragedy, but it reminds me of my own sister's death."

His eyes narrowed and his grip on his fork tightened, turning his knuckles white. "At least you have your sister-in-law's wedding to look forward to. Watching her wed Prince Evander should bring some much needed joy to this palace."

Anger rose inside of her, making her want to punch Rainer in the face. He'd said that just to irritate her.

"With regards to the murders, I will keep you safe and warm in your bed tonight. You'll be too busy enjoying your time with me to worry that pretty little head of yours about anything else." His eyes gleaned with mischief. He'd not only said that to see her reaction, but Evander's as well.

"Is that so? Will you be coming to me after you're done

with Heather? Or is she too sick to entertain you, so have no choice but to bed me instead of her this evening?"

Dead silence filled the room. Sabine might have gone too far with that comment. It had just slipped out of her mouth before she could think better of it. This was one of those instances Axel was always warning her about how she needed to play the game and be more subtle. *Oops.*

"Heather's sick?" Axel asked. "Is she okay? Is there anything I can do?"

Rainer's eyes remained fixed on Sabine's. It looked like he was thinking of all the ways he'd make her pay for that comment. It had been stupid to say it, but her temper had gotten the better of her. If she were back home, she'd run out of the room and to the stables. She'd take her horse and ride until it was too dark to see. Then she'd spend the night out under the stars, not coming home until everyone had worried so much about her that they'd forgotten her transgression. But she was neither at home nor was she a child any longer. And the man who sat across from her didn't like to be challenged, yet she'd done just that.

Not once did she dare look Evander's way through this conversation. The true threat in the room was him, not her, regardless of the way Rainer was behaving. If Evander wanted to, he could kill every single person in this room in under ten seconds. The only one who'd put up any sort of a fight would be Rainer. However, Sabine had no doubt Evander would best him.

A servant entered, delivering a letter to Rainer. The king sat there, not taking his eyes off Sabine for an uncomfortable minute, before plucking the letter from the servant and reading it. He handed the letter to Evander and stood. "Anton, please escort Lottie to her room. See that guards are posted outside for her protection. I want at least two sentries assigned to her until she leaves for Avoni or until the assassin is caught."

"Consider it done," Anton answered.

"If you'll all excuse Prince Evander and me, we have a matter to attend to." The two men exited the room.

Anton stood. "Sister, let's go."

Lottie shoved her chair back and stood, glaring at Sabine. "My brother has been nothing but kind to you. You might want to try to show a little respect."

"Yes," Sabine said, "he's been so kind to me. He even gave me this lovely necklace." She pointed to the bruise around her neck.

"That was your own fault."

Anton placed his hand on the small of Lottie's back. "Enough," he said, ushering her out of the room.

The second Axel and Sabine were alone, he began laughing.

"What's so funny?" she demanded.

"*You*. Never a dull moment."

Harper entered the room. "Your Majesty." She curtseyed. "I have news." She came closer to Sabine, whispering in her ear. "Neron died from poison. Dregger has been named the new commander. A man was just arrested and is at the military cavern. Something about having poison on him. He's going to be questioned."

That must have been why Rainer and Evander left. "Thank you, Harper."

"I'm going home to check on my family if you're okay with that?"

"Yes, of course. I'll see you tomorrow. Be safe."

Harper hugged her and left.

Axel stood. "What are your plans for this evening until that husband of yours comes to visit your bed?"

"I have no plans and I doubt Rainer will come to me tonight."

"Can I ask you a personal question?" He leaned against the table and folded his arms.

"Maybe."

"Has my brother ever come to your bed?"

Her face warmed. "Why do you ask?"

"I know it's none of my business, but I see him at Heather's room every night. I doubt he's doing double duty."

Sabine wanted to crawl into a hole. Her entire life, she'd always been the one men looked at during parties. The one they tried to steal a moment with, a touch of the hand, maybe even a kiss on the cheek. Now here she was, married to a man who didn't even want her. Not that she cared because she'd rather not have to sleep with him. Regardless, his relationship with another woman still hurt. Even if Sabine didn't love him. Even if she found herself drawn to another man.

"Do you understand that in order for him to keep the throne, you must have his child?"

She stood, her chair scraping the floor as she did so. "Yes. I am well aware."

"You've consummated your marriage, haven't you?"

Closing her eyes for a minute, she took several deep breaths, trying to calm herself down. When she focused back on Axel, she said, "I have everything under control."

He pushed himself upright. "If you say so." Sliding his hands in his pockets, he headed for the exit. At the threshold, he peered over his shoulder. "You look like you need to relax. Do you want to do something fun?"

"That depends on your idea of fun." She folded her arms, not sure what he had in mind.

He chuckled, the sound low and deep. "Oh Sabine, don't

tempt me." He exited the room. "Are you coming?" he called out from the hallway.

A distraction sounded like something she could use at the moment. Against her better judgment, she hurried after him.

He led her to his suite. Opening the door, he waved her in.

"Rainer made it very clear that I am not to be alone with you."

He lifted a single eyebrow. "Is he afraid you won't be able to control yourself around me?"

She shoved his arm. "Don't be stupid."

"Captain Drew, will you and one additional guard accompany us?" Axel asked.

Sabine entered Axel's sitting room, Drew and another guard remaining near the door. The sun had set but no candles had been lit. "It's rather dark in here," she said.

"Just the way I like it."

"I can't even see your sofa."

"You don't need to," he said. "Follow me." He reached out and took her hand, leading her to the corridor off to the side—the one she assumed led to his bedchamber.

"You and I must have very different ideas of what is fun," she said, trying to pull her hand free.

"Where do you *think* I'm taking you?" he asked.

"I won't go to your bedchamber with you."

He barked out a laugh. "I'm not taking you there, especially with your two dogs following. I'm not that sort of man."

"They're my loyal guards, not dogs. Be respectful."

Shrugging, he said, "If you insist." He tugged her along.

Since her guards were with her, she decided to follow to see what, exactly, Axel considered *fun*. He led her past two doors to the end of the corridor and down a stairwell. At the bottom, the moon illuminated the room which contained a pool similar to the one in Rainer's suite. Half of the pool extended under the floor they'd just come from, while the other half stretched out beyond the roofline. The moonlight reflected off the water. In a land such as Lynk, where it never got cold, having a room with one wall missing made sense. Although, from where Sabine stood, it looked as if the pool hung out over the mountain. She shivered from the mere thought of it.

Axel began removing his shirt.

"What are you doing?" Sabine demanded, glancing back to make sure her guards were still nearby. Both remained at the bottom of the stairwell.

"What does it look like I'm doing? I'm going for a swim." He tossed his shirt on the floor. Wearing only his pants, he jumped into the pool, water splashing Sabine. When Axel surfaced, he laughed, wiping the water off his face.

Even though she had two guards with her, she didn't think it appropriate for her to swim in a pool with Axel at night. Instead of joining him, she sat at the edge of the pool, sticking her legs in the water.

Axel floated on his back.

"Why'd you bring me here?" she asked, trying to figure out his angle. It could be anything from actually caring about her as a sibling to wanting to upset his own brother. She honestly didn't know with him.

"You looked like you needed to get away," he said, still floating. "Like you could use a friend." He rolled over and went under the water, swimming toward her. When he surfaced, he was a foot away from her legs. "Are you going to come in and join me?"

She shook her head.

"Suit yourself." He came to the edge of the pool, next to her, placing his arms on the side as he watched her. "Do you want to talk about anything? Like what made you so upset?"

"I'm not upset." Just irritated and sad. Her mind had been going crazy trying to come up with a plan to stop the war. One that might actually work.

"I know my brother can be difficult," Axel said. "I'm sorry for everything. If you ever want to talk, I'm here."

She raised her hand to gently touch the bruise on her neck. *Difficult* wasn't a word she'd use to describe Rainer. And talking about him was out of the question. She'd decided that as soon as she figured out how to stop this war, she was leaving. Staying here with Rainer wasn't an option. It was only a matter of time before his temper snapped, and he killed her. If only Lottie had been found guilty of treason. Then Lottie and Rainer would be dead. Sabine's problems would be solved. Instead, things were even more of a mess than before.

"Thank you, Axel. I appreciate everything you've done for me. If you don't mind, I'm just going to sit here and think." The soft breeze, the moonlight, and the water were calming.

Axel lifted himself out of the water. He walked over to the wall where a shelf held a handful of towels. Grabbing one, he dried his face. "I'm going upstairs to change, then I'm leaving to meet someone. Stay here as long as you like."

"Thank you. For everything."

"Any time. Goodnight, Sabine." He left.

Sabine sat there, kicking her legs in the water. "Drew?"

"Yes, Your Majesty?"

"Are the rest of my guards standing outside of Prince Axel's room?"

"They are."

"Can you have them move so it's not obvious I'm in here?"

"Yes, Your Majesty." He turned to head up the stairwell.

"One more thing," she called out after him. "I'm going to swim."

"Then we'll give you some privacy." Drew and the other guard left, leaving her alone in the pool.

This reminded her of being home. Of her and Alina swimming late at night in the small lake outside their castle. Her parents had forbidden them from swimming in it, saying it was unladylike. However, after watching their four older brothers swim, Alina and Sabine had decided they would too. So they wouldn't get into trouble, they waited until their parents had gone to bed, then went out at night and swam.

Smiling at the memory, Sabine undid the holster around her thigh, setting it and her dagger aside. She slid into the cool water, feeling an instant relief from the muggy weather. She swam out to the end, to the part not covered by the roof. Since her dress material was thin, it was easy to swim. At the edge, she peered over, seeing the mountain drop straight down.

An arm snaked around her waist and a hand slid over her mouth. Sabine frantically grabbed at the hand, trying to pull the fingers back so she could scream.

"It's me," Evander whispered in her ear. He released her. "I didn't want to scare you and have you scream."

"Well you did scare me," she hissed as she turned in the water to face him. "What are you doing here?"

"I came to see you."

She surveyed the stairwell.

"Your guards are busy," Evander assured her. "We're alone."

At the word *alone*, her face warmed. She suddenly realized Evander didn't have a shirt on. Not only that, but her wet dress was practically see-through. She'd have to keep her body under the water. Feeling overly exposed, she swam to the other side of the pool, the part that was covered by the roof. Evander silently followed her.

"Why did you come to see me?" she asked, wondering if

it had something to do with the letter Rainer had received tonight. Maybe he had something to tell her.

"What sort of a silly question is that?" He splashed water at her. "I like spending time with you."

"How'd you find me?"

"It wasn't hard. I just had to follow the trail of guards in your wake." His head bobbed above the water. "Why all the questions?"

Instead of answering him, she decided to float on her back as Axel had done. The moon didn't shine on the water in this part of the pool, so she was fairly concealed by the darkness. Closing her eyes, she floated, reveling in the quietness of everything.

One of Evander's hands slid under her back, suspending her body in the water while his other hand came and traced a line from her forehead to her lips, down her neck, between her breasts, and to her belly button. She shivered.

She finally looked into his eyes. "What are you thinking about?"

His focus was on her body. He shook his head.

"Tell me," she prodded.

His hand traced from her naval to her neck. "I'm thinking that I want to kill Rainer with my bare hands for doing this to you." His fingers traced over the bruise around her neck. "I'm thinking I hate myself for not stopping him from hurting you." His fingers went to her lips. "I'm wishing you had run away with me." He moved his body so he stood above her head, his hand no longer supporting her. "I'm thinking how beautiful you are." His hands came to either side of her face, resting on her cheeks. "And I'm thinking about kissing you."

Her breath caught. He moved into her line of sight, staring down at her as she floated in the water. He pinched his eyes shut.

She bent her body, going under the water. When she surfaced, she faced him. He stood there, his chest and head above the water. "Being here with you is dangerous," she whispered. "I should go."

"I'm not dangerous to you."

A small laugh escaped her lips. "You are." She neared him, placing a hand on his shoulder. Just as he'd done, she traced a line along his skin. Only, she traced a finger from one shoulder to the other. She went behind him, tracing a line across his back. When she came to his front again, her finger went up to his lips. "You're the most dangerous person I know. I've never met anyone who tempts me like you do."

He closed his eyes. "Sabine," he whispered.

"I need to go before I do something stupid."

He reached out, clutching her wrist. "Don't go back to your room."

She peered into his eyes. "Why?" Was this because of what Rainer had said at supper? About coming to her bed tonight?

His hands went to her waist, pulling her to him. He leaned his forehead against hers. "It's not safe for you in your room at night."

Terror slid through her. "Because of the assassin?" she asked.

He didn't say anything.

Frustration filled her. "Do you know who the assassin in the dungeon is?" She knew he did. The real question was if he'd share that information with her.

"I do," he answered carefully. "Why?" His grip tightened on her ever so slightly. His fingers felt like fire, making her want to melt into him.

She forced herself to focus because she needed to know if the man in the dungeon was responsible for the deaths that had taken place in the palace.

"When I went to the dungeon to speak with the prisoner, I saw he had the tattoo of your assassin guild." Hopefully, Evander would explain things so she wouldn't have to prod him for more information. If he felt anything for her, he needed to be truthful.

He released her and let out a breath. "You went into the dungeon?"

She nodded.

"You need to be careful when dealing with people like him."

"But he's one of yours." Evander hadn't denied it. "You're the leader of the Crimson Cloaks." And as the leader, that meant he was responsible for his assassins and their actions.

"I didn't send him here," Evander said. "I need you to know that." His voice held a hint of panic to it.

"Is he acting of his own free will?" Because that thought scared her.

"No."

Then he had to be acting on behalf of the king. She didn't realize the king could give orders to the assassins. While King Kai had told her he'd sent a group of assassins to Lynk, she mistakenly assumed Evander was still the one giving the orders, not the king.

"I guess it's a good thing he's in the dungeon." She waited to hear Evander's response, eager to have him either confirm or deny the man had been captured on purpose.

"When you went to see him," Evander said, "did you tell him who you are?"

"He guessed."

Evander submerged under the water. When he surfaced, he wiped the water from his face. "So he knows what you look like," he said more to himself than to her.

"Is he responsible for the deaths we've had in the palace?"

"What makes you think that? He's locked in the dungeon."

"If it's not him, and it's not you, then there's another Avoni assassin on the loose." Which very well might be the case since the king had implied there were several assassins in Lynk. She just didn't know if they were working separately or together.

Evander didn't say anything. His silence scared her. She went under the water and swam to the edge. Even though it was muggy out, she was starting to get cold. Before getting out, she twisted to face Evander.

"Will you please tell me your family's plan?" Maybe they could work together.

"My father never tells anyone the entire story. We only ever know bits and pieces. That way, if one of us is compromised, the plan isn't. Or, if someone sells the information, he can trace it back to the traitor based on what was said."

"In other words, you don't know?"

"I don't know all of it. I've managed to figure out a lot of the pieces just from being here." He swam over to her, placing his hands on either side of her body, trapping her against the edge of the pool. "You're in danger."

"It's a good thing I have you here to protect me," she whispered, sliding her hand onto his chest.

"Your plan failed," he whispered.

She flinched.

"I thought you'd figured it out," Evander said. "I thought Lottie would be convicted of treason and Rainer would be dead. Our problems would have been solved. For a brief moment, I thought I might be able to have you. I thought wrong." His hand took her jaw, tipping her chin up. His lips hovered next to hers. "He doesn't love you, he doesn't respect you, and he doesn't deserve you."

Her heart felt as if it had been split in two. "I know."

His lips gently brushed hers. "Please be careful. Don't take unnecessary risks. Keep your guards with you at all times."

She nodded.

His hands gripped her waist and he lifted her out of the water, setting her on the edge. She stood and got a towel, wrapping it around her body.

Evander joined her, doing the same. After he pulled his tunic back on, he went over and picked up her dagger and holster. He knelt on the floor, sliding a hand up her leg to her thigh.

She gasped. The feel of him made her warm. He smiled as he attached the holster to her leg. Then he leaned forward, kissing right above the dagger. Sabine almost fell over. He chuckled and stood.

"What I wouldn't give for a night alone with you." He kissed her cheek. "I need to go while I still can. Goodnight."

Before she could respond, he turned and ran up the stairwell.

Drew joined her a moment later. "Ready, Your Majesty?"

She nodded, not ready at all. Her breath came too quickly, her face felt flushed, and she felt unsatisfied.

After returning to her room, Sabine peeled off her wet dress and put on plain pants and a tunic—something she'd train in. Then she exited her room and joined her guards.

"I'm thinking you should sleep in the guest wing," Drew said. "I was originally thinking of the servants quarters, but there are too many people and variables to account for."

"The guest wing works." Sabine didn't care where she slept tonight, so long as it wasn't in her room.

Most of the oil lamps had been turned down for the night, casting the palace in a soft glow she wasn't used to. As they traversed through the corridors, she didn't notice any other people. Turning a corner, she spotted a handful of guards outside a room to the left.

"Who's down there?" Sabine whispered.

"I don't know," Drew answered.

She motioned for her guards to wait there while she went to speak to the sentries on duty. As she approached, the men all stood a little taller, a little straighter. No one looked her way but with their masks on, she couldn't see their facial features anyway. She was about to ask who they were guarding when she noticed the door was half-way open. Peering inside, she spotted Rainer sitting on a chair, hunched over, clutching the hand of a woman. It had to be Heather. The scene almost made her feel sorry for the king. Slowly backing up, she returned to her guards.

"Everything all right?" Drew asked.

She nodded, unable to speak for fear that if she opened her mouth, a scream would come out.

When Sabine awoke the next morning, she was surprised she'd not only fallen asleep, but slept well. Six of her night guards had remained in the room with her. After getting out of the guest bed, she headed to the royal dining room for breakfast. Along the way, her night guards were replaced with her day ones. It was a seamless transition, thanks to Drew, who appeared to be managing everything.

Before she entered the royal dining room, Drew joined her. "Good morning, Your Majesty." He motioned to the side, so she joined him. "I wanted to let you know that there's been another death," he said, his voice low so it wouldn't carry.

"Who?"

"Commander Dregger. He'd only been sworn in

yesterday." He ran a hand over his face. "This is the third commander this week."

"I can't believe three murders have taken place right under the king's nose." She found it hard to believe the king was killing his own men, but she couldn't rule anything out at this point.

"Technically, two. They're still calling Commander Felix's death a natural one."

"Given the state of things, I suppose we should stop appointing new commanders until the assassin is found."

"I agree. However, you should also know that without an officially appointed commander, the position falls to the king."

In that case, they had to announce one. "Thank you for telling me."

No longer hungry, she had her guards escort her to the military cavern so she could train.

When she entered, she found it quieter than usual. Only a dozen people were training instead of the hundred or so that were normally there. Sabine spotted Captain Higman heading her way. Before he could pass her and head into the tunnel leading to the palace, she stepped in his way, forcing him to stop.

"Yes, Your Majesty?" he said, annoyance seeping through his voice.

"Where is everyone?"

"That is nothing to concern yourself with."

She raised her brows. "That's not how you speak to your queen."

His eyes narrowed.

She could see the words he didn't say written on his face: *you are just a woman and have no authority over me.* Thinking back, Sabine didn't recall seeing him that day the soldiers swore their allegiance to her.

"Forgive me, Queen Sabine," Higman said, his voice dripping with disdain, "I was told not to discuss the matter with anyone, including you."

"Well," she said, stepping closer to him, "as your queen, I command you to answer me."

"I'm sorry, I cannot." He moved to step around her.

"Captain Drew," Sabine said, waving him forward. "Arrest Captain Higman for insubordination."

"My pleasure, Your Majesty."

Higman held up his hands. "I don't have time for this. If you need information, discuss the matter with the king." He stepped around her and went into the tunnel.

"Let him go," Sabine murmured, rubbing the sides of her forehead, a headache forming. "Captain Drew, please find out what's going on."

He nodded.

Sabine headed to the training area. Two of her guards began working with her on basic hand-to-hand combat techniques. They focused on what to do if someone came at her and put her in a chokehold.

About thirty minutes later, Drew returned with Evander in tow.

"What's going on?" she asked, looking between the two of them.

Evander finally answered. "Your husband sent the army south to the border. There are only a handful of officers left. Once my wedding to Lottie takes place tomorrow, Rainer and the officers are heading south to declare war."

Her time was up. If she was going to do something to stop this war, it had to be today.

Chapter Twenty-One

Sabine couldn't stand there in the middle of the training facility having this conversation with Evander. The empty room allowed their voices to carry and anyone could be lurking nearby. Just because the army was gone, didn't mean that all threats were.

"I am going to visit Harta." Sabine inclined her head to the side and Evander nodded, following her. They went to the corridor leading to the dog kennels. "What's your plan?"

"I'm going to marry Lottie tomorrow and return to Avoni. Once I'm home, I'll discuss the matter with my king."

In other words, his hands were tied. Otherwise, he wouldn't have referred to his father as the king. The other part, the part about Lottie, she tried not to think about it. She'd just pretend it wasn't happening.

"Do you have anything to say?" he asked as they stopped before the closed door.

"No. I don't have a plan yet." Neither to stop the war nor the wedding. She threw open the door, irritated that a woman she despised, who'd ordered her sister's death, got to marry the man she loved. It wasn't fair. And since her plan to end Rainer had failed, her hopes for stopping the war were rapidly diminishing. She had no idea if Rainer would honor his promise to protect her family or not.

Stepping into the kennels, she found them empty. "Where are the dogs?" She peered over her shoulder at Drew who remained at the threshold.

"I don't know," he answered. "But if I had to guess, I'd say with the army."

Without saying a word, she hurried to the door at the end, opening it and peering inside. She cursed. Most of the boats were gone.

"What is it?" Evander asked, trying to see around her.

"Captain Drew is right," she whispered, unable to imagine Harta with the soldiers, preparing for war.

"Drew—I need a minute alone with the queen." Without waiting for a response, Evander gently pushed her into the lava tube, closing the door behind them.

"What are you doing?" Only a single torch hung on the wall, casting the area in dark shadows.

Evander shoved Sabine against the wall, his mouth suddenly on hers, demanding. Warmth flooded her. She grabbed his waist, pulling his body flush with hers. His tongue slid into her mouth. Then it changed. He moved slower. His hands came up, cupping her face as his lips moved over hers. When he pulled away, he rested his forehead against hers, his breathing fast.

"Evander?" she asked, wanting to know why he'd kissed her.

He didn't say anything, he just kept looking at her.

And that was when she realized this was a goodbye kiss. She shook her head. "You can't leave." Not with Lottie. Not with a war on the horizon. And not with her heart. "Stay here and help me stop this war." She wanted him to choose her which was selfish considering she'd chosen Lynk over him.

"You know I can't. I'm sorry, but I have my own orders to follow." He pressed his lips against her forehead.

She closed her eyes, savoring the smell and feel of him.

He released her and took a step back. "Once I leave with Lottie tomorrow, I won't be able to protect you."

She shivered. "I understand." If there was going to be any sort of royal assassination to stop the war, it would either be tonight or tomorrow after the wedding.

Opening the door, Evander ushered Sabine back into the kennels where they found Drew and the rest of her guards waiting. They exited the corridor and entered the main portion of the cavern.

Anton was headed straight for them. "Evander, we need to talk."

"The army is headed to the border," Evander said. "I thought you had a plan to stop it."

"My plan fell through," Anton replied, his voice irritated as he rubbed his palms against his eyes. "My brother is hellbent on ending the League."

"I told you that's what this was about." Evander folded his arms.

"I sent letters to Carlon and Nisk letting them know."

Evander nodded. "And what of Bakley?"

Sabine could kiss him for remembering her family and kingdom.

"My hands are tied due to the marriage contract. However, I personally sent a letter to Otto."

"I need to speak with my men and send word to my parents. Avoni must be warned." Evander turned to face Sabine. "Your Majesty," he said, taking her hand and placing a kiss on it. "It has been a pleasure getting to know you." His eyes bored into hers, as if he wanted to say more but couldn't with Anton there. He released her and left without a backward glance.

Over the course of the past few weeks, there had been many times where Sabine had experienced true fear. However, right now, a fear like she'd never known consumed her. The approaching war, her family's safety, and the thought of never seeing Evander again terrified her.

Sabine had just reentered the main portion of the palace when a man's scream pierced the air. Drew quickly ordered one of her guards to find out what was going on. Closer to the residence wing, another scream rang out followed by the sound of something breaking.

As Sabine made her way toward her room, the screaming intensified. The sounds were coming from somewhere to the right, so she headed that way as if pulled by a string. Turning into another corridor, she heard a crash followed by an eerie silence. Up ahead, a handful of guards stood by a door. Dread filled her. She'd been here before—last night when she'd spotted Rainer in Heather's bedchamber.

As she got closer, she heard someone crying. When the guards noticed Sabine, they stepped aside. It felt like slow motion as she moved toward the door, unable to stop herself yet afraid of what she'd find. But she had to know. At the doorway, she froze at the sight before her.

Inside the bedchamber, Heather was sprawled on the bed, the sheets around her stomach drenched with blood. Cutler clutched his wife's unmoving hand, hunched over her arm, crying. Rainer stood off to the side, heaving deep breaths, chunks of wood from a broken armoire, shards of glass, and flowers scattered around his feet. A healer hovered near the foot of the bed. Claire stood in the corner holding a balled up sheet with splotches of blood, staring at her sister, her eyes wide with shock.

"What's going on?" Sabine asked as she stepped into the room, trying not to gag with the metallic smell of blood permeating the air.

The healer turned toward her, bowing. "Your Majesty," he said softly. "Heather is dead."

A snarl erupted from Rainer as he began pacing, raking his hands through his hair. "I want to know who killed her."

"Your Majesty, no one killed her," the healer said. "It was a complication with the pregnancy. Her body couldn't handle the baby."

Cutler let out a sob, the sound of his pain stabbing Sabine in the heart.

"Why's there so much blood?" she asked.

"When I realized she was about to die," the healer said, "I delivered the baby to try to save one of them. Neither survived."

Sabine glanced at Claire again, this time realizing a tiny, lifeless baby was wrapped in that bloody sheet.

"Her death is your fault!" Rainer shouted, pointing at the healer.

The man paled. "I'm sorry, Your Majesty, but it's no one's fault. These things happen."

"If there's nothing further to be done, you're excused," Sabine said to the healer as she stepped out of the doorway, giving him room to exit.

Relief filled his face as he gathered his instruments and left.

Someone needed to inform Heather's parents. "Claire, your parents should know what happened. They'll probably want to be here. I think you're the best one to deliver the news." And Claire needed to get out of here before she passed out.

Nodding, Claire set the dead baby on the bed next to Heather before rushing out of the room.

Sabine went over to Cutler, rubbing his back. "I'm so sorry," she murmured to him. Then to Rainer. "I think Captain Cutler deserves a few minutes alone with his wife to say his goodbyes."

"You don't tell me what to do," Rainer snarled. "He shouldn't even be here."

"Neither should you. Heather is not your wife." She could feel, rather than see, the guards tense behind her.

"The baby is mine." He pointed to his dead child.

Her words had been too harsh—she'd need to rein in her temper. "I'm sorry," she said. "You're right." She rubbed her temples, a headache starting.

"This is your fault," Rainer said to Cutler. "You did this to her."

Cutler raised his head, looking at the king. "I neither got her pregnant nor insisted she travel in her condition to the palace. If you'd just left her alone, she'd be at *my home* and she'd be alive. If anyone is to blame, it's *you*."

Though Sabine agreed with him, she didn't say it. Continuing to rub Cutler's back, she tried to soothe and comfort him.

Rainer started to come toward Cutler. Sabine moved to cut him off. "Let's give him a minute alone," Sabine said to the king. "Then you can come in and say your goodbyes."

"I shouldn't have to bury another person that I love! My mother, my father, and now Heather?" He gripped his hair in anguish.

Sabine almost felt bad for him. "I know, it's not fair." She wanted to try to calm Rainer down so he didn't lash out and hurt someone. His temper felt like a volcano that would erupt at any moment.

"No, it's not fair," he sneered. "I should have been able to marry Heather." With his hands on his hips, he began pacing again. "I will destroy the League." He glanced at the dead bodies. "Even if it's the last thing I do, the League will end. I will make the rules. I won't bend to someone's will ever again." He stormed from the room.

Shock filled Sabine.

"Your Majesty?" Drew asked, coming to her side.

"Please have someone get Lady Regina. She needs to be here for her son."

Rainer's scream echoed through the palace, making Sabine jump.

She exited from the room, wanting to give Cutler privacy. "Keep an eye on him," she ordered the guards stationed there. Needing to get away from the smell and the sight of Heather, the baby, and the blood, she left that wing of the palace. Her hands began shaking.

Given Rainer's state of mind, and knowing he intended to head south tomorrow to join his army to start a war, Sabine had an opportunity to do something to stop him. She just had to figure out what. "Captain Drew."

"Yes, Your Majesty?"

"Have someone apprise Prince Anton, Prince Axel, and Prince Evander of the situation. Tell them I want to speak with them immediately. I'll be in the library."

He instructed one of her guards to convey the message.

She made her way to the library, trying to come up with a plan. By the time she got there, she still hadn't thought of a single feasible idea. Sitting at the table near the window, irritation filled her. She'd never learned about battles, strategies, or any such things. Those had been reserved for her brothers. The lack in her education was affecting her ability to lead the people of Lynk. Even though her parents hadn't thought she'd sit on the throne, they should have given her the same opportunities to learn as her siblings had.

The sun shifted across the sky, and still she sat there waiting. It felt as if too much time had passed. One of the three princes should be here by now.

A guard Sabine didn't recognize approached, speaking with Drew. After a minute, he left.

"What's wrong?" she asked.

Drew pursed his lips. "I've just been informed that Princess Lottie and several other officers are dead."

She blinked, trying to comprehend what he'd just said, struggling to wrap her brain around this information. "What happened?"

"It seems someone entered the palace and killed almost every officer." He gripped his hilt, his knuckles turning white. "Captain Cutler, Captain Lithane, and Captain Higman are the only high ranking officers alive. As well as myself. Everyone else is dead. Lithane is going to the dungeon now to see if the prisoner is still in there. No one can find Prince Anton, Prince Axel, or Prince Evander. I think you should consider leaving the palace. I'll take you to the royal castle."

She started pacing, hands on her hips, her mind reeling. So many deaths in such a short amount of time. "How was Lottie killed?" Given that the princess was dead and the two princes were unaccounted for, she had to consider that an assassin was in the palace with the intent of killing all members of the royal family—herself included.

"Princess Lottie's throat was slit."

Definitely an assassination. "And the others?" She wondered if Heather dying was truly a coincidence or part of some grander plot.

"Poison."

It was interesting that Lottie was killed in a different fashion than the others. Almost as if she wasn't originally one of the targets. As if she'd been killed as an afterthought. Or for revenge. While Sabine was secretly happy Lottie had gotten what she deserved, she couldn't let anyone know she was grateful for the princess's death. She chewed on her thumbnail, wondering who killed her, a sinking suspicion it might have been Evander.

"Has the king been informed?" she asked.

"Someone went to find him, but I don't know if the news has been delivered."

Given the king's state and the fact that no one could find the princes, she was truly alone. Suddenly, an idea formed. A crazy, dangerous one. "Has another commander been appointed?"

"No."

A smile spread across her lips. It was time she beat Rainer at his own game, and she knew just how to do it. "I have an idea."

Chapter Twenty-Two

S abine rushed through the palace, thinking about everything she needed to do to pull this off. There wasn't much time before Rainer figured it out. That, and he'd head south tomorrow to join his army and start the war. Time was of the essence.

"Captain Drew—please have someone get the remaining captains and bring them to my room immediately."

He began barking out orders.

Once in her bedchamber, Sabine grabbed a bag and crammed clothes in it. Then she quickly changed into thicker pants and a plain tunic. After strapping a dagger to her leg and sliding another one into her boot, she was ready.

A knock sounded on her door. She shoved her bag beneath her bed before Drew admitted Cutler, Higman, and Lithane.

"The four of you are the highest ranking members of our military right now," she began. "We have no commander appointed since the last three have been murdered." No one responded. Holding her head high, she forged on. "Therefore, I am appointing myself as the commander of the army."

It was no surprise when Lithane said, "Forgive me, Your Majesty, but that is something that King Rainer should do."

"The king's sister, lover, and baby all died. He is grieving. I think he deserves to let me handle the military today and tomorrow. Once he's recovered, he can take over."

Cutler nodded. "I agree." His eyes were still red.

"As do I," Drew said.

She observed Lithane and Higman. "The king sent his army south. He is leaving tomorrow to join them. I need the two of you by His Majesty's side to carry out his orders and to support him in this difficult time."

"Why do we need a commander?" Lithane asked.

"Neither prince is accounted for and every officer in the palace—except for the four of you—is dead," she said, her voice harsh. "I will not sit here like a helpless queen and allow our army to fall apart. I will be appointed commander, and I will ensure our army remains fierce until the king is able to lead it." She hoped that was enough to gain their trust.

Neither looked convinced. "Look," she said, trying to calm her voice. "Someone is killing those in charge for a reason. I believe this assassin wants to stop the war. I fear the king and I may be next. It is imperative we remain strong and carry on."

Lithane pursed his lips. "Fine. I agree."

"I do as well," Higman said.

"Excellent. Captain Drew, will you do me the honors?"

"Yes, Your Majesty." He came and stood in front of her. "Please kneel."

She did as he said.

He placed his hand on her shoulder. "As the highest ranking official in the palace, I do hereby appoint Queen Sabine Manfred to the position of commander." He handed her a set of keys. "These are the commander's keys."

She took them and stood. "Thank you." Now she needed to get out of here before Rainer caught word of what she'd done. "Captain Lithane, you will maintain control of the palace guards. Your chief concern is protecting the king from an assassination attempt." She didn't care if the king was assassinated. However, she needed Lithane on her side right now so she could buy herself some time. "Captain Higman, you will take control of the surrounding town. We have an assassin nearby. Find him. Captain Drew, you'll remain with me as my guard. Captain Cutler, given your loss today, you may have time to grieve. Dismissed."

Lithane and Higman left.

Sabine withdrew her bag.

"Commander," Cutler said, eyeing her bag. "I'd prefer to travel with you and assist in any way I can. I don't want to remain here."

The more soldiers she had on her side, the better. "Fine, but we're leaving right now."

"And the rest of your royal guard?" Drew asked. "Will they be coming with us?"

"No. I want them to stay here and keep up the ruse that I'm still in the palace. Have Harper act as my decoy. I need them to buy us as much time as possible. We must reach the army before Rainer does. If he catches wind of this, my plan fails."

Once they'd gathered the necessary supplies, they headed through the tunnel to the military compound. Sabine led Cutler and Drew to the kennels. Inside, they went to the door at the end, the one leading into the lava tubes.

"Since the dogs and most of the boats are gone," Sabine said, "I'm assuming this leads to the army. It'll be the fastest way for us to get there."

"Smart," Cutler said. "The army will have used the lava

tubes at the bottom of the mountain. That'll be the way the king goes as well."

She'd been hoping the king would have to travel by foot. "How much longer is that way?"

"It depends on how fast they get down the mountain. I'd say at least half a day? Maybe more?"

"The water is moving fast," Drew observed. "Once the boat is lowered in, there won't be much time for us to get situated."

"I don't want anyone to come after us this way," Sabine said. "Since there are three boats left, we'll release two, then we'll use the last one."

The two men inspected the boats, ensuring there weren't any problems with them before releasing the extra ones into the water. Then they put the last one in, holding it in place. Sabine tossed their supplies in before stepping in and taking a seat in the middle. Drew then sat in the front, hanging on to the ledge as he did so.

"Here goes nothing," Cutler said as he joined them, sitting in the back.

Drew and Cutler let go, and the boat immediately took off through the dark lava tube.

Having no idea how long they would travel like this in the dark or what they would find at the end, Sabine tried to remain calm and not think about the ginormous mountain above them. The likelihood of it collapsing on them had to be small. This tunnel had to have been here for years.

"Your Majesty—" Drew began.

"Let's forgo the formalities," Sabine said. "Just use names, no titles, while we are traveling and it is just the three of us."

"Very well. Now that we're far enough away our voices won't carry," Drew said from in front of Sabine, "we need to talk about the assassinations."

It seemed strange to have a conversation when they couldn't see each other's faces. Given what she knew of Avoni assassins, she wouldn't be surprised if an assassin dropped down from the ceiling of the tunnel and landed in the boat with them.

"I verified the prisoner is still in the dungeon," Drew said.

"Any indication he's been getting out at night?" she asked, not knowing if it was even possible with the locks and guards present.

"No. Which makes me wonder about Evander. What do you think, Cutler?"

Sabine was curious what Cutler had to say.

"Evander's a kid. He can't be more than what? Twenty? Twenty-three at most? And he's a prince."

"He has a reputation for being ruthless," Drew said. "Though I didn't see anything to indicate that during his time in the palace."

"I've heard stories," Cutler said. "Once I saw the guy, I began to wonder if those stories were even true. Maybe they were made up just to scare people?"

"What kind of stories?" Sabine asked, not sure if she really wanted to know.

"I heard someone threatened his father, the king," Cutler said. "Evander broke into the guy's house and killed everyone inside—the husband, wife, four sons, and over a dozen servants. After slitting each one's throat, he hung them by their ankles, securing each to a rafter. Rumor is he made the husband watch. Saved him for last."

Her heart beat so loudly she could hear it over the rushing of the water. The story was horrific. Suddenly, she wanted to know if it was true. Could he have killed that many people in such a cruel way?

"I was surprised the king allowed him into the palace,"

Drew said. "But he did have men watching the prince at all times."

Evander would have known the king had men watching him and been able to avoid detection if he needed to.

"I thought the men were trying to catch Evander with the queen," Cutler quipped.

"We're off topic," Sabine said. "We're supposed to be discussing the assassinations."

"I want to know if you think Evander killed the commanders," Drew said.

She knew he was asking her because of her friendship with the prince. Drew had seen enough to know there was something between the two of them.

"Is he capable? Yes, without a doubt he could have pulled it off. Did he do it? No, I don't think he did. However, I do believe an Avoni assassin committed the murders. But with regard to Evander, no, I don't think he did it."

"And what about Lottie?" Cutler asked. "Do you think Evander killed her since her death was different from the others?"

"I'm not sure. He was supposed to marry her tomorrow. He could have married her, left the kingdom with her, then killed her and said she died of natural causes."

"True," Cutler said.

"But it's rather convenient, don't you think?" Drew asked.

As horrible as it was, Sabine didn't mind Lottie's death, so she hadn't given it much thought. Lottie deserved to die because of what she did to Alina. A trickle of fear slid through her. Evander knew Sabine felt that way. Had he carried out his own brand of justice on her behalf?

"And Heather's death," Cutler said. "I know the healers said her body wasn't able to handle the baby and she'd been sick for days. But the timing is suspicious."

"Again, I'm not saying it wasn't an assassin from Avoni," she repeated. "But I don't think it was Evander."

"Are you implying that there's another Avoni assassin on the loose?" Cutler asked.

"I think there is another assassin in Lynk." She didn't need to share any details beyond that.

"Then we all need to be extremely careful," Drew said. "The assassin could be anywhere."

In the darkness, Sabine had no way to keep track of time. She ate when she was hungry and slept when she was tired. When not doing either of those things, she had nothing to do but think. The blackness surrounding her seemed to breed doubt and negative thoughts. If Evander was involved in the assassinations, was she okay with that? She honestly didn't know. He'd told her countless times that his father had a plan in place. It made sense that Avoni's plan involved killing people since it seemed that was all they were capable of doing. The issue she had was the number of people they'd killed all in the name of stopping a war. Truth be told, it was the same reasoning she'd used when she had Lottie arrested knowing her siblings would face the same fate. Sabine had told herself that a few deaths to save many justified those deaths.

It felt like days passed. Just as her mind and body had reached the limit for what she could take on this journey, a faint light came from up ahead. The lava tube expanded, and the water opened onto a small beach before narrowing and exiting through a large opening off to the side. The boat hit the sandy bottom and Drew jumped out, pulling the boat farther onto the shore. Sabine and Cutler climbed out. No one spoke as the three of them lifted the boat, carrying it over to the side where dozens of boats had been stacked.

They grabbed their sacks of supplies and headed to the exit. It was too bright for them, so they remained where they were, letting their eyes slowly adjust. Once they were able to handle the light, they exited. Clouds covered the sky making it difficult to tell the time of day. Cutler led the way, taking them south and eastward. They didn't talk as they traversed over rocky terrain which eventually leveled out. They continued until nightfall, then made camp.

The next morning, they traveled until just after midday when the land opened to a large field covered with tents and soldiers. To the south, the wall separating Lynk from the southern kingdoms loomed tall and imposing.

"I didn't expect so many soldiers," Sabine whispered. There had to be thousands of them in the valley. Way more than she'd ever seen in the cavern.

"Lieutenant Aaren is most likely in charge," Cutler said. "We'll go straight to the command station to speak with him."

A tent larger than the others stood in the middle of the camp with a blue flag at its peak.

"Just remember you are not only the commander but the queen," Drew said. "You bow to no one. Cutler and I have your back."

She turned to face him. "Thank you for everything you've done for me." Sometimes he reminded her of Otto the way he offered advice. Since she was young and inexperienced, it was nice to know others cared for her well-being and success.

They made their way through the camp, passing tents and soldiers—some eating, others training, and a few standing on guard. At the large tent, Cutler went in first to make sure the area was secure. Once he deemed it was, he held the flap open for her.

"Lieutenant Aaren," Cutler said. "May I present Queen Sabine Manfred."

She stepped into the room, Drew behind her.

"Her Majesty has been appointed as our commander," Cutler added.

A man in his late twenties with dark hair and eyes stood. "My queen and commander." He bowed. "Welcome. We weren't expecting the king or officers until tomorrow."

Thankfully they'd maintained a one day advantage. She stepped farther into the room. A large table took up most of the space. Maps were strewn over it along with a few knives and daggers.

"There have been a handful of assassinations at the palace," she said. "Have there been any incidents here at camp?"

"Not in the past week," Aaren answered. "However, before that, there were several."

Dogs barked, reminding Sabine of Harta and the other dogs from the kennels. She would have to seek them out when she was done here.

She went around to Aaren's side of the table, observing the map stretched out before him. "What instructions did the king give you?"

"We were told to prepare to invade Carlon and Nisk."

She loosed a breath.

"In three days."

She peered up at him. "So soon?"

He nodded.

"Well," she said, tapping her finger on the map. "There has been a change of plans. Please gather the lieutenants. I wish to speak with them so that I can explain everything." She would tell them to pack up and go home. There was no need to have an army sitting here, especially with the wall guarding Lynk. And she would have to find a way to inform the other kingdoms that Lynk would not be attacking. The League also needed to know that Lynk would continue to abide by the laws they'd set forth.

"Consider it done." Aaren bowed then left.

Alone with Drew and Cutler, Sabine let her shoulders droop. "We have to assume Rainer will be here tomorrow," she said, still looking at the map as if it held all the answers. "That means we need to get this army packed up and on the move today."

Cutler clasped his hands behind his back, shifting his weight from foot to foot. "May I speak freely?"

"Don't you always?"

He came forward and looked at the map. "Even if we get this camp packed and on the move today, as we head north, we can only move so fast. The king will find us."

"I agree," Drew said. "We have to figure out how to deal with opposition."

"Can the king strip me of my title as commander?" She assumed he could.

Cutler nodded. "We could start destroying weapons," he offered. "Ruin supplies. Make it difficult for the king to continue with his plans."

"I like that idea," Sabine said. "We can send the soldiers home. Scatter them. Make it hard for the army to be gathered." The more she thought about it, the more she liked this plan.

Aaren ducked inside the test. "Queen Commander Sabine, are you ready for everyone?"

"I am." She tried not to laugh at her mouthful of a title.

Aaren held the tent flap open, and about two dozen soldiers strolled in. They stood shoulder to shoulder taking up most of the space in the tent. Sabine glanced at their faces. Three were women and the rest were men. Most looked to be in their late twenties or early thirties.

Holding her head high, she said, "Thank you all for coming to speak with me. I assume Lieutenant Aaren has told you I am not only your queen but your commander. We've had some unexpected events and there has been a change of plans."

One of the men raised his hand.

Sabine gestured for him to speak.

"Excuse me, Your Majesty, but what happened to Commander Felix?"

"He died in his sleep."

A collective murmur rippled through the tent as everyone expressed their shock.

"Before the commander died, we spoke. He told me he didn't want to go to war with our neighboring kingdoms. I agreed with him."

"So we're not going to attack the south?" another soldier asked.

"No," Sabine replied. "We are not going to war." Now she had to get them to destroy their weapons, pack up, and head home. Peacefully.

The tent flap opened and someone strode through. "That's not entirely true," Rainer's voice cut through the tent as he strolled toward Sabine who still stood at the table. "Now that I'm here, I will take over command of the army. And we will be going to war." He slid his arm around Sabine's waist, pulling her to his side. "Hello, wife. Nice to see you here." He kissed her forehead.

Sabine froze in shock.

Chapter Twenty-Three

For Rainer to be there already, he had to have left the palace shortly after Sabine did. Since he didn't seem surprised to see her, he must have figured out her plan.

Her forehead burned where his lips had touched her. She peeked into his hard, unyielding eyes. His grip on her waist pinched to the point of being painful.

"Now that I'm here," Rainer quipped, "everything will proceed as planned."

"No," Sabine said, shaking her head, refusing to let him ruin everything. She'd given up too much, sacrificed too much. "There will not be a war. I forbid it."

He chuckled, the sound low and rumbling. "Honey, I know the idea of a war scares you since you're so fragile. That's why you'll let those of us who've trained and know how to fight handle this." He pinched her side harder.

She flinched, trying to move away from him, but he held firm. Two of the women in the tent noticed his hand on her side.

"I've been appointed the commander of this army—not you," Sabine said. "I'm in charge."

"Even as the commander," he replied, his voice smooth as silk, "I still outrank you. I'm in charge of the commander. My word goes. I think it's cute of you wanting to come here and help. But you are out of your league."

This could not be happening. Every time she had a plan she was sure would outmaneuver Rainer, he did something to turn it on its side.

"We don't need to go to war," she insisted. "This is madness." Maybe the other lieutenants would agree with her. Maybe they could all convince Rainer to stand down.

Rainer leaned toward her, whispering in her ear, "Madness is thinking a little girl from Bakley can come into Lynk and control the army. You have no idea what you're doing or playing at." Rainer straightened and faced those present in the tent. "Return to your units. Spread the word that we'll attack tomorrow as planned. Dismissed."

Everyone filed out of the tent except Drew. Sabine had no idea where Cutler had gone. Maybe once Rainer entered the tent, Cutler left because he couldn't stand to be around the person responsible for his wife's death.

"Captain Drew," Rainer said, "you're relieved of guarding the queen. I'll take responsibility for her safety from now on."

Drew's eyes locked on Sabine's. She knew he didn't want to leave. However, if he disobeyed the king, Rainer would kill him. Even though she didn't want to, she nodded at Drew, letting him know he should go.

He hesitated a moment before giving a curt nod and exiting the tent.

Now that the two of them were alone, Sabine said, "You're insane." She tried shoving away from Rainer but he didn't release her.

"You have caused me all sorts of problems. I'm done playing games with you." He grabbed her arm, twisting it behind her back and forcing her out the tent. "Smile or I'll kill you right now," he whispered in her ear. He kept her body against his so no one would realize what he was doing to her. The two of them entered the adjacent tent. This one contained a large bed and several opened trunks filled with clothes and various weapons. A fur rug covered the floor.

Rainer shoved her onto the bed and cold fear sliced into Sabine.

"I'll scream," she said, scooting back, trying to put space between them. She needed to get the poison tipped dagger from her boot.

Rainer loomed over her. She tried not to make any sudden movements. Her hand slowly slid down, only inches from her weapon. He snatched her wrist, yanking it up. She cried out in pain. Grabbing a piece of rope, he tied her wrist to the top of the bed. Then he grabbed her other wrist, doing the same.

"It doesn't have to be like this," she said, panic setting in now that both her wrists were attached to the bed. "We can work together instead of fighting one another."

He shook his head. "Since the moment I met you, I knew you'd never work. You're too independent and opinionated."

"You can't kill me," she reminded him. "You need your heir to maintain the throne."

"See, that's where you're wrong." Kneeling on the bed, he put his hands on either side of her body, hovering over her, his face mere inches from hers. "If I go to war and end the League, I can change the rules." A sadistic smile slid across his face. "I can do whatever I want." He leaned even closer and whispered in her ear, "I can even kill you."

"King Rainer!" someone shouted from outside the tent.

"Don't worry, I won't make your death easy. You've caused me so many problems and so much pain, I will take my time and enjoy it." He went over to the tent flap, lifting it.

"Your Majesty, we found a man snooping around the camp," a soldier said. "He's from Avoni and he has several weapons on him. We think he's one of the men responsible for the assassinations."

"Excellent," Rainer said. "Let's go." He left the tent without another word.

Lying there staring up at the ceiling, Sabine knew she had to come up with another plan to get out of this mess. Only, her plans didn't seem to work. And this time, she couldn't think of a single idea to help. Unless Drew or Cutler came in and untied her, she was going to die. The realization that she couldn't save herself was almost too much. Tears filled her eyes.

Sabine must have fallen asleep because when she peeled her eyelids open, darkness blanketed the tent. Someone had just entered, which must have woken her. A figure went over to the side and lit a candle, revealing it was Rainer. Setting the candle down, he turned and sat on the side of the bed next to Sabine.

"Prince Evander has come for you," Rainer said. "My men spotted him on the outskirts of camp." He chuckled, the sound dark. "I assumed he had a thing for you."

Confusion swirled within Sabine. There was no way Evander knew she was here. If he'd come to the camp, it was for something else. A shiver wracked her body.

Rainer ran his finger over Sabine's forehead, along her cheek, and over her bottom lip. She had to refrain from biting his finger and spitting in his face.

"Don't worry that pretty little head of yours," he said.

"We're setting a trap. Tomorrow I will kill you in front of Evander. He will watch you die like I watched Heather die."

"Evander isn't responsible for Heather's death," she said. "He had nothing to do with it."

He tilted his head to the side. "You're defending him?"

"I'm sorry Heather died."

His eyes narrowed. "No, you're not. You never liked her." He stood. "Try to get some sleep. You'll need your energy for tomorrow."

Sabine jolted awake to men shouting out orders. She heard several people yell the word *dead*. She wondered if they'd been attacked or if Evander had done something. Darkness surrounded her, the lone candle no longer lit. She was still in bed, her wrists bound. Angry voices came from right outside her tent. It sounded like they were next to her head, on the other side of the tent's fabric wall.

"She is the acting commander," a voice said. "That means she must be killed."

"I gave specific instructions that the queen was not to be touched in any way," another voice said. This one seemed angry, deadly, lethal.

"And the king gave me instructions. I can't return home until the commander is dead."

"I'm changing the orders."

"You can't. You know that."

There was a shuffling sound and a thump.

"If something happens to me, there will be another."

"You will *not* touch the queen. That's an order."

A low chuckle sounded. "Then say the words."

"You are bound by oath and blood."

"Then it is done." There was a shuffling noise. "I'll let the others know. If the king is displeased when I report, it's your life—not mine."

"Agreed."

Sabine's heart pounded with the possibility that Evander was on the other side of the tent. She was about to call out to him when someone slipped inside her tent. The person got closer.

She was about to say *Evander,* thinking it was him, when a hand slid over her mouth.

"Shh," Drew said. "Don't say a word. We're under attack and several people have been killed." He released her and cut her bindings.

She sat up, wanting to make a run for it.

Drew motioned for her to stay put, then he turned to face the tent's opening.

"I need to get out of here," she whispered.

He shook his head. "It's too dangerous to leave the tent." Withdrawing his sword, he stood there guarding the queen.

Rainer shoved the tent flap back and stormed inside. "He's going to pay." The king's hair was disheveled, there was a cut across his face, and his clothes were rumpled. It looked like he'd been in a fight. "What are you doing here?" he asked Drew.

"With all of the assassinations last night, I came here to protect the queen. It's a good thing I did, since she was tied up."

"You're dismissed. Leave."

Drew slid his sword in its scabbard then exited the tent.

"Who's going to pay? What happened?" Sabine asked as she sat up on the bed.

The king glared at her. "The assassin that we captured got away. He killed three dozen of my men."

"What about Evander?" she asked, wondering if he'd been involved in the killings, especially since she thought she'd heard him last night outside her tent.

"Evander is the one who rescued the assassin."

Sabine found it hard to breathe as the realization set in. Evander had rescued the assassin, but not her. Her first thought was that he didn't know she was here in this camp. But he did. The conversation she'd overheard all but confirmed that he knew she was here. Yet he'd done nothing to save her. It sounded like he'd prevented the assassin from killing her—but saving her? Rescuing her? She wasn't part of his plan and that stung.

"Let's go." Rainer grabbed Sabine's arm, dragging her off the bed and out of the tent.

Fog coated the land, concealing the tents more than twenty feet away. Rainer pulled her along. The camp seemed deserted. When they reached the center where a platform stood, she realized why the rest of the camp had felt empty— it was because everyone was here.

Rainer dragged her along a narrow pathway leading to the platform. When they reached it, he yanked her up the steps. At the top, he gripped her arms. Another soldier joined them, tying Sabine's wrists together in front of her body. Several of the soldiers murmured, probably wondering what the king was doing with the queen. Then the soldier removed both of Sabine's daggers and exited the platform. When Rainer and Sabine were the only two standing on it, Rainer shouted, "If you want to save her, show yourself!"

The soldiers gathered closest to them pulled out their swords and turned so their backs faced the platform as if guarding it from a threat.

Evander was nowhere to be seen. She thought it rather

bold of Rainer to stand out in the open, so exposed. However, she didn't see any archers among the soldiers. She also didn't see any areas where one could potentially hide and shoot an arrow toward Rainer.

Sabine had an inkling of a plan. "Listen to me," she said loudly, her voice carrying over the hundreds of soldiers gathered. "Every life here is valuable. We do not need to go to war—"

Rainer backhanded her across the face, causing her to fall on her arm. She cried out in pain.

Someone in the crowd moved, as if to help her.

Rainer ordered Aaren, who stood at the bottom of the steps, to arrest that soldier who'd moved. Aaren rushed forward and grabbed the person, yanking back the man's hood, to reveal a Lynk soldier.

"It's not him," Aaren said, letting him go.

Rainer cursed. "Where is he?" He stepped toward Sabine, placing one of his boots on her back, forcing her to remain on the floor. He withdrew his sword, the slice of steel ringing through the air. "Last chance!" he called out. "Show yourself, or she dies!"

It felt as if time slowed.

Sabine tried to get to her knees, but Rainer only stepped harder on her.

"I guess he doesn't care for you," Rainer said. "Pity there is no one here to save you." And with that, he swung his sword down, right toward Sabine's neck.

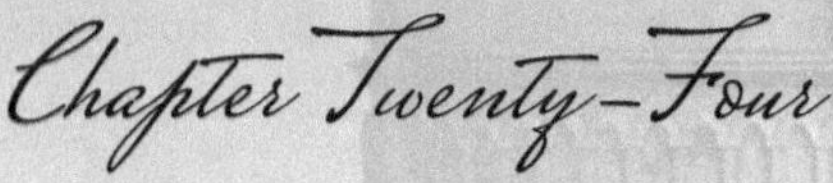

Chapter Twenty-Four

Sabine squeezed her eyes shut, waiting for the sword to strike her. Something large and solid hit her body, knocking her out of the way.

"Protect the queen!" Drew yelled, running toward the platform, too far away to do anything himself.

A loud *thump* resounded, and Sabine twisted her head to see Cutler lying next to her, blood pooling around his body, his chest carved open from Rainer's sword. He heaved deep, garbled breaths as blood flowed from his body.

"Cutler!" Sabine screamed, understanding that he'd thrown her out of the way and taken the hit himself. He'd saved her life. "No! You can't die."

"It's...okay." His voice was barely audible. "I'll...be...with...her...now." He looked at Rainer. "I'll...finally...have...her...to...myself." His head lulled to the side as he took his last breath.

"He's dead," Sabine said, shocked. "You killed him." She glanced up at Rainer who had straightened, lifting his sword again to strike Sabine. Rage filled her. This man took and took without a thought or care for anyone other than himself. He didn't deserve to rule Lynk, let alone live. She rose on her knees, defiance lighting up her eyes.

"My queen!" Drew's voice cut through the air.

Her eyes met Drew's. He was still too far away to help. His face contorted in a mixture of fear and rage. He held up a dagger, showing it to her before throwing it her way. It landed right next to her hands, embedded into the platform, hilt up.

Right when Rainer started to swing downward, she grabbed the dagger, withdrew it and twisted, slicing his abdomen. Blood gushed from the wound. He stumbled, his sword striking right next to Sabine.

Before Rainer could lift his sword again, Drew finally reached the platform, jumping onto it and plunging his sword into the king's back. Sabine shoved his body away from her, and he collapsed onto Cutler, dead.

The king was dead.

Rainer was dead.

Sabine started shaking. She was alive, and her husband wasn't.

Images bombarded her. The first time she'd met Rainer, the two of them dancing together, him teaching her how to defend herself, their wedding at the castle. Then other memories flooded her. Him grabbing her neck, trying to strangle her. His cruelty to others.

She heaved in a gulp of air, tears filling her eyes.

Soldiers stormed onto the platform, surrounding her.

Voices filled the air.

"He just tried to kill the queen."

"He killed Captain Cutler."

"The king is dead."

"Protect the queen."

Her entire body shook violently.

"Your Majesty," Drew said, coming to squat before her. "Are you harmed?"

She looked into his eyes. "Is King Rainer really dead?" she asked, her voice barely audible.

"He is." He gently placed his hand on her elbow, helping her to stand. "Are you bleeding anywhere? Do you need a healer?"

The blood on her clothing was from Cutler, not her. "I'm fine."

Drew severed her bindings. "Let's get you out of here and get you cleaned up."

She shook her head. While she wanted to be away from these bodies, she needed to address the soldiers standing here. There seemed to be too much confusion. Forcing her uncertainty and terror down, she rolled her shoulders back and stood tall.

"Thank you Captain Drew for saving my life. I'm not sure why the king was so upset."

"What do you want us to do with the bodies?" Aaren asked.

"Wrap King Rainer's body up to be transported back to the palace. A service will be held for him there so he can be buried with his deceased family members." Her hands were shaking.

"And Captain Cutler?" he asked.

"I'd like to honor him here." That seemed to be the right thing to say as soldiers immediately got to work building a pyre next to the side of the stage. Then she spoke louder so everyone could hear. "There has been enough death and bloodshed. After honoring Cutler, we will dismantle the camp, pack up, and return home to our families. We will not go to war."

Drew and Aaren dropped to their knees, bowing their heads in supplication. Everyone else began doing the same.

Four men came forward, lifting Cutler's body and carrying him to the pyre. His body was placed atop the wood. Another soldier came forward, handing Sabine a torch.

"I am thankful Captain Cutler was brave enough, honorable enough, and loyal enough to step in to save my life at the expense of his own. His sacrifice won't be forgotten." She lowered the torch to the pyre and it immediately caught fire, engulfing Cutler's body.

She stood there, surrounded by hundreds of soldiers, as they all paid their respects to the captain.

There had been far too much death. Poor Lady Regina—she'd lost not only her husband and daughter-in-law, but now her son. Sabine didn't think the woman had any family left.

That could have easily been Sabine in those flames. Rainer had been so close to ending her life today. But Cutler had saved her. When she'd first met him, she'd feared him. Disliked him. Wanted nothing to do with him. But they'd formed an alliance of sorts over the Heather situation. He proved to be loyal, trustworthy, and a friend.

She wiped her tears.

The following hours were a whirlwind of activity. The soldiers began dismantling and packing up the camp. A messenger was sent to the other gate to inform the soldiers camped there to return home.

Though most soldiers kept their distance, a few thanked the queen for not sending them to war.

Sabine had a lot of work ahead of her. Work that she would have to handle and figure out on her own. Gone were the days of being confined to her room and thought of as only a decoration. She was in charge of Lynk and needed to make sure she appeared strong. The last thing she needed was some sort of insurrection. However, most of those who opposed her rule were dead.

Once she appointed a new commander, Sabine left with Drew and a dozen soldiers. She wanted to ride quickly to the palace and stay off the main roads. If what she'd overheard last night had been real, then she thought the Avoni assassins had left Lynk. She was safe. But just in case, she wanted to be smart and not let her guard down.

They made it to the palace without incident where she was greeted by Captain Higman and Captain Lithane along with Prince Anton and Prince Axel. She told them what happened and about Rainer's death. No one seemed particularly sad. She dispatched a letter to the League informing them of what had taken place.

With news of the king's death, many nobles began leaving the palace and returning to their private homes. Most preferred to stay there during the cooler months. Sabine hadn't noticed it getting any colder.

She spent the following week going through Rainer's rooms and learning as much as she could. She saw little of Anton and Axel.

When the soldiers returned, she gave most of them leave to see their families while requesting some stay to ensure the safety of the town and palace. New officers were appointed. With the return of the soldiers meant the return of the dogs. Harta was now back with Sabine, in her room, keeping her company. Life seemed to be moving on.

Sabine hadn't heard a word from Evander. With so much going on in Lynk, she tried not to let it bother her. At least she had enough to do to keep her mind occupied.

At Rainer's funeral, she didn't say a word about him. She'd simply had his body buried with the other royals who'd gone before him.

A letter arrived from her parents asking her about attending Viktor's wedding. Sabine wrote back that she would love to visit home and see her brother married. She could be there in a few weeks if they would wait that long.

Drew said he would see to the proper accommodations for her travel.

She'd taken to eating in the royal dining room. After a couple of nights, Anton started joining her. Then Axel as well. At dinner one night, Sabine informed the princes that she would be leaving in a week to attend her brother's wedding. She asked Anton to oversee things while she was gone.

"I have to meet with the League in a couple of days," Anton replied. "Axel might have to rule for me."

She didn't much care which brother ruled so long as one of them did.

"Why'd you ask him and not me?" Axel inquired while sipping on his wine.

"Since he's a League member, I thought he'd know more about how things are handled." In truth, she thought Anton was more reliable.

"I'm hurt," Axel said, bowing his head.

Sabine rolled her eyes. "You're not. If you were left to rule this kingdom, I'm pretty sure you'd be bored." While she had seen him take multiple women to his room, she recalled the masquerade and him telling her how he'd planned the entire event for Rainer. Maybe she didn't give him enough credit.

"I'm retiring for the evening," Anton said as he stood. "I need to leave first thing in the morning to make the League meeting on time."

Sabine bid him goodnight.

"Do you plan on always having that beast in here when we eat?" Axel asked, pointing to Harta.

A servant came in, giving each of them a slice of chocolate cake for dessert.

"She is not a beast," she chided Axel. "Harta is my friend. And where I go, she goes." While gazing at her dog, giving air kisses, her napkin fell to the floor. She bent over and picked it up. When she straightened, she found Axel closer than she remembered him being.

He chuckled and took a bite of his cake. "Friend or not, it's still a creature and not human."

"Leave my dog alone." Harta nudged her arm. "Don't worry, girl, I won't let him kick you out." She picked up her fork, and Harta nudged her arm again. "Watch it," she scolded the dog. "You're proving Axel right on this matter. Behave." She cut a piece of cake, lifting it to her mouth. Harta slammed against Sabine's chair, making her drop her fork. "What on earth?"

Harta started barking and moving from side to side as if agitated.

Looking at her plate, Sabine examined the cake in greater detail. A bit of yellow powder had been sprinkled on the plate next to the cake. It brought her back to her dining room in Bakley when she'd trained with her mother on how to spot poisons. One of them had been a yellow powder often used on food.

"Don't eat it," Sabine said to Axel. "There's poison on it."

"Are you certain?" He set his fork down. "I've already had a few bites." His face paled.

"Guards!" she called out.

Drew entered. She quickly explained about the poison.

He took the plates. "I'll fetch a healer, then speak with the kitchen staff and your taster—if she's still alive." He left.

Sabine stood and paced about. Someone had tried to kill her. Maybe the Avoni assassins hadn't left. A thought occurred to her. "Is that assassin still in the dungeon?"

"I don't know," Axel replied. "I'll have someone find out." He spoke to one of her guards.

Her arms were shaking. She peered down at her dog. "Thank you, Harta." Her dog had saved her life. She'd been too complacent—a mistake she wouldn't make again.

"Are you okay?" Axel asked.

"I'm fine." Although, something about this seemed sloppy. A trained assassin would have noticed the powder on the plate and wiped it off. The poison would have only been on the food so as to be undetected. It reminded her of the assassination attempt at the seamstress's room. Evander had told her there was no way that had been an Avoni assassin. She had a feeling this one wasn't either. Regardless, she needed to know about the man in the dungeon.

A few minutes later, Drew returned. "Nothing is amiss in the kitchen. Your food taster is alive and well."

Glancing at Axel, he seemed fine as well. "The healer?" she asked.

"He is getting a handful of antidotes together, then coming to the royal wing," Drew said.

The other guard returned, panting. "Your Majesty," he said. "The prisoner in the dungeon is dead."

If it wasn't the Avoni assassin in the dungeon, then she didn't have any suspects.

"You look like you're going to be ill all over the table," Axel said.

She'd thought this was over. She couldn't live her life like this with the threat of death around every corner and at every meal.

"Come on," Axel said. "I'll show you where Rainer kept his good whisky."

With Harta trotting close behind, Sabine followed Axel out of the dining room.

Chapter Twenty-Five

Axel opened the door to the royal suite. Sabine still considered these rooms Rainer's. After returning from the army camp near the border, she had gone through them, but she hadn't removed any of the king's personal items yet. Eventually, she would have his brothers come in to take his things away.

Drew remained in the hallway. "I'm going to have someone walk Harta and give her a treat as her reward for saving you," he said.

"Thank you." Sabine closed the door then sat on the sofa. Now that Rainer was dead, she didn't have to worry about having a guard with her for proprietary reasons.

Axel meandered over to a cabinet, pulling out a bottle and two glasses. "How are you really doing?"

Sabine didn't know how to answer that. The past couple of weeks had been a whirlwind. So much so that she hadn't had time to sit and think. It was all about maintaining control and making sure things moved forward. Her sole focus was on the kingdom, not on herself or her feelings.

"How are *you* doing?" she countered. "You lost your

brother and sister. That's a lot." Since being back, she hadn't had a personal conversation with either prince. At supper, most everything revolved around the kingdom's matters. This was good that the two of them were finally getting a chance to sit and talk without anyone around to overhear them.

After pouring whisky into the glasses, he gave one to Sabine before taking the other and sitting on the sofa across from her. "I've been better." He took a sip.

Sabine held the glass, twisting it in her hands. "While I didn't love Rainer, I am sorry he's dead." Instead of rotting in the dungeon where he belonged. "I'm sorry for your loss." But not sorry she'd stopped the war and managed to keep the League in place.

He lifted a single shoulder in a semi shrug. "I've been thinking," he said, taking another sip. "What if we married?"

Of all the things he could have said, Sabine hadn't expected that.

"You look shocked." He chuckled, setting his glass on the low table and resting his elbows on his thighs. "Consider it —you need guidance. I can give you that. I know you don't love me, but you didn't love Rainer either. At least we're friends."

Twisting the cup between her hands, she tried to comprehend what Axel was offering.

"I don't have a lover," he continued. "I won't take one. I would like the freedom to dally here and there, but never in front of you or the court. I would never disrespect you like Rainer did."

Until now, she'd never considered the possibility of marrying Axel. A part of her had hoped she could still be with Evander. But she hadn't heard from him since Rainer's death.

"Our law dictates you marry and produce an heir," Axel

said. "You should marry someone from Lynk since you're not from here. I make sense."

What he said was true and it did make sense, but her heart screamed against it. After going through everything she had with Rainer, she wanted to marry someone she truly loved. It was naive, yet it was what she wanted.

"What do you think?" he asked, his voice hesitant.

"I don't know."

He stood and moved to sit beside her on the sofa. "Sabine, talk to me. What's wrong?"

"There have been so many changes lately." Focusing on her hands instead of looking into his eyes, she felt ill at ease being this close to him having never thought of Axel this way. He'd always been a friend and brother-in-law.

"What's holding you back from agreeing to marry me?"

"I don't love you."

"And I don't love you. But that doesn't mean we're not perfect for each other. In time, we can learn to love one another." He eyed her. "This isn't because of Prince Evander, is it?"

Panic crept in. "What do you mean?"

"It's obvious you have feelings for the man, but you know you can never be with him, right? He's from Avoni. A Lynk queen from Bakley can't rule Lynk and marry someone from Avoni. You have to see that. You must marry someone from Lynk."

What he said made sense.

A knock resounded on the door. "Your Majesty," Drew called out. "The healer is here."

"Come in."

The healer entered, Drew right behind him.

"I'm fine," Axel said. "You don't need to examine me."

"Poisons can be tricky," the healer said. "Sometimes they

take hours to work. If there's an antidote, I need to administer it before the poison kills you."

"Axel, please let him look you over," Sabine said. With the recent assassinations, each body had been found in the morning. Maybe they'd been poisoned at supper then died a few hours later in their sleep.

The healer approached him, looking in his eyes, mouth, and ears before listening to his heartbeat. "You appear healthy," the healer said as he started to pack his bag. "No signs of being poisoned." Suddenly, he went still, his eyes widening.

"What's wrong?" Sabine demanded.

The healer stood and took a step back, away from Axel. "I was told the poison found on your plate was a yellow powder?"

"Yes, that is correct." Sabine set her glass on the low table and stood, facing the healer.

The healer's eyes darted to Axel before settling back on Sabine. "There is a yellow residue on the prince's sleeve and a bit on his pants."

The room suddenly seemed very quiet. Sabine looked at Axel wondering if he'd poisoned her dessert or if he had gotten the poison on his clothes from his own plate. "Did you try to kill me?" They were friends, not enemies. However, something deep inside of her knew the truth.

Axel rolled his eyes. "Don't be ridiculous. Why would I ask you to marry me if I wanted you dead?"

A deep foreboding filled her as everything began to make sense. It felt as if her heart would burst out of her chest. He probably only asked her to marry him because his attempt to kill her had failed. "You want to rule Lynk." The realization shocked her since he'd always appeared so aloof.

Axel pushed to his feet, running his hand through his hair as he inched closer to Sabine.

"I need you to move away from the queen," Drew said, withdrawing his sword.

"I didn't try to kill her. I like the queen and don't want her dead."

"Then why do you have poison on you?" Sabine asked.

"The healer is lying," Axel said.

"I can obtain a sample of the yellow substance and test it," the healer offered.

Something flashed across Axel's face. In the blink of an eye, he lunged for Sabine.

Without thinking, she withdrew her dagger, nicking his thigh as she stepped away from him, out of reach.

"Not enough to do damage," Axel said, a sly smile spreading across his face.

"The dagger was poisoned," she informed him.

Drew had managed to move up behind Axel. His sword now pointed at the prince's neck.

Axel crumbled to the floor, unconscious.

"You almost gave me a heart attack," Drew said. "Next time, you can trust that I will handle the threat." He knelt next to Axel, feeling his pulse in his neck.

She shrugged. "I didn't think. I just acted." She slid the dagger back in its sheath. "Thanks for that weapon."

"I'd say I'm glad it came in handy, but I'm still shaken by watching you defend yourself."

She smiled, thrilled she'd saved herself for a change. "What are we going to do with Axel?"

"He's going to be taken to the dungeon." Drew stood. "As is Prince Anton."

"Did Anton have anything to do with what happened?" The thought that Anton could have been working against her as well was almost too much to bear.

"Prince Axel just tried to assassinate you," Drew said.

"The healer here is a witness. That means Prince Anton will be punished accordingly."

Guilt filled her. If Anton was innocent, she didn't want him to suffer the same fate as Axel. It didn't seem fair. However, the law was the law.

Sabine stood in the dungeon before Axel's cell. When she'd been in Avoni, hunted by Ex, she'd known true fear. The assassin had been unrelenting and lethal. When an assassin had tried killing her at the seamstress's room all those weeks ago, the attempt had been sloppy. Sabine remembered Lottie discussing it with the assassin that night in the Avoni delegation's suite. He'd said the situation hadn't been handled as he would have liked. When Sabine brought it up to Evander, Evander had said there was no way that it had been an Avoni assassin who'd tried killing her at the seamstress's.

What happened last night at supper reminded her of that. Sloppy. She knew it wasn't someone from Avoni. If it had been, she'd be dead. Given that poison had been found on Axel's sleeve, she had a feeling he was the one who'd tried killing her in that seamstress's room.

Axel sat on his cot as if he had all the time in the world. As if he wasn't in a dungeon.

"Why?" she asked.

"You're going to have to be a bit more specific," he said.

"Why did you try to kill me? Twice."

He smiled. "You finally figured it out." He stood.

"Why?" She needed to understand. Drew had found a couple of handwritten notes in Lottie and Axel's rooms indicating the two had been working and plotting together.

"What do you plan to do with me?" he asked, taking a step closer to the bars that separated them.

"I haven't decided."

He smiled again. "My offer is still on the table."

She rolled her eyes. Like she would marry him after he'd tried killing her. Twice. "Just answer my question. Please." She added the *please* hoping to appeal to his ego. Hoping to get him talking. Hoping he'd tell her the truth.

He sighed. "Honestly?"

She nodded.

"Rainer was a self-serving prick who didn't deserve to be king. Killing you was a way to get rid of him. Lottie was easier to manipulate and manage. I could have more and be more with her on the throne. Pure and simple."

"Then why last night?" she asked.

"With you gone, the royal throne would have been mine." He shrugged. "You're from Bakley. You don't deserve to rule over Lynk."

There was something wrong with him. "I feel sorry for you." She turned to leave.

He chuckled. "No need. I have a plan to get out of here."

The hairs on the back of her neck stood on end. Glancing over her shoulder, she sighed. "I feel sorry for you because you neither had nor know what a loving family is." She left him standing there, calling after her.

Drew joined her. "Your orders, Your Majesty?"

"I'd like to say he is to remain here in the dungeon, but I fear for my life. Even with him locked up."

"I agree. I'll take care of it."

She nodded and stopped before Anton's cell.

"I heard my brother tried to kill you. Is that true?" He was sitting on the floor, not looking her way.

"Yes." She folded her arms, watching him.

"Do you know why?"

"Yes."

"Do you think I'm involved?"

"Honestly, I don't know." After extensive searches of his room, nothing had been found to indicate he was involved with Lottie or Axel's plans.

At that, he looked at her. "Have I given you reason to think I want you dead?"

"When I first came to Lynk, I didn't like or trust you." Axel always felt safer to her since Anton kept a wall up between them.

"I didn't trust or like you either," he admitted.

"Axel tried killing me. Twice."

Anton's shoulders slumped, making him appear defeated.

"Did you know?" As the head of Rainer's spies, it seemed likely Anton would be aware of what was going on.

"I had my suspicions. But then the Avoni delegation arrived and things got muddled. Complicated. I wasn't sure. I don't think I really wanted to know the truth."

She happened to believe him.

"At first I wasn't sure of your intentions," Anton said. "For Lynk and my family."

"I've always wanted peace and what's best for all kingdoms." And she'd wanted love. Friendship. Loyalty. She hadn't found any of that with the Lynk royal family. "So where do we go from here?"

He shook his head. "I guess I'll suffer the same fate as my brother."

"Is that what you want?" she asked him, curious. Did he want things like love and a family? He never spoke about it to her.

He shrugged.

"What do you want?"

"No one has ever asked me that," he admitted.

"Well, I'm asking."

"I want peace. I'd like to downsize my spying operation. I don't want to have to marry if I don't want to. And I'd like not to have to train every day—I don't enjoy it."

Sabine laughed. "Anton, I think we can arrange that."

His brows pulled together. "What are you saying?"

Leaning against the bars, she said, "I wrote to the League. If you die because of your brother's actions, then Lynk has no one to serve in the League. Therefore, the League has granted you a special pardon. You will not suffer your brother's fate."

"I'm not going to be executed for treason?"

"Are you guilty of treason?"

"No."

"Then you've done nothing wrong and do not deserve to be in here." She turned to Drew. "Let him out."

Drew unlocked the door.

Anton slowly rose to his feet and came to stand before Sabine. "I can't believe you wrote to the League on my behalf."

"I wrote to them about that and one other matter that we need to discuss."

"Which is?"

She chewed on her thumbnail, trying to figure out how to broach this with him. "I never consummated my marriage with Rainer."

"No one has to know."

"I told the League. I asked them what my options are." She'd known she'd be stripped of the crown and wouldn't be able to rule. Before she wrote to them, she'd prepared herself for that outcome.

He released a large breath. "This complicates things."

"It does. The League has decided to pass the Lynk crown to you."

"But I'm not in line for the throne."

"Your mother was the queen. You are the legitimate heir."

This was the part she was afraid to bring up. "I hear you have a woman friend. And a five year old son." The woman he'd been seeing was a commoner in town. Anton hadn't told anyone her child was his. Sabine had only discovered it when she'd read through Felix's notes. He'd been helping Anton funnel money to the woman and child for years.

Anton ran his hands over his face.

"Since you have an heir, your son can take over for you as the League member once he's of age."

"I don't know about this. I never planned on ruling."

Neither had she. But things happened in life and they had to adapt. "The League has granted you the royal throne and the right to marry the commoner. You may declare the child your heir. It's a better option than me ruling. I'm not from here. And, honestly, I can't marry someone from Lynk. You have to understand that. I don't belong here."

Anton took her hand, squeezing it. "I don't think you understand what all you've done for Lynk. You are a true queen."

Chapter Twenty-Six

Once everything had calmed down, Sabine traveled south with a handful of guards who'd volunteered to escort her. Anton had been sworn in as the new king of Lynk. The people had been sad to see her go. However, once she gave her full support to Anton, people began to come around. After he married the commoner, everyone fully embraced him.

It felt like she hadn't been home in years, even though it had only been a few months. So much had changed that she no longer felt like the same person who'd left here, determined to seek revenge for her sister's death.

When the carriage rounded the bend revealing her family's castle in the distance, tears filled her eyes. She'd missed this more than she'd realized. Things had been so busy lately that she hadn't had time to think about her life here in Bakley. Seeing her family's land, she knew that she'd made the right decision by leaving Lynk. Now that she understood what it meant to be a queen, she wanted to thank her mother for all she'd done for her family and her kingdom.

The carriage pulled through the gates and onto the road leading to the castle. Her family stood on the front steps, waiting for her. An overwhelming sense of gratitude, love, and something else that she couldn't pinpoint overwhelmed her. When the carriage came to a stop, she almost shoved the door open, wanting to throw her arms around her parents. However, she refrained from doing so. Not only was she no longer a child, but she was the princess of Bakley and needed to act accordingly.

Drew opened the door and held out his hand for her. Before she could take it, Harta jumped out of the carriage, thrilled to finally be able to run around. Smiling, Sabine took Drew's hand, gingerly stepping down onto Bakley soil. "Thank you for escorting me," she whispered to her loyal guard.

"It has been a pleasure serving you, Your Highness." He bowed.

"I wish you nothing but the best," she said. "Both you and Harper." She knew her guard and lady's maid had formed an attachment to one another. She hoped it worked out for them—they deserved happiness.

His face flushed. "Thank you, Your Highness." He closed the carriage door and gave the order to head out. Now that he'd brought her home, he would return to Lynk with the soldiers who had accompanied them.

Not bothering to watch the carriage leave, she turned and faced her family, Harta obediently at her side.

She shifted her cape behind her shoulders as a genuine smile stretched across her face. Front and center, her parents, Franz and Elsa, stood arm in arm. To their right were Karl and his wife, Jesamine, along with their boys, Haron and Beck. Jesamine's stomach looked like a small melon had been placed under her dress indicating she was pregnant. On her parents' other side, Rolf had his arm draped over his wife who held their sleeping baby. Otto and Viktor stood next to them.

Suddenly, everything felt right in Sabine's life.

Elsa opened her arms, and Sabine ran into them, squeezing her mother. The next thing she knew, the entire family had piled in for the hug. Tears of joy streamed down her cheeks. She was home with her family—the people who loved her most in the world. Harta ran circles around them.

The wedding was held the following day in the chapel on the castle's property. Everyone from town had been invited. So many came that people were forced to stand around the edges and at the back. Flowers decorated the aisle. The marriage binder stood on the dais with Viktor off to the side, awaiting his bride.

Sabine and her family sat in the first row.

A group of musicians began playing, and everyone stood to watch Carin enter the chapel at the back, wearing a beautiful soft white dress in the traditional Avoni style, with pale pink roses embroidered along the hemline. A cape with long sleeves matching the dress lay atop her shoulders. She walked down the aisle, joining Viktor.

Sabine watched the two of them, remembering her own wedding day to Rainer. This ceremony felt vastly different from that one. Here, friends and family gathered to watch and support this union. This wasn't done in secret or in haste.

Once the ceremony was complete, everyone headed over to the castle's great hall to celebrate.

Sabine used the opportunity to slip away for a moment.

First, she went to the garden where she plucked a single white rose. Then she headed to the royal family's cemetery. She went to Alina's grave, pleased to see a bouquet of lavender had been left on it.

Kneeling, she ran her hand over the headstone. "My dear, sweet sister." She laid the single rose on the grave. "I made a promise to you. I promised to find who murdered you and to avenge your death. It wasn't as easy as I thought." Taking a deep breath, she tried not to cry. "I found out Rainer's own sister, Lottie, wanted the throne. She hired an assassin, and the assassin poisoned you. I'm so sorry. So, so sorry. The assassin is dead. Lottie is dead." Sabine kissed her fingers, then brushed the kiss onto the headstone. "Axel is dead. Rainer is dead." So much death and for what? Power? It seemed so silly and petty.

"You didn't deserve this. I miss you. Every day." Sabine stood, wiping the tears that slid down her cheeks. "I hope you've found happiness wherever you are." She headed to the castle, back to the wedding celebration, to celebrate the joining of two people in marriage.

It was funny how life continued on. When Alina died, Sabine found it hard to live, hard to breathe, hard to carry on. But she was forced to, and so she did. Her family would never be the same. Life would never be the same. But Alina wouldn't be forgotten.

Inside, she found the celebration in full swing. People were dancing in the middle of the room while others sat eating at the tables around the perimeter.

"Sister," Viktor said, coming to stand at her side. "Have you met my wife, Carin?" He pointed his chin to the dance floor where Carin was dancing with their father.

"I have." She wondered how Carin felt about coming to Bakley and marrying Viktor. "How's it going?"

"I never thought I would marry for political reasons." He lifted a single eyebrow. "But I think I lucked out. Carin is beautiful, funny, witty. We seem to get along."

"That's all well and good, but remember—she's an assassin." She tried to keep her lips from pulling into a smile. "I wouldn't tease or upset her too much."

Viktor's head tilted toward Sabine. "Thank you for that information. I will keep that in mind every night when I sleep by her side," he deadpanned.

At that, Sabine burst out laughing. She missed joking with her brothers.

The song ended and Carin and Franz came over and joined them. Viktor took his wife's hand and he twirled her into the medley of dancers.

"Can I have a turn with my baby girl?" Franz asked.

"I would love that."

The song that started was a slower tune, giving them the opportunity to talk.

"I'll give you a full update tomorrow when we have a chance to speak in private," Sabine assured him.

"I'm more concerned with how you're doing."

"I don't want to talk about anything related to Lynk right now. Today, I just want to celebrate and be happy with my family." Tomorrow she could tell him all that had happened.

"I can understand that." He filled her in on the town gossip, her nephews' antics, renovations to the stables, how her horse missed her, and how her mother seemed to be doing much better.

Sabine took it all in. The familiar faces, the fragrant flowers, the feel of home.

Someone tapped her shoulder, and she glanced to see who it was.

Two green eyes were staring right at her, amused.

"Evander?" She spun around to face him.

"At your service," he said with a bow. "I came for my sister's wedding." The corners of his lips pulled up as he fought a smile. "It's good to see you, Princess Sabine."

"I'll let the two of you finish this dance," Franz said. "I'm going to go find my wife." He patted Sabine on the shoulder before leaving.

"Dance with me."

Her heart picked up, beating faster as she put her hands on Evander.

"I hear you're missing a husband," he said, amusement sparkling in his eyes.

"I am." She wanted to ask him why he didn't save her that night in the army camp.

"Is the position open?"

Her brows pulled together in confusion.

"Because if it is," he went on, "I'd like the opportunity to fill the role."

"You want to be my husband?" she asked, dumbfounded by this turn of events.

"More than anything. I want to marry you. I want to be your husband. I want a life with you. Say you'll marry me." His eyes sparkled with amusement.

She pulled back, searching his face. "I thought you left me," she whispered. "That night, at the army camp…"

"I left with my men," he said. "I knew you could take care of yourself. That you didn't need me to save you."

"I thought you didn't care about me."

"You have to know," he whispered. "You have to know how much I love you."

She threw her arms around his neck, yanking him to her. "I love you, too."

He chuckled, the sound light and happy. "That's good to hear. Because I have no intention of letting you go."

His lips came down, gently kissing hers.

They were in public, kissing. And it was okay. She wasn't married. She was just Sabine, the princess of Bakley. And she could do as she pleased with whomever she pleased. It just so happened she loved Evander.

And planned on spending the rest of her life with him.

The End

OTHER BOOKS BY JENNIFER ANNE DAVIS

True Reign:

The Key

Red

War

Reign of Secrets:

Cage of Deceit

Cage of Darkness

Cage of Destiny

Oath of Deception

Oath of Destruction

Knights of the Realm:

Realm of Knights

Shadow Knights

Hidden Knights

Reigning Kingdoms

Sword of Rage

Sword of Desire

League of Rulers

The Queen's Crown

The King's Sword

The Royal Throne

The Order of the Krigers:

Rise

Burning Shadows

Conquering Fate

Single Titles:

Evil Lurks Beneath

The Voice

The Power to See

ABOUT THE AUTHOR

Jennifer Anne Davis graduated from the University of San Diego with a degree in English and a teaching credential. She is currently a full-time writer and mother of three kids. She is happily married to her high school sweetheart and lives in the San Diego area.

Jennifer is the recipient of the San Diego Book Awards Best Published Young Adult Novel (2013), winner of the Kindle Book Awards (2018), a finalist in the USA Best Book Awards (2014), and a finalist in the Next Generation Indie Book Awards (2014).

Visit Jennifer at:
www.JenniferAnneDavis.com

facebook.com/AuthorJenniferAnneDavis
x.com/authorjennifer
instagram.com/authorjennifer
bookbub.com/authors/jennifer-anne-davis
goodreads.com/jenniferannedavis
pinterest.com/authorjennifer
tiktok.com/@authorjenniferannedavis